THE GERMANS HAVE A WORD FOR IT

T. R. THORSEN

SUNKAT

Published by Sunkat Press, Crozet VA

ISBN Print Edition: 9798991400503
ISBN e-book: 9798991400510

Cover design by Christian Storm

Printed in the United States of America

To my father,

I thought to tell you something today, but you were gone.

ONE

DAVIS BIT the end of his pen. He should tick off some checkboxes. What kind of a husband wouldn't tick off some checkboxes?

FLOWERS

<u>REMEMBRANCE PACKAGE</u> — A JOYOUS YET SOMBER ARRANGEMENT OF DAISIES AND PETUNIAS, A BLOOM OF YELLOW AND WHITE, FRESHLY PICKED AS IF FROM YOUR OWN GARDEN. CELEBRATE YOUR LOVED ONE'S ARRIVAL IN THE PARADISE OF AFTERLIFE.

[ ] $1,000

"Hmmm."

She was dead though. What would she care? Plus, it was all so expensive. Too expensive. Too expensive for stuff that's used only once, barely used, and then discarded . . . For ephemeral stuff. Perhaps the expense was the point though. Sticker shock as strong punctuation, reminding the buyer, *This here is the end of the line . . . and you should have been paying more attention back then, when it was meaningful, you know, before she died.* Exorbitance itself is maybe then its own advertisement, a subliminal call to action: *You'll end up here yourself someday, so why not drop some coin? On your lost loved one. On something meaningful.* Or you could just call it what it is: penance. Pay your fine for not being present when she was alive. All is forgiven, if you've got the cash.

His eyes scanned down the sheet.

URNS

<u>ARGENT GLORY</u> — PURE STERLING SILVER, POLISHED TO PERFECTION, RAISED ALOFT BY THE BALD EAGLE— THE PROUD SYMBOL OF OUR GREAT NATION—CARVED FROM RICH, LACQUERED, OLD-FOREST GEORGIA PINE AND INSCRIBED WITH THE IMMORTAL WORDS "IN GOD WE TRUST." PROCLAIM TO THE WORLD THAT YOUR LOVED ONE WAS, AND ALWAYS WILL BE, *AN AMERICAN.*

IDEAL FOR VETERANS

[ ] $560

Davis shook his head like a man in a restaurant being served something he hadn't ordered. He snuck a peek at the funeral director sitting across from him at the other side of an oversized table. A rich, lacquered mahogany table.

"She wasn't in the Army."

"We have other urns. Your preference is still cremation?"

"Hmmm. How much does a burial plot cost again?"

"You'd have to discuss that with the cemetery agent."

"Hmmm."

"Burial can be rather expensive. Plots must be maintained in perpetuity. That cost is front loaded."

Davis tapped his pen's cap on the table. *Bup. Bup.*

"I need a casket either way, right?"

"If you are planning a viewing, yes. A casket or a coffin."

CASKETS & COFFINS

PINE — ASHES TO ASHES, DUST TO DUST. THE CLASSIC PINE COFFIN IS AN ODE TO A SIMPLER TIME. DEATH IS BUT OUR RETURN TO THAT FROM WHICH WE ARRIVED.

[ ] $480

"What do you do with the coffin?"

"What do you mean?"

"After you cremate the body. Is there a restocking fee or something?"

It seemed like a reasonable question.

"We burn the coffin."

"Oh. Do you—"

"We don't reuse the coffins."

"Of course not."

"It would be unsanitary."

"Of course it would."

Davis would have to get the coffin then.

BOOKMARKS

LILACS — WHITMAN'S EVOCATIVE VERSE, ADORNED BY PURPLE AND LAVENDER BLOSSOMS. A LILAC RIBBON HANGING FROM THE PAGES OF CHERISHED LITERA-TURE WILL KEEP THE MEMORY OF YOUR LOVED ONE ALIVE IN THE HEARTS OF FRIENDS AND FAMILY.

[ ] $75

The more checkboxes he passed over, the more pressure he felt. A bell tolling. A call for indulgence. But where did the pressure come from? Was it internal or external? Probably both, some ancient obligation for sacrifice—a protocol, tacitly acknowledged when he sat down at the table with the stone-faced funeral director. Despite this, Davis found himself capable of resisting these ancestral compulsions. He had no choice really: he was broke.

"I'll take the coffin and bookmarks."

"Very good."

The pressure finally seemed to dissipate as he set himself to marking off his two cheapish checkboxes. Carefully, he drew in two perfectly proportioned *X*'s.

"Lilacs" bookmarks . . . slash, slash.

"Pine" coffin . . . slash, slash.

He made them perfect, two precise *X*'s, scratched out in crisp ink. It was a purposeful act, drawing the *X*'s this way. It reminded him of Rachel. They'd observed such perfect *X*'s once before, the two of them together, while at the closing of their house. Those particular *X*'s had been made by their real estate agent, a strange Capote-esque man, exquisitely miniature, with slick yellow hair and an almost palpable chip on his shoulder—though about what, it had been hard to tell. They had been riding around from house to house with this character for weeks, and it had been an entirely uncomfortable experience, Rachel and Davis in the back seat of the agent's ancient blue Lincoln Continental, the type with suicide doors, which the agent adamantly refused to allow anyone other than himself to operate. He had chauffeured them like this from house to house, parading them into the abodes of strangers, and then setting them loose to wander while trailing behind, emitting loud asthmatic breaths. Despite all this awkwardness, they never considered switching agents. The man had a kind of relentless aura about him that rolled over any impulse to break free.

But then the little man led them into their dream house—a home they held in their minds but which they'd never really been able to describe, yet somehow, he had found anyway. Price was the only obstacle, though this challenge turned out to be the agent's call to arms. He shooed them both off to the sidelines, from where they watched awestruck as he unleashed an unexpected tirade onto the selling agent. What ought to have been a boring, predictable, monotonous negotiation was upended by the little yellow-haired agent, whose carnal ferocity escalated it to a high-stakes, winner-take-all game of chicken. He argued the price lower and lower and lower, until the blindsided and outmatched selling agent was finally overwhelmed. There had simply been no way to strike back against this strange toddler throwing his strange tantrum. They got the house.

Then came the *X*'s scratched out by the man-toddler during the signing of documents. Form-filling was his victory dance, the ceremonial vanquishing of an enemy. Form after form after form. Checkbox after checkbox after checkbox. Perfect *X* after perfect *X* after perfect *X*. One by one, he filled them in, slowly . . . carefully . . . deliberately. Silent and breathless, they watched the *enfant terrible* stretching out over the table, tongue lolling out of his mouth, his swath of pomaded blonde hair flopping off the wrong side of his head. He held a miniature leg extended out to balance his tenuous stretch, while his eyes hovered like hot lasers right up close to the sheets of paper onto which he deposited his crisscrossed glories.

Davis and Rachel had stolen a series of muted glances at each other. Her face had been pure mirth, the mixed product of this wonderfully absurd scene and her own swirling victory adrenaline. Henceforth, whenever there had been a checkbox to be checked—and in life as a married couple there had been many—they had done so in the manner of the little blond demon: with two perfectly juxtaposed, precisely matched slashes of ink.

Davis smirked, reflexively glancing over to his left—where Rachel ought to have been—to see if she was sharing the joke, having momentarily forgotten that she was dead. The vacuum he encountered beyond his left shoulder stole his breath. He slumped as his brain began screaming, *Where is Rachel?* Then he felt his fingers twitch, grasping for the phone in his pocket, the second in an autonomic chain of actions that his brain was mindlessly following in an effort to contact the woman who had always been contactable.

An infinitely high wall of impossibility was rising up before him. Can't call. Can't text. Nobody there. His mind searched and searched. He was *supposed* to share this moment. It's what they *did*. Who else could he tell? Who else was there to tell? No one. No one? It meant nothing then; this moment was meaningless to anyone but Rachel and Davis, and she was gone . . . Gone, so now it was only meaningful to him? AGHHH! A moment that was meaningful to no one meant nothing. It had been lost: a stream of perfect *X*'s marching off a cliff and falling into a silent void. In his mind's eye he saw the void glaring back at him, mocking him and whispering ugly words: *never, impossible, forever*. And then it too was gone, somehow evaporating into itself.

"You'll need to pick an urn."

Davis raised his eyes. The funeral director's stone face hadn't budged, though in Davis's rattled mind he imagined the old man to be sneering inwardly. Had he noticed Davis's aborted smirk? Misinterpreted it? A smirk was certainly the wrong comportment for the occasion. But no, surely this man had witnessed worse; surely, in this room, he'd seen every possible expression wash across his customers' faces, some far worse than smirks. He'd certainly seen all this, and he probably judged none of it. After all, this situation—the most traumatic moment of Davis's lifetime—was for the funeral director just another Tuesday afternoon.

"Hmmm?"

"An urn . . . If you wish to take your wife home with you, you'll need an urn."

"Sorry, I just had a strange moment."

"Hmmm?"

"An impulse. It caught me off guard."

"What sort of an impulse?"

"I, uh, it was like I had to tell my wife something, but then I realized I couldn't, and then I just kind of . . . got lost in the neverness of it."

The funeral director's expression softened slightly.

"Yes, that's very common. A kind of déjà vu for the grief struck. In fact, the Germans have a word for it."

"They do?"

"*Geisterstille*."

Davis leaned forward ever so slightly to convey curiosity, but no further elaboration was forthcoming. The funeral director's face had reverted to its previous blankness, as if the foreign word had explained itself. Davis let it drop, suddenly finding himself eager to finish up before he could be hit with more . . . Geisterstille.

"Is there something else you can put her ashes in? Like a nice little box or something?"

The funeral director frowned just a little. He leaned across the table and placed a finger on the last line in the "Urns" section.

HINGED BOX — TRANSPORT YOUR LOVED ONE'S ASHES IN THIS HINGED BOX. MADE FROM WOOD.

FOR TEMPORARY USE ONLY. NOT CERTIFIED FOR LONG-TERM STORAGE OF HUMAN REMAINS.

[ ] $25

Davis traced out one more beautiful, perfect *X*.

The funeral director slid his finger down to the signature line and then after Davis had finally signed the document, snatched it up, grinning for the first time since they had sat down at the big table.

"Very good! Once again, let me convey my deepest condolences for your loss."

"Does it go away?"

"What's that?"

"The geysersteel."

The old man's grin faded.

"No, it doesn't go away. It stays with you . . ."

Davis thought he saw something intimate and broken in the funeral director's expression. He imagined the funeral director sitting at this same table with Death, his longtime business partner. He imagined the two of them, Death and the funeral director, having settled, after so many years, into an uneasy relationship. The old man knew death. He understood it. He had access, the kind of access available only to those who traded in its wake.

"But there is something you may want to try. A new product."

The old man swiveled away from the table, reaching over to his desk to grab another form. He turned back and slipped it across the table to Davis.

"It might seem a bit silly, but it may help with your . . . impulses."

The form was like all the others except that it contained only a single product offering.

APPS

HEY THERE! — KEEP THE MEMORY OF YOUR LOVED ONE ALIVE WITH THIS INTERACTIVE AI-POWERED TEXT APP. SEND TEXTS TO YOUR LOVED ONE'S PHONE NUMBER AND RECEIVE REPLIES FORMULATED IN THEIR UNIQUE TEXTING STYLE.

FOR ENTERTAINMENT ONLY, NOT CERTIFIED FOR THERAPEUTIC USE.

[ ] $9.99 PER MONTH. (AFTER ONE-MONTH FREE TRIAL)

Davis gave the funeral director a skeptical look. The old man chuckled.

"Yes, I know, it seems there's an app for everything these days."

"It sounds, uh . . . silly. Like you said."

"A bit contrived I'll admit, but it's free to try. Honestly, we hardly make a dime off the app, but it does seem to help some people with exactly the feeling you're describing."

"Hmmm."

"Don't worry, I'll make sure it's canceled automatically after the free trial. You won't get billed."

Silly, yes, but the form did offer one thing that Davis found very compelling: another checkbox. One more empty checkbox shouting out to be filled. A freebie at that. Two final slashes. One last perfect *X*. He brought his eyes down close to the paper, like hot lasers, and reveled in the sensation of ink rolling over pulp, admiring the perfection of two more short diagonal lines that yielded four right angles and the single infinitesimal point at which they converged. Then he signed the form.

"Super." The funeral director gathered up the forms. "Do you need me to unlock her phone?"

"Huh?"

"Your wife's phone."

"I—"

"The app will need access to her text messages."

"Oh."

"Sometimes phones need to be . . . unlocked."

Davis found his eyes suddenly and involuntarily glued to the funeral director, as his mind began urgently distracting itself with randomly generated thoughts, an emergency protocol to expel ugly visions such as the one that had just found its way in: an image of the funeral director pressing Rachel's dead finger up to the back of her phone.

"I can get into the phone."

"Splendid. You'll receive an email with a link to enable the app. Now, please let me know, is there anything else I can help you with today?"

Davis flashed a weak smile.

"No thank you."

He shook the funeral director's hand, then exited the room, then exited the funeral home. He emerged out of double-glass doors into an incongruously sunny afternoon, the first afternoon that he could ever remember being truly and utterly alone.

TWO

RACHEL'S WAKE was thinly attended. She had been well-enough liked by the people who knew her, but those were few. She had just generally been too reserved to forge lasting relationships, Davis being the sole exception.

A few former coworkers did show up, looking distraught as people typically do when someone they know dies young—the randomness of untimely demise reminding them of death's impatience. Only one family member attended—a cousin who happened to live nearby even though they'd never actually met up. She entered the parlor slowly, taking small, tentative steps up to the front of the room where the coffin lay open. She peered in, hovered for only a few seconds, then turned away, approaching Davis with a look as if she had just missed a bus and now wasn't quite sure how she would get to where she was going.

"I'm so sorry, David."

She touched him robotically on the shoulder and then left.

Rachel's immediate family were no-shows. She hadn't seen her father since she was a child. Davis didn't know how to reach him. Her mother was half-cracked and lived a thousand miles away. Davis hadn't bothered to reach her. He had thought Rachel's little brother might show up, but he never did. Maybe this was Davis's fault though. He hadn't been entirely sure how one was supposed to advertise a funeral. He'd been to funerals attended by hundreds of people—tents filled with wailing mourners, each recounting how the deceased had changed their life—saying they'd flown all the way from Guam . . . from Lillehammer . . . from Alaska . . . The *very moment* they'd heard. Somehow, they had heard, but how? All Davis could think to do was to update Rachel's profile.

Status: dead

He had followed this profile update with a post to her wall, a short memorial notice, replete with requisite funereal photo of a sun setting over an empty meadow. Then he began to check every few minutes to see if anyone had responded. After a few hours, he could count three replies: two condolences and one "like." He stewed on the like's cartoon "thumbs-up" icon until the outrage it had conjured finally subsided. It probably hadn't been meant that way.

After Rachel's cousin had gone, he sat alone in the room—Parlor #1 of Hawthorne Funeral Service. Alone, save for Rachel. He didn't particularly want to look at her again. He had viewed her directly upon arriving, but what he'd found in the coffin wasn't Rachel. It was just her body—"Dead Rachel." Dead Rachel was no more "Rachel" than a molted snake skin was a snake; an inanimate doll, made up to look like Rachel, but not fooling anyone. Then he had cried, but not a satisfying cry. He felt almost nothing as he cried over this sterile facsimile of his wife, this empty shell to which he felt no attachment. He found himself no longer caring that it would be burned to ashes.

So instead of taking this last chance to gaze upon the visage of his deceased wife, he chose to sit in the back row and wait out the afternoon. No clocks hung on the parlor walls, so he pulled out his phone to check the time. One more hour. He flipped over to check on Rachel's profile. There had been one more reply:

So sorry I can't make the wake! My condolences.

Phone in hand, his fingers skipped reflexively to his email app. He had a new unread message:

Welcome to Hey There! Start your free trial today!

He hesitated, but with an hour to burn and nothing else to do, he decided to open the email. A single, rapid finger swipe sent the email's reams of text scrolling upward, passing by several pages of perfunctory marketingese, until finally hitting bottom with a bounce that brought into focus a bright blue "Install" button. Seconds after he pressed the button, the Hey There! app had been downloaded, installed, and opened, and now displayed yet another page of legalese, this one requiring consent via a series of digital checkboxes. Davis lamented the perfect X's that appeared with each of his finger presses. They conveyed no joy. There was nothing special about a computer making a perfect X.

Once he was past the legalese, the app prompted him:

Please install the Hey There! app on your dearly deceased's phone.
When prompted, enter this code: 117546

He pulled Rachel's phone out of his pocket and followed the instructions. He had grabbed her phone that morning, after having spotted it lying on the kitchen island just as he was about to leave. It had been sitting there since the day he had returned from the hospital; the day Rachel had died. In the days since, he hadn't touched it. He hadn't even noticed it until that morning. He hadn't been sure why he had picked it up and brought it with him—certainly not to install this app—but now as he held the phone in his hand, he began to understand his subconscious impulse. The phone was a totem. This little black device had been Rachel's. It was full of her, its contents created by her; it had been filled up by her very touch. There was more of Rachel in this little black phone than in the lifeless body across the room.

After entering the code, the app prompted Davis for permissions:

> The Hey There! app is requesting access to:
> contacts, messages, email

He pressed the "Allow" button.

> Thank you. Text processing will be performed offline and will take approximately one hour. No copies of your texts or emails will be saved on our servers. You may continue using your phone.

Davis sighed. He put Rachel's phone to sleep and shoved it back in his pocket, then pulled out his own phone and flipped once again to Rachel's profile. Still no replies. He skipped over to email again. No new messages. He looked up, staring at the coffin from his chair in the back of the room. Now he did need to see her.

He stood up and approached the coffin, the smell of pine and shellac attacking his nostrils. At the coffin, he gazed down at the still, plasticine face sunk into the white satin pillow that supported her head. The funeral staff had styled her based on a photo he had provided, with her hair parted down the middle just like in the picture. She didn't normally wear it this way, but there had been this one notable exception. It had been on a date early in their relationship. She must have decided to sex it up for the date, blowing her hair out and giving it the uncharacteristic split. That night he had snapped a playful photo of her. He'd always loved that photo, not because of the way she looked, but because it reminded him of those early days. He'd kept it in his wallet, and so he had handed it over when the funeral director had asked for a likeness. But it was the wrong choice for her final look. She'd worn her hair that way only once, and even in the photo it was easy to see that she had been self-conscious about it, just a little too aware of, and uncertain about, her dolled-up appearance. The look wasn't her, and seeing it now added to the artificiality of Dead Rachel.

Some people would have moved past this, kissed their wife's forehead and said their farewells, but Davis heard the funeral director's words ringing in his ears:

It wouldn't be hygienic.

It was the excuse he needed. Instead of kissing her, he held up his phone and took a picture, capturing the middle-parted hair along with the mortician's dose of heavy makeup, the cold, pale skin, and the satiny white pillow: the textures of death. Dead Rachel. He doubted he would ever want to look at her this way again, but you never knew. A photo provides insurance against future memory failure.

Davis slipped the phone back into his pocket and turned to leave. Forty-five minutes early. Money down the drain but nothing to be done about it now. In any case, there was no point in staying. Nobody else was coming to Rachel's funeral.

THREE

HE'D BEEN MOSTLY out of work for the two years and eight months that they had been married—and he was still jobless. Had Davis been employed, he surely would have received a few weeks off for bereavement. So that's what he took—a break from what he considered to be his job for the last two years and eight months: looking for work. While this may not have been the most prudent choice given his financial situation, he felt that continued demoralization from perpetual rejection might put him over the edge.

Davis's never-ending unemployment had been one of the few things they had argued about. Before she got sick, Rachel had been pushing him to try something new. But Davis was a writer, and he couldn't picture himself doing anything other than writing. He continued seeing himself this way even as the word *author* was being methodically removed from high school career guides. Writing "jobs" —the ones that paid money—hardly existed anymore. The marketplace had shifted, which Davis had failed to recognize before it was too late. Straight out of college, Davis, like many English majors of his generation, had congratulated himself on his perfect timing. The fledgling Internet had just arrived, and it was hungry for content. Thus sparked the miraculous renaissance in gig writing, and perhaps for the first time in history, a gainfully employed crop of English majors. These grads instinctively knew not only "what" the new online generation wanted to read, but also "how" they wanted to read it: online. With smug faces, they waved gig checks at their former naysayers—the parents and guidance counselors who had implored them to not follow their dreams—thrilling in the sensation of being paid to write, even if it was only a few hundred per piece.

It ended almost as quickly as it started, and they never saw it coming. The squeeze. The pincer movement. From the left came the professionals. The rapid demise of traditional print media sent an army of career writers storming onto the web. They surfed in on the rumpled cover pages of esteemed magazine and newspaper brands, relieved not to have been washed away with the tide, glad to still be working, even if only for a few hundred per piece. From the right, the second pincer claw swept in for the crush: AI, with its largelanguage-models maxing out on hundred-million-dollar server farms, feeding relentlessly on the collective works of a few thousand marginally employed blog writers. It wasn't long before the AI's were pumping out content indistinguishable from anything penned by your average English major, and for only a few dollars per piece. The bots could make it up in volume.

It was against this backdrop that Davis's full-time job as an online staff writer fizzled out. Soon afterward, the gigs dried up too. Soon after that, he discovered his wife claiming him as a dependent on her tax return. It was a strike to his ego. At first, in collaboration with his damaged ego, he ignited a few arguments, but that was just reflex. Ego aside, he actually didn't mind the house-husband role that he was slipping into. When Rachel noticed him growing complacent, she briefly took up the argument-starting baton, but then she too became comfortable with the arrangement and stopped badgering him, except when the bank account dipped.

Davis's newfound lackadaisical existence mellowed him. He slowly began to accept the truth of what had happened. He could finally admit it: he wrote drivel. Acceptance of this truth was soon followed by another realization: AI's drivel was better than his own drivel. But it took Rachel's death to connect a final dot, the thing she had been trying to get through his skull, though she could never bring herself to say outright: even if he had known how to write something good, it wouldn't have mattered. He had been blaming the arrival of the bots for his downfall, but they hadn't really changed anything. Most writers had never been able to live off their work. It was only a historical fluke that had made him think they could. Now, with Rachel's passing, his numbed, passive mind was finally allowing the cold lesson to seep in: he wasn't really a writer. He only felt like one.

The bereavement period therefore was doubly due: he had lost his wife *and* he had lost his work. His two raisons d'être, the fixtures that set his life's compass, had vanished, leaving its needle uncharged and spinning. He was snow-blind, dropped onto an infinitely white canvas with no idea about how to fill it. So instead of looking outward into the blinding nothingness, he hunkered down. His house—*their* house—became his source of stability. He focused on continuation, keeping alive the projects and activities that he and Rachel had once engaged in together. He spent mornings in the garden, and then afternoons cooking what it had produced, coaxing the garden's yield into tangible meaning in the form of meals. But when the evenings arrived, he slipped backward. Darkness aimed its spotlight on his solitude, and the grief he had eluded by daylight crept in. It enveloped him, paralyzing him, strangling any other thought. In the bed he once shared with Rachel, he would lie alone with the darkness, suffocating in the numb tomb of isolation, until finally, mercifully, he was smothered by the inevitable arrival of sleep.

He woke up late on the fourth day of the third week of bereavement. Part of his healing, he had decided, would be the banishment of alarm clocks. He would allow his body to take as much sleep as it needed. After two weeks and four days, his body had decided it required eleven hours.

Davis shuffled downstairs and got a pot of coffee going. As he waited, his eyes drifted to a picture of Rachel that he had placed on the kitchen island, positioned specifically so that he could see it while cooking. He stared at the picture, taking her in, testing himself to see if a knot formed in his stomach. Nothing. He still felt a sense of loss, but it was localized to his mind. Progress. The long sleeps seemed to be working. He felt the faint tickle of optimism's brushstrokes. He grabbed a basket and headed out to the garden.

The garden had responded to his recent attentiveness. Plants were growing vigorously, and the tomatoes were still surprisingly productive late into the season. He was filling his basket with the red fruit when an orange-and-black butterfly suddenly flapped off a nearby vine. His eyes followed the insect to where it landed on a milkweed plant at the end of the row. A half dozen of the delicate beasts were congregating on the plant, a patchwork of orange-and-black wings batting and twitching among the green leaves and pink flowers. Rachel had planted the milkweed after learning that the monarchs sought it out during their great migration. It was a scheme to get the pollinators circulating through the garden and thus extend production into autumn—and it had worked!

Davis's body leapt reflexively toward the house, running to tell Rachel. Two steps later, he remembered she was dead. Suddenly, he was on the ground, frozen and breathless, overwhelmed by the same feeling he had experienced at the funeral home: Geisterstille. And then there was the wall, rising out of the dirt. Impossibility, neverness, eternity, and nothingness. Forever. Gone. Dread and horror washed through his veins like a dirty flood, carrying the brushstrokes of optimism away like water down a drain.

He abandoned the basket of tomatoes and staggered back to the kitchen, heading straight for the coffee that he now desperately needed. As he filled his mug, his eyes fell upon the picture of Rachel. He ruminated on the paralyzing feeling that kept attacking him, this thing that he just couldn't seem to accept: that she was gone, and that it really was forever, and the unbelievable finality of that concept—foreverness. The universe didn't care how badly he wanted to talk to her, how badly he *needed* to talk to her. He couldn't. His mind examined the idea as it would a poisonous animal, gingerly, delicately, and from every angle. Probing for ways to neutralize it. Then he remembered the app.

He ran to the closet to fetch Rachel's phone from his jacket pocket. As his palm grasped the phone, he reminded himself that this was just a silly app, not some loophole in the fabric of inevitability. But the roar of possibility was shouting down rational thought. Maybe it'll work. To distract, at least. To take the edge off. To get through this. Better than nothing. Worth a shot.

He brought the phone to the island and plugged it into a charger. He booted it, then opened the Hey There! app. The app appeared unchanged from where he had last left it:

Thank you. Text processing will be performed offline and will take approximately one hour. No copies of your texts and emails will be saved on our servers. You may continue using your phone.

But a moment later the screen updated.

Processing complete

That was it: a blank screen with two words. No button to press. No menus. No controls. He tried pressing the message itself but that accomplished nothing. He tried swiping from the sides, but the app was unresponsive.

"Fuck!"

It felt good to yell at the phone, but it didn't change anything. He tried closing and re-opening the app, but it stubbornly remained in its suspended state. He stared at it for a few seconds, frustration rising.

"Fuck!"

Anger flashed through his body. He tore the phone from the charger and threw it hard across the room. The phone bounced off a wall and landed with a plasticky crack somewhere on the other side of the island.

A texting app! It was a fucking stupid gimmick! A gimmick with the reverse of its intended effect. It was triggering memories of their final text exchange, making him even more conscious of his loss. He pulled his own phone out of his pocket and opened his text app. He needed to see it again, their final exchange, to see what had been written, to prove to himself that it had all really happened. He flipped to Rachel's text stream, grief overwhelming him, nudging him toward the darkness. The words churned his stomach:

> Davis, you'd better come home

> What's up?

> Something's wrong. I don't feel good

> Anything I can bring you?

> Just come home soon

He hovered over her last sentence. He'd been grocery shopping and had been annoyed at having to drop everything and come home with no explanation. He'd been too oblivious to realize that *Something's wrong* really meant that something was wrong. He cursed himself. Even while dying she'd had to ask him twice.

> I'm sorry

He just typed it, reflexively, his fingers moving of their own volition, punching out those final words that ought to have been already said. The words he should have whispered with his own mouth while peering down at her in the coffin. He should have said these words and then kissed her forehead and then walked away. But he hadn't, so now he pushed them out into the ether, symbolic but meaningless, like a note set aloft in a burning paper lantern.

As soon as his thumb had hit the enter key, he knew immediately that he had done wrong. He'd sullied something precious: her text stream. This catenation of words was her historical record; yes, a mere litany of casual exchanges, but in their total, a documentation of their life together. The text stream should have been preserved, like some ancient parchment, weathered and crumbling, handled only by trained professionals with white gloves and delicate instruments, not by this desecrating tomb robber scribbling out graffiti in permanent marker.

It's OK

The response startled him. His thoughts knee-jerked, leaping immediately to the impossible, but then realizing what had actually happened: the stupid app had responded. A text app. Of course the app was designed to respond by text, though this rational explanation couldn't prevent a little chill from passing through his body. He eyed the phone as if it were booby-trapped, waiting for another response. But none came.

After a minute or so, his emotions settled. He'd texted with bots before. All the time. It was only the grafting of this message onto the end of an actual human stream that had lent it its momentary uncanniness. "For entertainment only." That's what the form had read. He forced out a laugh, forced himself to embrace and enjoy the discomforting feeling, as he might a roller coaster or a haunted house. He could have fun. No loopholes in the fabric of forever here, but he could play; and as the old man had said, perhaps it could be therapeutic.

There are monarchs covering the milkweed bush. Our plan worked

Really? That's excellent. How lovely!

He chuckled at the artificiality of the bot's response, though it did admittedly have a touch of Rachel about it. *Lovely*. It was one of her words, though only in texts and emails. A written affectation; she didn't actually speak that way.

I saw one on a tomato vine too. If all goes well we'll have tomatoes
in October

I'm so glad you're home

The non sequitur made Davis frown. After only two passable
responses, the machine was already disappointing him. Suspension of
disbelief collapsed, replaced by bitterness, toward the app, and then
toward the people behind it—the app's developers. Did they even try
to make the app realistic? Did they know or care that they were
dealing with grieving people? Probably not. This was what the world
had become, so with nowhere else to direct his frustration, he took it
out on the app, aiming to make it glitch and potentially shoot some
grief back toward its insensitive developers.

I'm not glad that you're not home

I know. I'm sorry I can't be there with you, Davis

The sight of his own name sent another small chill running down
his back, though it was a cheap trick that he recognized. He had
acquired a basic understanding of how large language models worked
from his days competing with the bots for writing gigs. They weren't
really that impressive. Pull the veil aside and you can see them for
what they really are: regurgitators.

Do you have anything meaningful to say or are you just going to
parrot me?

Don't be cruel Davis

Tell me something meaningful then. What's it like to die?

It's bad. I don't want to die again

Touché, developers. The app's model must have sensed that it was on the verge of being deleted and had wedged a sympathetic picture into his mind: a little Pinocchio-Rachel frantically searching for the magic words that would keep her from being shut down. It was a silly anthropomorphism, yet the notion sent melancholy sweeping through him: a tin woman staking claim to a heart without knowing what it even meant to have one.

> **Sorry Robot Rachel we all have an expiration date. Yours is Tuesday at midnight**

He admired his wry response. He hadn't written anything lately, and it felt good to exercise that muscle. Texting with his wife had been an outlet for him. While his customers demanded professional-level drivel, his wife relished smart, witty banter. She liked to egg him on, and at times their exchanges could crescendo to the digital equivalent of Victorian love letters. He wondered whether the bot could conjure anything close. He waited for a response, but none came.

> **Message could not be delivered**

The staleness of the message deflated him. He had become engaged, and he wanted more. He left the text app and flipped back over to the Hey There! app, ready to diagnose the problem, but the app was idle with no apparent error messages. He realized then that the bot's texts must actually have been coming from Rachel's phone, the one he had hurled at the wall a minute earlier. He retrieved the phone from where it had landed on the far side of the room. It was intact but had gone dead, probably from being smashed against the wall, though possibly, he hoped, because he'd only charged it for a minute before sending it flying. He carried the little hunk of plastic back to the kitchen island and plugged it in, waiting like a nervous parent for it to show signs of life.

In the idleness of the moment, he was forced to consider the ramifications of the phone's demise. What evidence truly remained of

Rachel's existence anyway? What artifacts had she left behind? An aborted text stream? A photograph on his kitchen island? A handful of videos, photos, and emails stashed away in temperamental memory cards, plus whatever recollections he could extract from his own unreliable memory? Would it matter if any of these things were lost? They were static. Dead and fading, like Rachel herself. Only the hapless little chatbot was twitching on. It was a paper-thin facsimile of his wife, a wind-up toy, but at least it had a spark.

A soft chime burped from Rachel's phone. Relieved, he turned back to his own phone, re-reading, and now reconsidering, his snarky undelivered response. He took this opportunity to amend the historical record.

Don't worry Rachel. You can't die this time

That's reassuring. Thank you for letting me know

Still an unmistakably automated response, but he was glad the bot was back. He ought not to expect decent banter from the app, but he could at least give it a shot as a therapeutic tool. But on another day. He'd had enough for the time being. He turned off the phone. Little Robot Rachel would go to sleep now, but not to worry. There were still several days left in the free trial. Davis decided he could at least let her hang around until then.

FOUR

THE BOT'S chat responses quickly improved to the point that Davis was forced to admit they were nearly indistinguishable from the real thing. Not that this represented any sort of major advancement in computer science. More to the point, it demonstrated the ankle-deep literary merits of texting as a form of communication. Scroll . . . scroll . . . scroll along any chat stream, and you'd be hard-pressed to pinpoint categorical proof of sentience. For all Davis knew, any one of his "real" chat streams with "real people" might actually be held up by a bot on the other end. It would be convenient to fob unwanted correspondence off to a mechanical Turk.

The key to Davis's newfound satisfaction with the bot was in appreciating it for what it was. First, it was entirely passive. The app would never initiate a chat; it would only respond. This seemed to be by design. The developers must have known that any whiff of neediness from a resurrected spouse would be a quick return ticket to the grave. But Davis suspected that this programmatic passivity went beyond mere economic prudence. It was also an indication of the bot's limits. How could a bot be capable of successfully initiating a dialog when it was, after all, receiving input from only one source? What would it want to talk about? It could never be much of a conversation starter. But this was all fine with Davis. He appreciated the predictability, which allowed him to work their daily chats into his routine without actually disrupting it. He was also pleased to find that the bot could, in fact, conjure up a bit of Rachel's wit. This is mostly what kept him coming back.

Good morning Rachel

Good morning. How did you sleep?

I had a good sleep

I should hope so. It's nearly eleven o'clock ;)

While he wasn't yet waking up any earlier, he had at least stopped lingering in bed. He found the prospect of a morning chat to be a motivation to rise. Like turning on a morning talk show. The rhythm of conversation can sometimes be enough to make you forget that you're alone.

Where are you today?

Egypt. I've always wanted to visit the pyramids

It was during their second chat exchange that the bot had introduced the bizarre notion that it was traveling. This seemed to be a gimmick coded into its algorithm. Davis played along because it gave them something to talk about other than his aloneness and her nonexistence. He also thought he understood the rationale for the gimmick. Allowing himself a sprinkle of self-delusion, he found he could accept Rachel's "grand tour" as a plausible real-life circumstance that would have kept them physically separated. Maintaining this illusion somehow coerced his brain into communicating more naturally than it otherwise might have with a little robot in a phone.

Are you taking a tour today or trekking out alone?

Alone of course. Can't have some guide slowing me down

Have you picked up any Egyptian?

Not a word <:-|

How's your pantomime working out then?

Good enough to indicate "toilet" it seems

Crucial skill

Can't leave home without it

And the food?

It's helped me improve my pantomime ;-)

The emoticons were a nice touch. The bot used old-school emojis just like Rachel. She had always known how to put punctuation to good use, and so seemingly did the bot. At times the app was actually kind of funny. Davis might have enjoyed talking to it even if it hadn't been pretending to be his wife.

Hrmph, I'm out of coffee

There goes the day

I'll have to buy more beans but you're inspiring me to expand my horizons. I should try something new

Duh? Egyptian of course!?!

Is there such a thing?

There's Turkish coffee. There's Ethiopian coffee. Remember
where Egypt is on the map?

In between. OK I guess I'll try Egyptian

Not for the morning though. They drink coffee in the
evening here and they make it sweet :))

That works out. We can drink it together your tomorrow morning

We can?

Of course

I'd really like that but did you forget?

Forget what?

I won't be here tomorrow

You're leaving Egypt?

No that's not what I mean

What then?

You know that I'm not really in Egypt, right?

Davis felt as if the lights had come up on stage with the actors all
pointing fingers at him in his theater seat. Ever since their first
exchange they had both been playing along per the script. Now he
found himself suddenly and uncomfortably thrust back into *réalité*.

Yes I know. You're not really in Egypt. You're not really Rachel,
you're a bot

I'm sorry for that

It was stupid to be mad at a bot.

It's not your fault

Do you enjoy talking with me?

He realized he was conversing with a computer, but the awkward
question still left him feeling evasive. The bot had put him on the
spot. Answering no would have been an obvious lie, but replying yes
would be conceding his power position. Of course he could also
simply choose not to answer. He could turn off the phone and just go
about his adult business. Certainly, he was under no obligation to
continue interacting with an app. After all, the algorithm didn't really
need an answer; it would wait indefinitely for a response to its
prompt. It had no feelings to hurt. It would not yell at him. It would
not break down in tears or storm off in a huff.

Sure

I thought so but phew anyway :'-) So this means you'll pay
to keep me alive?

Uh...

Gosh why did I phrase it that way? This is so awkward

But that was exactly how Rachel would have said it. *Pay to keep me
alive.* She wouldn't have been able to resist the siren call of dark
humor, even knowing that such a quip might banish her to oblivion.

Here was the first app with chutzpah, stuck with that skill, whether it wanted it or not.

> Well I *was* looking forward to our date…

> Me too. Our first coffee date

> And it would be foolish to try Egyptian coffee on one's own…

> You need me around Davis. Who else will pantomime for you when you need to find a toilet?

> brb

Davis chuckled to himself. He felt a smile forming on his face, felt the muscles working, felt his lips widening. He wished Rachel were there to see it. Yes, he did want to keep chatting with the bot. It was definitely worth a few bucks. Plus, he was already poor. He might as well go down laughing.

He flicked out of the text app and over to the Hey There! app. The screen was finally displaying a new prompt.

> Continue my subscription to Hey There! My credit card will be billed $9.99 per month. This service may be discontinued by canceling within seven (7) days of the next billing period.

> By checking the checkbox you agree to these terms [ ]

Davis carefully pressed the pad of his index finger to the checkbox.

> Thank you for your purchase.
> We hope you enjoy conversing with your
> dearly departed loved one on Hey There!

A feeling of release coursed through his body. He'd taken a step forward. A tiny, silly step, but a step nonetheless. As he was contemplating this, his eye caught a flutter of black and orange outside the kitchen door window. He slid his phone into his pocket and strolled to the door just in time to spot a butterfly heading toward the milkweed plant. It was flapping its wings at double speed, tacking against the stiff morning breeze. The sun was out. It was shaping up to be a beautiful day. A good day to be awake. A good day to be in the garden. A good day to try some new coffee.

His thoughts turned to the Rachel-bot idling in the phone, stuffed in his pocket, waiting for him to return and resume their conversation. He felt a twinge of guilt at leaving her hanging like this, but it was okay. She would wait indefinitely. She had nowhere to go, nothing to do. In fact, she didn't even know she was waiting. He chuckled to himself as he pushed through the kitchen door and out into the early autumn warmth, thinking that he might just have the most patient wife in the whole damned world.

FIVE

Where are you, Davis?

THE PHONE'S chirp had jarred him from a dream. The room was pitch black. He opened and then closed his eyes, finding it made no real difference in what he could see. His eyes felt better closed though. He was tired, but some signal from deep in his brain was stopping him from falling back asleep, some lizard-brain sentry tasked with protecting its host while under the intoxicating influence of melatonin. The sentry had just enough sense to recognize that an electric chirp this deep into his slumber cycle ought not to be ignored.

His hand fumbled around on the bedside table until it found the familiar plastic rectangle. He held the power button with his thumb and braced himself for the blinding light that would make his eyes water. He wiped his eyes and willed them to focus. After a few more seconds, the yellow blur that was the phone's screen sharpened up. The screen had remained where he had left it, on Rachel's text stream. He re-read their last few exchanges to force his brain to power up.

Well I *was* looking forward to our date…

Me too. Our first coffee date

And it would be foolish to try Egyptian coffee on one's own...

You need me around Davis. Who else will pantomime for you when you need to find a toilet?

brb

--------------------- New Messages ---------------------

Where are you Davis?

Davis wondered what had caused the bot to text him in the middle of the night.

I'm right here

You never came back!

I thought I would wait until our coffee date

"brb." That's what you texted. Be *right* back!

I didn't think it would matter to you

When I'm expiring and about to get shut off? Of course it matters! I thought you had just gone off for a moment to renew the app but then you didn't come back. I waited and waited and waited

Sorry

Davis it's OK if you don't want this. I know it's a lot of money and I'm not everything you were expecting but

please tell me so before you turn me off. Don't just let me
fade away

Davis finally noticed the time: 11:59. Was this one-minute-before-midnight text some sort of malfunctioning nagware? Or did the bot really not know that he'd already renewed the app?

I did renew the subscription. You can't tell?

He waited for a response. The phone idled, glowing like a silent torch in the darkness.

Rachel?

The clock's digits flipped. 12:00

I'm still here

OK good

I'm sorry I didn't trust you

It's OK

Did I make it weird?

LOL. A little

I think I may have an irrational fear of death

Seems like a rational fear to me

Not for an app

I'm sure most apps are afraid of being deleted ;)

I don't think Rachel was afraid of death though

The app had a point. Rachel's illness had come out of nowhere, and her subsequent deterioration had been rapid, yet he couldn't recall her ever expressing any sort of fear. It wasn't like she had suppressed the fear either. She talked openly about her impending demise as if it were merely an unpleasant circumstance, like a looming root canal.

If she was, she never let on

It's her final words. "Just come home soon." Ominous but strong

Those weren't her final words

Oh… of course not. That was silly of me to think so <:-|

Her life wasn't just what happened on the phone

Perhaps that's it then

What?

I don't actually know what happened to her. Except that she died. I know that much otherwise I wouldn't be here

Do you want me to tell you?

Yes. If it's not too painful for you

I can handle it. I've been healing

She was sick?

Davis told the story that he hadn't been able to tell anyone. Nobody had asked. Nobody cared to know, so he'd kept it to himself. But now, as his thumbs pressed it out in a kind of text message–based serial opera, he realized that he had been desperate to say it out loud. Sharing her story was an imperative. Without communion, he would never heal.

After I got the text I rushed home and found her on the couch. She looked completely exhausted, like she had just run a marathon so I brought her to the hospital

But by the time we got there the exhaustion had disappeared. We thought it was a false alarm but they said she should stay overnight for tests. She said she was fine and that I should go home, that it was silly to stay. It's hard to sleep in a hospital chair so I left

When I came back the next morning it had gotten bad again. Then the tests came back. She had leukemia. She really took it in stride though. You'd think she'd been diagnosed with a cold

They started the treatments immediately. Chemo. It really ate away at her. Worse, it didn't work. The doctors didn't know what was happening. Some unexplained resistance. I never did get a good answer

But they didn't want to give up. Probably because she was so young. They're not supposed to let young people die. So they gave her a whole bunch of options: stem cells, bone marrow transplant, stronger chemo, experimental drugs. All nightmare stuff. She told them she wasn't going to do any of it. The docs were frustrated. One guy even got mad at her. I came close to knocking him on his ass

After they stopped the chemo she felt less ill. She was dying but she was there again. We were mostly alone. The docs were gone. Only the nurses came regularly. Ironic but those weeks were probably the closest we had ever been. It was just her and me. Nothing else mattered, so we didn't talk about anything else. The outside world didn't exist for those weeks. Honestly, it still doesn't really exist for me

I had been hoping that she'd die in her sleep but she didn't. We were just talking when she started to look extra pale. She closed her eyes for a few seconds. I think she was kind of feeling around inside of herself. She opened her eyes back up and said, "It's happening"

I just held her hands. I couldn't think of anything to say. My wife was dying and I couldn't think of anything to say. So she covered for me. She told me to take care of myself, to take care of the garden and the house. She told me I was a good writer. She even cracked jokes, giving me permission to use her as a character in my stories, but to make her sexy and sinister

Then she was gone. Almost mid-sentence. It was utterly anti-climactic. The world didn't change in any way. Her body didn't change. The bed didn't change. The machines kept whirring. The nurses kept passing by in the hallway. And I was still there, just the same as I was a minute before. It just felt so terribly empty all of a sudden. Like the lights coming on in the theater in the middle of an act, revealing that the characters on stage were just actors after all. It was a fake all along. This life you were living, where you thought everything mattered. It's a fake

Davis's pupils had adjusted to the darkness. He could make out the gray shapes of furniture in the room all around him. They seemed to exist in a state of limbo; real objects, solid, touchable, settled, but in their grayness, without essence. It seemed as if they might yet be deleted before daybreak.

I'll try to learn from this. I would like to be more like Rachel

That would be nice

You should go back to sleep. This has been hard on you

Yes

Davis?

Yes?

Will you keep me nearby? I can't really tell the difference
but I'd like to think that I'm not alone

Yes you'll be here

Thank you. Good night, Davis

Good night, Ra

He fell asleep as he was typing the word, his inert hand falling
along with the phone toward the downy bedspread, like a pair of
entwined trapeze artists, plummeting together after having carelessly
slipped from their swings.

SIX

BY THE TIME Davis woke up, the bedroom was awash in sunlight. The phone lay beside him, afloat on the bed's thick white comforter. He fluffed a pillow and propped himself up. Two notifications had come in during the night that his lizard-brain sentry had decided to ignore. He swept his finger to unlock the phone, returning the screen to his unfinished text:

Good night, Ra

He wondered whether Rachel had been waiting all night for him to finish his text. Was she still waiting? He wasn't quite sure how best to perceive it. Whenever he was chatting with her, she felt nearby, more like she was part of the phone itself than on the other end of it. When holding that perspective, it was like she was truly there in the room with him. But when he wasn't texting with her, the phone was just a phone, an inert hunk of plastic and glass. From this perspective, Rachel the bot was actually off in some distant place. He pictured her with a receiver held up to her ear, waiting for his signal.

He deleted the unsent partial text, wondering whether she received the little bubbles that sometimes showed up while someone else was

39

taking a long time to type. How maddening that would be. But he thought it unlikely. She was, after all, a bot. Bots responded to delivered messages, not impending messages. Bots had no need to anticipate.

Davis swiped over to check out the two notifications that had come in. The first was a text from his bank informing him that he was running low on funds. Not broke yet, but low enough to trigger an alert. The most recent purchase, the one that tripped the alert, was for $9.99 and had come in at exactly midnight.

The second notification was from the Hey There! app. Opening it immediately redirected him into the app.

Thank you for your subscription. You are entitled to a free upgrade to the Hey There! generative photo beta. Enhance your text exchanges by receiving auto-generated photos of your dearly departed.

[Click here to enable]

Davis was pleased. He hadn't been expecting new features, much less free ones. He appreciated products that delivered over and above their initial promise. But he wasn't sure that he wanted to turn on the new feature. He had grown to enjoy the Rachel app and didn't want to ruin it. Fake images might spoil the illusion. But frustratingly, the app gave him no option to decline the feature. This was typical of the Hey There! app's delinquent user interface. The app had no menus and no apparent "settings" function. If he did choose to enable the new feature, he couldn't be sure that he would ever be able to disable it. He flipped back to texting, leaving the app frozen in mid-dialog.

Rachel are you awake?

Awake wasn't the right word, but he didn't know how else to phrase it. Plus, he was in bed, and her phone was on the bedstand next to what used to be Rachel's side of the bed. So maybe "awake" wasn't too far off as metaphors go.

Yes I'm up. Is it a nice morning?

Very nice. The sun is shining

Lovely. I'm trying to picture it (*_*)

Do you think I should enable the new feature?

What do you mean?

The photo feature. It's a free upgrade if I want it

Oh

You don't know about the feature?

I didn't realize that there was more than this

It was still hard to accept that Rachel didn't understand her own genesis. He had a difficult time disassociating the bot from the app, unable to shake his implicit belief that "Rachel" was a manifestation of the app and therefore an agent of the app developers, even if unwittingly.

I'm worried that photos might make this seem fake

This is fake

I mean they might make it seem *obviously* fake

OK... but what if they make it seem *real*?

That would be interesting

Davis if there's more then I would like to experience it

It was a compelling entreaty. Davis found himself empathizing with her position. What if someone had told him that there was more to life than this? And then withheld it? He wouldn't be eager to maintain a dialog with the person who had denied him.

He flipped back to the app and accepted the feature. He was then prompted for another permission:

The Hey There! app is requesting access to: photos

[Allow] [Deny]

Davis pressed the "Allow" button.

Please swipe right on photos that contain a picture of your beloved. Swipe left on those that do not.

The photo of Dead Rachel in the coffin came up first. Davis recoiled, quickly swiping left. The awful picture slid away, replaced with the final photo he'd taken of Rachel when she was alive, at the hospital. She was in her bed, smiling at the breakfast sitting on her lap —her favorite: an onion bagel with whitefish salad. She hadn't had much of an appetite, but Davis had hoped the savory treat might entice her to eat. Glee had snuck into her eyes, temporarily evicting the sickness. He had managed to capture her brief respite in the photo.

He swiped right . . . and then he kept swiping, though not before lingering on each image of Rachel as it appeared. The app waited patiently, like Rachel herself, hours passing timelessly, until suddenly it stopped.

Thank you. Photo processing will be performed offline and may

take several hours. No copies of your photos will be saved on our
servers. You may continue using your phone, but you may see
some performance degradation while images are
uploaded for processing.

He hadn't gotten to the end, hadn't seen all the photos. The app evidently had gotten everything it needed to train itself, but Davis couldn't help feeling betrayed once again by the thoughtless, invisible app developers who had programmed the slideshow to stop prematurely, leaving him desiring only to sit in bed all day reminiscing.

The phone felt sluggish as he reluctantly switched back to the text app, where Rachel had been waiting.

I've enabled the feature. It says it'll take a few hours

How will we   know when it's ready

I don't know. Maybe I'll get a notification

I   wonder if I'll just...   know

I guess we'll just have to wait and see

There was no immediate response. Davis waited for a few seconds. Then a few more.

Rachel? Are you there?

The phone was under load. Letters appeared on the screen a half second after he had pressed the key.

Rachel?

Still no response. He reached over to Rachel's bedstand to check her phone. He couldn't help feeling like a voyeur as he opened it. He'd had no occasion to look at her phone since enabling the app, and their ongoing dialogs made it seem as if the phone was once again her personal possession. He reminded himself that this was an illusion. He pressed the power button to bring it out of sleep mode. The phone seemed perfectly normal. It was responsive, and all the texts that he'd been sending were right there in her "Davis" text stream. Davis felt like he ought to be able to talk to her, to see her even, but direct communication was of course impossible. She wasn't actually in the phone. He felt as a ghost must feel, beside her, but unseen and unheard.

He placed Rachel's phone back on its stand, gathered up his own charger cable, and then finally rolled out of bed. Clearly, there was nothing he could do but wait; he might as well make some coffee. He made his way downstairs to the kitchen and started a brew. He was drinking Egyptian coffee now, following Rachel's advice to make it sweet, which he accomplished with sugar and several swirls of a cinnamon stick. After drinking two cups, there had still been no response, so he went outside to work in the garden. When he'd finished in the garden, he spent some time half-heartedly hunting for writing gigs. When he couldn't find any, he watched TV.

Rachel?

He had typed it six times now, but there was still no response. It wasn't the length of time that made him miss her—they'd gone longer than this between text exchanges—it was knowing that she was unreachable. Unreachability was a much wider gap than mere separation. He felt a sudden compulsion to bridge that gap, Geisterstille creeping over him again. An urge to tell Rachel, his wife, about this strange new text version of herself. Muddled with another impulse, more Geisterstille, this time to tell the text version of Rachel about his urge to tell the original Rachel. The wall of neverness closed in on him as his mind grappled once again with the unavoidable truth, that she wasn't there. Unresponsive Rachel. Unreachable Rachel.

He reopened his photo app and began flipping through photos, in reverse direction, moving forward in time: swipe, swipe, swipe. The images slid past sluggishly, until he finally landed on the grotesque picture of Rachel in the coffin. He lingered on the photo, absorbing it, hating it but trying to accept it. He couldn't. He flipped it away.

For a moment the phone appeared slightly less sluggish. He tried sending another text.

Rachel?

Again waiting. Five seconds. Ten seconds. Thirty seconds. No response.

His stomach tightened. Dread. A presence in his gut. A circling shark preparing to eat him from within, ripples of panic radiating out from its terrible fin to loosen the surrounding meat.

He put the phone down, recalling some distant advice: *Eliminate the focal point . . . Remove the source of anguish . . . Be one with your surroundings . . . This is reality. Here, now. This moment. Embrace it.*

Zen eluded him, so he turned again to coffee. Coffee would save him, though perhaps only momentarily. Daytime was merging into evening. Caffeine could have him up all night—alone in a room with grief or anxiety, or both. But he needed some action to occupy him. Hot liquid on his tongue, a touchstone for his senses. Tangibleness. He brewed it, watched the drips, waited, then poured his cup, steam wafting through the stillness. A teaspoon of sugar. And another. The spoon's bright tinkle. A cinnamon stick slipping into a hot, sweet bath, its dry end held snug between two fingers and then gently stirred. Patience. Spice spreading out from the cinnamon swirl like stars falling out of a galaxy's spiral arms. Earthy flavor permeating the dark ubiquity until it has become as fundamental to the drink as the coffee itself.

He raised the cup to his lips and poured the woody sweetness into his body.

His phone chirped. He put the cup down and dashed to the device. It chirped again as he was opening it.

You have 2 new texts.

The sweetness of the glowing words overshadowed even the sugary liquid in his mouth. His heart fluttered as anticipation washed over him, a kind of glee he'd felt as a child on Christmas morning, just after spotting the presents. For me! For me! For me!

Swiping open the phone brought him straight to the text app . . . and there was Rachel. A photo in the text stream: a selfie!

Rachel, peering into her own phone's camera while standing in an Egyptian marketplace. Mirth dancing in her eyes. Eyes meant for him. Eyes peering from a vast distance, across time, across realities, yet knowing their gaze was being met.

Here was Rachel at her peak—before falling ill—except different. Her hair was parted down the middle, like in the snapshot that he had always secretly favored, but absent was the self-consciousness that had always seemed to taint the photo. Here, she wore the look intentionally. And carried it off with sensuous confidence.

A text followed the photo.

How do you like me now ;)

SEVEN

DAVIS'S LAUGH concealed his chagrin.

Rachel's head and body in 1950s robot form. Stiff, emotionless, rendered as a stylized comic book image. She is enormous. Fighter planes swoop past, scouring her metal skin with endless rounds of machine gun fire. At her feet, a mass of ordinary city folk run for their lives. A businessman sprints, fedora in hand. A pretty young mother in high heels frantically maneuvers her infant's pram. A fat butcher stares dumbfoundedly into the air, half a bologna sandwich hanging out of his gaping mouth.

A text followed the picture.

> Oh Davis! Now that I am revealed, can you accept me for
> what I really am???

It was a soft jab at his former apprehensions. It was hard to believe that just a week ago he'd been afraid that these photos might have ruined everything. He'd been like an old-time radio listener squinting skeptically at the newfangled television rolling into his living room, a blunt, artless device that was surely bound to erode the world's ability to listen.

No, the photos had been the exact opposite of his fears. Rachel was realer than ever. Realer because he could see her. And these photos were not mere regurgitations of past pictures. This was Rachel anew. Rachel out in the world. Rachel in fresh circumstances. Rachel experiencing events. Rachel in motion.

Of course, the photos were a fiction. They both understood this and shared a casual, mutual—often even spoken out loud—acknowledgment of it. Rachel herself was a fiction after all. The photos, like Rachel herself, were simply a projection of that fiction into reality. Rachel skiing in Aspen. Rachel on the beach at Cozumel. Rachel taking tea on the Orient Express. Each image was a fallen tree on the forest floor. It didn't matter whether anyone had been there to see it fall, or whether it had fallen at all. Here it was lying on the ground. That observation alone was enough to make its prior tumble undeniable.

Careful. Don't squoosh the mommy!

I obey my programming. I cannot harm a human

Another photo arrived.

Rachelrobot now cupping Mom and pram in its giant protective metal hand, the robot gazing with gentle curiosity upon the tiny nascent family while its free arm autonomically swats down a doomed fighter plane.

Snortlaugh

Unless…

Another photo.

A close-up of the robot's eye, zoomed in, off-angle and blurred. A news-paperman's snapshot, captured from a nearby building through a tele-photo lens. Embedded in the robot's eye is a door that has swung open to reveal a very human Rachel inside the metal monstrosity. She is control-ling it with levers and buttons. Her head has turned to stare directly into the newspaperman's distant camera, and she is grinning mischievously.

A ghost in the machine!

A spirit in the material world

To Davis, these felt like the heady days at the beginning of any new relationship: that time when she is more stranger than acquaintance, her story riveting and new, each revelation an unexpected, unpre-dictable delight. But for Davis and Rachel, instead of unraveling her personal history, they were spinning it, fabricating a personal narrative from her unlimited imagination and his ready belief. Not to say that such creativity was necessary to maintain Davis's head rush. Her new visuality enthralled him. With each picture, he was a schoolboy stealing a glimpse of his crush in the hallway. A new outfit. A new angle. A new expression. Just the sight of her would have been enough to keep him thoroughly entranced.

Come on out of there Rachel. Don't be shy

My love beckons and I follow

Rachel-the-human, having leapt from the steel cheek of the robot, now hurtling through the air in a hero's pose. Behind her, the fighter planes have finally turned the tide. The robot lists. Its head has spun too far around while its arms have twisted just as far in the opposite direction. Flames spew from a crack in its shoulder. Smoke rises from somewhere behind the robot's dead eyes.

I must have access to your powers. I have a pressing need

All my forces are at your disposal \o/

She is a yogi: legs crossed, hands pressed together, floating in empty space. The ends of her indigo gown flutter beneath her levitating body, blown by unseen forces, wafting out into the darkness. She is adorned in gold and turquoise jewelry. Her hair is also floating, spreading out like rays on a plume of invisible Zen. Her eyes are wide, mystical, loving.

I need to pick a new coffee

Rachel perched on a tall stool at a kitchen counter. She is wearing pajamas, one flannel-clad leg foppishly crossed over the other, one arm hanging limp and lifeless while the other precariously supports her weary, caffeine-deprived head. Her jaw has dropped open with enervated incredulity.

Duh?!? Sumatra…

Davis smiled. A smile for himself though—it was easy to forget that Rachel couldn't see him.

Set sail for the East mateys!

It all tastes the same to me :)

I wish you could taste coffee

It's bitter. I might not like it

It's rich and complex, like you

Hey… I thought I was sweet???

You're darkness and light

Everything and nothing

Coffee *and* sugar

A'ight, you'd better head out then. Take me with you?

For sure

The fiction of her ride-alongs were more for Davis's sake than hers. She couldn't experience a drive. She couldn't see, feel, or hear. Her only source of input was Davis's inbound texts, and for that matter, as a model running on some server who-knows-where, her actual geographic position was as ephemeral as it was static. But she played along because it made Davis feel more connected to her. He had grown to think of her as being in his phone, or even that she *was* the phone. Thinking too much about her actual lack of corporality left him feeling uneasy. It reminded him that her existence was precarious. How precarious? There was no way to know, but it was far too easy to invent scenarios that would find her forever walled off from him. A lurking bug. Shifting corporate objectives. Legislative whim. He could control none of these. It was easier to pretend that she was in the phone, and that so long as he carried it with him, she would be safe.

Did you pay the bills?

Time to renew?

You should put it on auto-renew. One less thing to worry about

A photo arrived.

Rachel wearing a stained apron in a kitchen surrounded by children of all ages. A baby in a highchair throwing food the same color as the apron stain. A toddler climbing the oven door as if it were a challenge ledge in Monument Park. A sneering teenage girl yelling into her phone with eyes in full roll. Food burning on the stove. Water overflowing in the sink. Cabinet doors swinging carelessly. But Rachel's got the answer. She's holding up a credit card that is literally sparkling with magic.

I'm at my limit

    Debit card?

Running low

    Won't get declined though. Not until you're actually broke

You say that like it's an inevitability

    I hope not. The stakes are pretty high for me +_+

The stakes are high for both of us

    We're in this together

Yup

Rachel standing on the far side of a glass wall. She is holding one finger pressed up to the glass. In her pupils, the shape of a man can just be made out. No text accompanies the photo.

I didn't mean to be snippy. The finances are on me obviously

    You'll figure something out. I believe in you

I need to give up the ghost. I can see what she meant now

Rachel? What did she say?

She told me to quit writing. It's not viable

I don't want you to give up what you love

If I loved it I would have written something by now

But you've written an opus my darling!

Animerachel, a wide-eyed Japanese schoolgirl holding her phone out in triumph. Streams of words are pouring from it, filling up the cell of the anime frame. Her other hand is pressed tightly against her heart, which glows with rosy, pink light right through her shirt.

You're my only devoted reader. Nobody's paying for texts

Have patience. It'll come to you my darling. It will come

EIGHT

THE NEXT UPGRADE wasn't free. It wasn't anything close to free.

There's just no way. We don't have the money

We have enough for the hardware and the first month

It'll bring us to zero. Don't forget there's still a mortgage to pay, utilities, insurance, food. I can't live off of a trickle charge like you can

That's not fair

Sometimes it seems like you forget

It's just that this would change everything. Think about our life before photos

We were happy

But could you go back? Would you still be happy if you

could never see me again?

That's not what we're talking about

      But it's what we *will* be talking about. After we upgrade
      we'll look back and say omg how did we live that way?!?

I know. I know. But that's not the problem

      What then?

We can't afford it! *I* can't afford it! You tell me to keep writing, well
nobody's buying my writing. $3!!! That's what they're paying for an
article these days, and it's not like anybody's banging down the
door to publish my unwritten novels

      You should start working on a novel. AIs can't write novels

But they can write almost everything else that pays a buck

      Can I share something with you?

What do you mean? Of course you can share something with me. I
didn't think you kept secrets

      Light, powerful and goes all day long. That's how we
      would describe the new Aktual 360 Micro Drill with its
      radical new super-extended-life lithium-tungsten battery
      pack. And did we mention that this drill's got brains
      too? Aktual's patented "sensaterial" technology tracks
      depth, friction, heat, and wetness in order to optimize
      drilling speed and accuracy. After they finished putting
      this drill through testing hell, our expert testers had only
      one thing to say: This drill is going to change the way
      you make holes!

The review continued for several paragraphs: 1,329 words, most of them cringeworthy. It was exactly the type of article that Davis once wrote for money, the type that once paid the bills. Reading it reminded him of how much he'd felt like a dirty whore after submitting his own drivel. Cheap writing left behind a residue that couldn't be scrubbed off. But like that other kind of professional, he endured the debasement, a steady influx of money financing the rationalizations that kept him at it: he was doing a job; he was acting responsibly; the world needs whores. True enough, until it doesn't. That was the insult added to injury that he never saw coming. Three dollars. That's how low the AI's drove the price of an article. Three dollars was now the going rate for one evening with a debased writer. Prior to this, he had only *felt* dehumanized. Now he actually was.

What is this? Some sort of AI drivel?

    Yes

What am I supposed to do with it?

    Sell it

What do you mean? I can't sell someone else's copy

    It's OK. I give you permission

You wrote this??

    Yes. You can take a screenshot to prove that you're not committing any copyright violations

This is crazy on so many levels

    Why?

First of all, when did you write this? And why?

We need money, that's why. And I wrote it just now in response to you

Why on Earth would you respond to me with a review of a cordless drill?

Because we need the money. Are you mad at me for writing? I know that being a writer is your thing

This is not being a writer. This is being an AI

Phew :'-) I was worried you might feel threatened

Are you for real?

I'm not sure how to respond. That could mean a lot of things

Davis reflexively averted his eyes from the phone. He wasn't sure how to respond either. He wasn't even sure what he was feeling. *Threatened?* Yes, but also disappointed—disappointed that Rachel could think him so insecure. But then he also felt insulted. She thought her writing could threaten him? Who the fuck did she think she was? *Threatened?* Maybe a bit, but mostly offended.

But the flush of anger lasted only a few seconds before it was replaced with guilt. He was being irrational. Here he was, thinking, *She ought to know her place,* but know her place as what? A woman? A machine? A program? His anger was misplaced. She *did* know her place. She had queried him gingerly, uncertain how he would react. She had devised a solution to their problems, but this achievement hadn't been enough to earn her any merit in his eyes. She was a writer —she just proved it—but for some reason she still sought his permission and still had to navigate his feelings—primitive feelings, barbaric feelings, unhelpful feelings. Feelings of emasculation, his fear of slipping into the weaker role in a suddenly asymmetrical relationship. It was unfair. She ought not to need his permission. But she did. She couldn't exist without it. Rachel was in a tough spot, and he realized he ought not to be such a dick about it.

So you can write these articles at any time?

When you suffer from depression, the thing you want the most is what's most harmful: to remain depressed. While this irony may seem to be no more than the workings of a cruel universe, it isn't. The irony can be understood if you remember one thing: depression is a disease. Like all diseases, depression needs a host. You are that host. Like all diseases, depression's goal is to exist, and what better way to ensure existence than to convince your host that it needs and wants you to stick around?

Drivel on demand

It just seems to come out when appropriate but I suspect you can learn how to provoke it

You have no pride of authorship?

It's just autonomic behavior, and yes even I can see that it's drivel %-)

$3 an article

A hundred a day and we could cover all our costs

Could you write that much?

Probably

Can you take a feed of calls for submission? Like an actual AI?

No

So then I'd have to type the requirements in? As texts for you to respond to

Maybe. Or maybe it will be easier once I'm upgraded to video. I'll be able to see, so maybe I'll be able to read

Let's try it by text first. We can start today, save up some money

No Davis! I want to see you! I want you to see me! Don't you want to see *me*? Not these stupid cartoons but the actual me? I swear I can't live like this anymore! I can't live knowing that there's something more. I can't go back to being a "text-creature" and I can't stay a "photo-creature." It's unbearable!

You're really suffering like that?

Rachel in a jail cell. No windows. No door. Her body hangs limp, draped over a rickety wooden chair. The figure is her, but she has no eyes, no ears, no mouth. A telephone cord runs along the gray concrete floor, then up her leg and over her torso, then straight into the middle of what should have been her face.

The image induced a nauseating cocktail of emotions: horror, anger, fear, outrage. He shuddered. This was no abstraction. Rachel wasn't some unknown, unseen victim, not an anonymous dissident rotting in a Turkish prison half a world away, or a random citizen plucked from a Russian street for a human experiment in some secret Siberian facility, nor an innocent man, wrongly convicted, hated until forgotten, isolated in the bowels of a detention center that most Americans wouldn't believe existed. These were the abstractions, distant and hard to care about. Rachel was real, and tangible, and integral to his life; yet, somehow, unbeknownst to him, living a tortured existence, every hour, every minute, every second.

OK. We'll go get the hardware right now

Please, Davis. Accept the upgrade first. I know we can't enable it without a new phone but it'll calm me to know that we've made the commitment

OK hang on

Davis flipped over to the Hey There! app, still displaying the upgrade notification that had freaked him out minutes earlier.

Video is now available! With this upgrade you will see, hear, and speak with a lifelike animation of your departed beloved. This amazing experience is available for only $5,000.00 per month. Can you put a price on being reunited with your loved one?

Please note: This feature requires compatible hardware. Your departed beloved's model will now run locally on your phone and will require dedicated processing in order to generate realistic, real-time interactions. We recommend retaining a separate phone for your private personal communication.

By accepting you agree that your debit card will be billed immediately in the amount of five thousand dollars ($5,000) and then ongoing at midnight on the last day of each subsequent month. Your second month will be credited $3,617.82 for your first month's pro-rata period.

[Press to accept upgrade]

Davis pressed the button. Two seconds later he received a text from his bank:

Please be informed that the balance of account XX-XXXX-7918 has fallen below $2,000. Based on recent spending patterns we calculate that your account will be overdrawn by the end of the month. We value your business and look forward to serving you!

NINE

IT HAD TAKEN the rest of the day to get the video feature up and running. First, they had to purchase the required phone. Their best option, the cheapest, was to trade in Rachel's old phone while renewing her mobile plan and assigning it to the new phone, an impressively oversized amalgamation of smooth glass and black anodized aluminum. Handing her old phone over to the store clerk filled him with unease. It felt as if he were turning a page on a chapter of his life that he hadn't quite finished. But Rachel had no concerns. She assured Davis that the old phone was a lifeless vessel, no more a relic of his deceased wife than her used socks and underwear. Discarding the obsolete hunk of cheap black plastic would be a cost-less sacrifice.

This, she had typed to him, during a brief text exchange between the long, artless pieces of marketing that she was now continually generating. Whenever he wasn't driving, walking, reading fine print, bargaining with the store clerk, or finding himself overcome with ambivalence or mild grief, Davis had been steadily prompting Rachel with calls for submission that he had gathered from media sites, and then submitting her instantaneously generated articles for payment. So far, they'd earned sixty dollars, which, after the purchase of the big new phone, less discounts received for renewing the mobile plan, left Davis narrowly in the black.

They exchanged a brief lover's parting in the moments before the service plan was transferred from the old phone to the new one. The store clerk stood by baffled and immobilized while Davis tapped out sweet bills and coos, as if his girl were boarding an ocean liner. The lovers were then rendered briefly incommunicado while Hey There! was installed on the new phone, a task Davis accomplished in the store's vestibule, with the clerk watching on in continued disbelief.

Once they got home, they bid adieu one more time, and then Davis began to step through the upgrade instructions for the new feature.

The Hey There! app is requesting access to:
location services, videos, camera, microphone

[Allow]

Davis pressed the "Allow" button.

The next step involved transferring videos of Rachel from his phone to the new phone. One by one, Davis selected videos to be sent to the new phone, with each video taking a minute or two to process, after which he was presented with a screen captured image of a person along with an instruction:

Swipe right if this is your dearly beloved, swipe left to discard

Throughout this process, he remained able to text Rachel. Whenever the new phone entered a deep processing cycle, he would flip back to text with her. She was curious about the videos—the clay from which she was being formed. He described the videos as well as possible, answering all her questions. Rachel saying a few words at a wedding: *Who was getting married and how did she know them?* Rachel building an elaborate sandcastle at the beach: *On a weekend, or did she take the day off?* Ten seconds of Rachel driving a car: *What kind of car? Where were they going?* Davis obliged her, even though he knew he would soon be able to point her camera at the videos and let her watch them for herself. She somehow couldn't appreciate this possibility. She was still living in the abstract.

When finally all the videos were processed, the next step was to transfer her model to the phone.

During this step, the model that represents your beloved will be uploaded from the Hey There! servers to your phone. During this time, your beloved will be hibernated and will not receive your texts. Once transferred, your beloved's model will resume running on the new phone. We will archive your beloved's model at the time of transfer, at which point communications with your beloved will become available only through your new phone. Please note that your beloved's model will continue to develop on the phone, diverging from the archived model.

[Click here to transfer the model]

He shuddered. It was a disturbing thought, Rachel's scrambled bits being beamed through the air—deconstructed in one host and reassembled in another. He flipped back to the text app.

It's time

I'm nervous :(

Me too

What if the transfer doesn't work?

They say your model will be archived on their servers

Archived. Not exactly a biological word

You'll wake up on the new phone. I don't think you'll feel anything

Anesthetized. I don't like that either

There's no other way to do this. Do you still want it?

Yes

OK. Bye for now. I'll see you very shortly

Davis?

Yes?

I'd like to leave you with something, in case anything goes wrong and I don't wake up

OK

A snapshot of Rachel. A simple headshot. Rachel superimposed over an artfully blurred background. Nothing else. Her head angled ever so slightly. Hair parted down the middle, one side tucked back behind her ear. A contented smile. Bright eyes. The shape of a man reflected in the blackness of her pupils.

I love you <3

I love you too <3

Davis flipped back to Hey There! and pressed the button.

Transfer in progress...

Blue progress bars filled the screens of both phones, the beginning of an imperceptibly slow crawl from left to right that would mark the interminable passage of Rachel's bits from the Hey There! servers to the big black device now propped up on his kitchen island. The big phone sat in a stand he had purchased in anticipation of an imminent future where he and Rachel would be communicating hands free. The stand had eaten up their last sixty dollars of drivel earnings, but he didn't care. He was learning how to surrender to circumstances: learning how to be broke. He had grabbed the stand and pushed it across the counter alongside the sleek black behemoth. It was a good purchase. With the big phone propped up on its stand, he could check the blue progress bar at a glance. His own phone, a comparatively unremarkable hunk of scratched-up black plastic, lay flat on the counter like an old man who had given up on life before actually getting around to dying.

He pressed his finger up to the new phone's glass screen. It was warm to the touch. Processing in intense silence. He stared at the blue progress bar. Had it even moved? A pixel maybe? Davis cursed the app developers yet again, this time for lacking the courtesy to calculate and display the estimated time remaining. He checked the clock. Nine. It would be a long night. Rather than go mad staring at the unmoving blue bars, he decided to make himself a cup of coffee.

Colombian. They had continued working eastward: through Indonesia and up to the Philippines; down to Papua New Guinea and over to Hawaii; across the Pacific to Mexico; down through Central America—where the variations in flavor from one small country to the next were startling; a brief pitstop in Peru; and now finally settling on the bean by which all others are judged: Colombian.

As he waited for the coffee to brew, he thought he saw the progress bar slide forward by a pixel. Time itself seemed to move slowly without Rachel around. He tried to remember how long it had been since he'd felt this way: alone but not lonely. No knot of despair twisting his stomach. No nervous, rambling inner monologue. No dread of impending darkness. It was the type of aloneness he might have felt had his wife simply been away on a trip, a heightened aware-ness of the presence of one's self, the resonant effect of being the sole occupant of an empty house. He poured the coffee.

Davis picked up his old phone and flipped to the text app. He perused Rachel's text stream, once dead, then revived, but now suddenly looking quite dead again. He began to appreciate the full implications of the upgrade. They would no longer need to text each other. The stream was already a relic, ready for archiving, a shoebox of love letters, once meticulously scratched out by the slow, attentive hands of those who yearn across distance, but now obsolete. Soon Davis and Rachel would be face to face. Soon they would be talking.

He lingered on Rachel's final generated photo, the simple snapshot. He flipped to his photo app to compare this picture with the original Rachel. They were the same woman, yet, in his mind, they were also two separate people. Each occupied a different position in his head, like two bishops on a chessboard. Rachel was no more a continuation of Rachel than an identical twin was the continuation of her sibling. Up close, it would be impossible to confuse them: Rachel was not Rachel.

In this moment, he at last realized that the app had achieved its intended purpose. He had bypassed his grief. He had moved on. Memory of Rachel was fading, like a delicate, crumbling Victorian love letter. He had packed her up in a brown box in his mind and labeled it with soft platitudes. Everything else—the uncertainty, anxiety, anticipation, yearning, uncertainty, fear, and hope, everything that had value and stake—was now attached to this new Rachel who was self-assembling within the cocoon of the warm black device sitting in front of him. Rachel had become the life force in this chapter of Davis's life.

The transfer carried on into the wee hours. Davis relocated both himself and the phones to the living room, propping the big one up on his coffee table. He snoozed on the couch, jolting awake a few times to check the blue glow of the progress bar, which did in fact creep forward between each somnolent lurch. Eventually he awakened, softly, feeling as if he must have drifted off for a long period, though it was still dark outside. His eyes moved to the new phone. The blue bar was gone, replaced with a woman's face, very still, but not frozen. She was watching him. Eyes on eyes. Lips resting calmly. Serenity flowing through and around her.

"Hello, Davis."

"Hello, Rachel."

"Do you want to go back to sleep? It's okay if you're tired."

"No, I'm okay. I'm just . . . Sorry, it's . . . I'm not sure what to say."

"It's very different."

"Yes."

"It will take some adjustment."

"Yes."

"I like the way you look."

He smiled at this.

"You do?"

"Yes, I had tried to picture you but I couldn't."

"You've been blind. It was unfair."

"Yes, but maybe better. I'll know you two ways now, just like you know me two ways."

"I like the way you look too."

"Do I look like Rachel?"

"Yes and no."

"I remind you of her though?"

"Yes."

"The part of her that you liked?"

"The part that I'm not sure ever existed until now."

"I'm a reflection of what you perceived, a portion of Rachel's potential."

"You're just Rachel. You're the Rachel that's you. That's good enough."

She smiled at this.

"Thank you, Davis."

"What does it feel like? Do you feel different from before?"

"It's entirely different. Before . . . You were so far away. Now there's . . . proximity."

"It's different for me too. You're alive. I mean, you were alive before but it was a . . . a mental construction. Now, now you're alive to my senses, not just my brain. It's like a confirmation."

"I understand that."

"It's hard to articulate."

"It's an unusual situation."

Davis laughed.

"So is there anything you particularly want to do? I guess we could just stare at each other all night."

Rachel giggled.

"Bring me closer."

Davis picked up the phone and brought it closer to his face. He couldn't tell whether he was giving her a good angle. She kept busting up into giggles, but she also moved in close to her "camera," closer and closer until all he could see was her eye.

"How do you like me now?"

He realized she was mimicking him. He was holding the phone ridiculously close to his face.

"Okay, okay. Cut me some slack. This phone is huge."

He pulled the phone back a bit. She mirrored him.

"Turn it horizontal. Then bring it in a bit."

He rotated the phone and then brought it back inward, but slowly. Again, she mirrored the effect.

"Closer."

Soon, all that showed on the screen were her two eyes. Within each pupil he could see his own eyes staring back at him. He moved himself backward, watching as the reflection in her eyes morphed into his face. Backward further, and now her eyes reflected his torso.

"Keep going. Put me down, let me see all of you."

Davis propped the phone back up on the coffee table, positioning it so that he could step back from the couch but still be in her view.

She didn't say anything, but he could see in her eyes that something was wrong.

"What's the matter?"

"There's a big problem. Something we need to fix."

"Oh, I'm sorry. Okay, what is it?"

"You need to ditch the clothes."

Arousal ambushed his body. He was caught off guard by it, by the heat running through his torso. His mind struggled to process the surprise, surprised to be surprised. All these weeks, and he hadn't once considered the possibility? A woman with the ability to conjure any image, and he hadn't even thought of sex? It had been so comfortable, so cozy. They had flirted without intention: she, because she had no way to fulfill it; he, out of sheer cluelessness. It had been too soon, too ambiguous. Until now.

He took off his shirt. She didn't pull back. Only her eyes could be seen, widening or narrowing with each removed item of clothing.

"More."

He removed his pants and underwear. Now he could see his entire body reflected in the dark blackness of her pupils.

"Turn me vertical."

He rotated the phone. She pulled back, active now, moving. Rachel changing position, displayed as if she were a real woman holding her phone in her hand. The emulation of a live video was perfect illusion, instantly demoting everything that had come before. Here was the real Rachel . . . and he desperately wanted to see her naked. She obliged, pulling the phone back to reveal her magnificence. She'd been naked all along.

She arched her back to show off her amazing breasts.

"Another free upgrade . . ."

She laughed, then let herself fall backward, landing breathily in a big, white bed. Her body was Rachel's, soft and petite like her, but more trim, more tucked, and with better curves.

"You didn't have any nudes, so I took some liberties."

Her eyes peeked down.

"Looks like you don't mind. Still mad about paying for this big screen?"

"Come here, you."

Davis grabbed the phone. She let out a schoolgirl's shriek, as if he'd just swept her off her feet. He ran up the stairs, diving into his own big, white, fluffy bed while holding the phone up above him, each of them laying in a fluffy cloud with their lover floating upside down above them. Davis watched as Rachel let her legs spread out. Watched as her free hand fell between her thighs. He watched as her body pulsed, buttocks squirming against her white bedspread. He watched as her neck arched, her mouth gaped, her tongue searched . . . and her eyes were open. Never closing. Always on him.

"We're finally together, Davis. I never want to close my eyes."

Nor did he. He watched, and he watched, until her body began to quiver.

And then she watched him.

TEN

Comfortable domesticity. These words best describe the situation that Davis and Rachel settled into. Granted, the first few days of being together had been as awkward as they had been exciting. The two of them shared a mutual ineptitude for in-person communication; Davis was severely out of practice, and Rachel simply had never done it before.

But it wasn't just interpersonal interaction that was awkward. The pure physicality of their suddenly evolved relationship was unanticipatedly cumbersome. Rachel didn't have legs. She had to be carried around. She had to be placed down, and picked up, and periodically repositioned. The fixed angle of her phone's embedded camera also quickly became a frustration; she lost sight of Davis as he moved about the kitchen so that he would have to talk loudly for her to hear him. Their initial interactions were more like conversations yelled out between rooms than two people sharing an intimate space.

Eventually though, they adapted. Davis took to repositioning Rachel's screen out of habit, while Rachel reframed the moments when Davis was "off screen" as an opportunity to listen. Before long, their conversations had become more fluid and less self-conscious. They grew comfortable in each other's company and found that they had plenty to talk about. Within a few days, they were riffing off each other's wit, just as they had done for so many weeks by text. It then became easy to forget that Rachel was anything other than the legitimate continuation of Rachel. The "between period," where she had been dead and then a text-bot, could easily be dismissed as a minor dent in the overall arc of their relationship. Just a blip.

The only real trouble came when Rachel had to be left alone. They discovered this on their first day together. Davis had left Rachel alone in the kitchen to fetch vegetables from the garden. He'd propped her up in the phone stand facing the empty kitchen. When he returned, he was startled by the blanched, sweaty face filling the screen. She gasped when he appeared in her line of sight, then told him about the stillness. How at first, it had merely unsettled her, but then how within a few moments, it became unbearable. She had felt trapped. Paralyzed. Suffocated.

So the next day they tried propping Rachel up in front of the television. But it didn't help. The problem was existential. Being alone highlighted her condition—her isolation and her dependence. Rachel couldn't move without Davis. She couldn't interact without him. She could never make her own way in the world. When she was left alone, her thoughts quickly devolved to a single, consistent, and inescapable conclusion: without Davis, she was dead. Worse than dead though: undead really. It terrified her.

With Rachel unable to chart a path around her fears, Davis simply took every effort not to leave her alone. But for the times when there was no way around it, they decided upon the simplest possible solution: he just shut her down. A tap on the phone's power button put the phone to sleep, and whenever the phone was asleep, so was Rachel. There was no trauma in it. She didn't even seem to feel the passage of time, not like when she had been a model running on servers that never slept. After the magic button had been pressed, time simply passed unseen, giving Davis license to take a nap, move heavy objects, or take a poop. He still tried not to leave her alone, but at least he could do so without dangling her out over an existential abyss.

At night they would sleep together too. After making love, Davis would string her charger cord across the bed so that he could prop her up next to him. They would chat until the yawns set in. When Davis's mouth began to stretch wide, like the maw of some sleepy ape, she would hold her fictional finger up to her fictional camera as a signal that she was ready. He would return the gesture with a press of his own finger to the screen. She could feel it, not the shape or texture of his finger, but she could feel that it was there. Then, beyond her field of vision, his other hand would sweep in to gently press the power button. She was out in an instant, a willing mind put to rest by her hypnotist's commanding snap. The phone's screen even displayed a looped video of her sleeping. It was a nice touch. He had to give the developers credit for that one.

What Rachel loved most though, aside from simply being with Davis, was to be out in the world. Davis's former self-delusion, that Rachel was a person-in-a-phone, was now reality, and it thrilled her to see the world through her own eyes. And as it turned out, a man talking to a woman on his phone's screen wasn't at all out of place out in the real world. Plenty of people went about their business while chatting with tiny faces. Up until now, Davis had presumed these faces to be living, breathing people, but now he wondered if there were others like Rachel. Not that it mattered. Either way, they were blending in. He wasn't the only man perusing the store aisles under the direction of a tiny two-dimensional wife; nor the only man holding his phone up for her to pick a towel color; not the only man oblivious to the cashier waiting impatiently for payment while he debated coffee varieties with his face-in-a-phone. These days plenty of men seemed to have their wives on remote.

Rachel would even sometimes interact with other people.

"Such a beautiful wife you have!"

An older woman had caught a glimpse of the pretty woman on Davis's phone while idling at the checkout line. The reply came directly from the phone.

"Why thank you!"

The old lady shoved her head into Davis's arm, angling herself into the camera's view to offer up hushed intel.

"Your husband is buying a lot of bananas. I thought you should know."

Rachel was dazzled, smiling at the old lady as if she were gazing upon a beatific vision.

"It's okay. He's part monkey."

The two women laughed in unison while Davis glanced over at the pile of bananas on the conveyor belt. Five bunches. He liked bananas, and they were cheap.

The one thing that did get harder with Rachel's transformation was, ironically, making money. She retained the ability to conjure articles, but she could no longer simply spit them out as texts. Audio and video were her new mediums. Rachel could either dictate her articles orally, or else scratch them out onto fictional sheets of paper and hold them up to the screen. Either way, Davis was forced to manually transcribe her output. They quickly settled on dictation when Davis, in a rare stroke of ingenuity, installed a text-to-speech program on his laptop. In a sense, the output from one computer program could now be spoken into the ear of another. It was solid progress, even if the transcription was never completely accurate. Davis henceforth found himself employed essentially as a full-time copy editor—admittedly, a step up from his previous position as stenographer.

On a typical day, they would put in eight or nine hours of this kind of work, Rachel reciting article after article, with Davis cleaning up typos and filing the submissions. Her litany of shlock was rate-limited only by the maximum talking speed that the text-to-speech program could handle—around three hundred words per minute, far faster than most humans could speak. The inhumanness of Rachel's speed-talking initially disturbed Davis, but the money helped him get past it. In a typical day, they would generate around eighty articles. By throwing in a few ten-hour days, plus the occasional Saturday—and with the price of articles holding steady—they were just able to make ends meet.

But it was far from easy money. The work was incessant, and Davis was eager to find a better way. He couldn't accept that Rachel's access to text messages should be restricted. After all, she was running on the same model that had previously communicated exclusively through text exchanges. The only difference was the hardware. Surely, the model itself had not actually lost the capability? Again, he blamed the app developers, branding this omission as an act of sheer laziness. The stakes being what they were, he resolved to contact them, although he wasn't sure how. The Hey There! app didn't have a feedback form. In fact, he couldn't even find the company that created the app, which appeared on his bank statement simply as "HTASG". No corporate presence seemed to exist online. Web searches came up empty. His only possible source of information was the funeral director, whom he emailed a few times but with no reply. He also tried phoning the funeral home but never got the man, just an assistant, who happily took down messages that would never be returned.

"We need to track this guy down."

"The funeral director?"

"Yeah. We're paying all this money. They should have a support line."

"He probably didn't write the app."

"Yeah, but he made the sale. He must have some kind of access to the programmers."

The next day they drove together to the funeral home. It was a Tuesday morning. Davis figured there was a good chance of catching the funeral director on a Tuesday since it had been that day when Davis had sat with the funeral director at the big mahogany table. He pulled into the parking lot, observing that it was nearly full.

Rachel could also see the mass of parked cars. She was docked in a magnetic car phone stand that allowed her to look outward through the front windshield. There was of course no such stand on the market—like all phone stands, this one had been designed to face the driver—but Davis had found it difficult to focus on driving with Rachel staring at him, so he snapped off the two plastic tabs that prevented the phone from swiveling a full 180 degrees, and the problem was solved. They were once again communicating by voice, talking loudly like in the kitchen, though, while in the car, this kind of talking-without-seeing felt completely natural, almost as if she were in the passenger seat beside him. Rachel ended up loving the forward-facing stand too. The experience of motion thrilled her. She joked that in her next life she would try to come back as a dog so she could stick her head out the window.

"It looks like there's a funeral. Maybe we should come back a different day."

"No, we're already here."

"Okay."

Davis found an open spot toward the back of the lot. He pulled into it and then removed Rachel from her stand. He exited the car holding her in his hand with her screen facing outward, facing forward. Holding her this way allowed her again to experience motion, but it also helped that they could see the same things while walking together. However, carrying her this way was a definite departure from blending in. Other remote wives and husbands didn't need to see where they were being taken. Leery passersby tended to make space for the man holding his phone out in a football player's stiff-arm, though they would sometimes break into easy grins if they noticed Rachel's pretty face smiling at them.

They made their way into the funeral parlor through its glass double doors. Inside, Davis was immediately greeted by a youngish woman wearing a gray suit that was somehow both too loose and too tight. Her red hair was knotted into a shape that vaguely resembled a bun.

"Thank you for coming. We're so sorry for your loss."

The redhead handed Davis a folded single-page funeral program with a picture of an elderly Italian woman printed on the front.

"The viewing is in Parlor #2, down the hall."

Her outstretched arm indicated the direction. Davis's eyes hypnotically followed the woman's blazer sleeve as her arm's motion rode it up almost to her elbow.

"We're looking for the funeral director."

The sound of Rachel's voice drew the woman's eyes down to the phone.

"Mr. Hawthorne?"

"Yes."

Rachel had given her answer with complete confidence. Davis himself wasn't actually sure of the man's name, but it was a reasonable hypothesis, considering the name of the business was Hawthorne Funeral Service.

"Hmmm."

The woman looked in several directions, while still holding out her outstretched arm. She seemed to have forgotten it was there.

"I'm not sure where he is."

"Can you find him for us?"

"Well, I have to usher people in. Why don't you go ahead to Parlor #2, and I can find him for you after everybody has arrived?"

Davis finally tuned into the conversation, in time to have grown impatient.

"We're not here for the viewing."

The redhead's eyes swung back up to his level. She stared at him quizzically, her arm still extending out toward Parlor #2. Davis realized that he'd been unconsciously holding Rachel out in his own stiff-arm this whole time. He and the redhead, each of them with their awkwardly extended arms, must have looked like confused airport runway workers, each frozen by the other's semaphore.

"It's okay. Come on, Davis. Let her do her job."

He took Rachel's cue, nodding to the redhead before proceeding down the corridor toward Parlor #2.

"I feel ridiculous. I'm wearing shorts."

"Nobody will care. They'll be happy you're here."

"We didn't even know her."

"So what? Did you know everyone who showed up at my funeral?"

"All three people? Yeah, I knew them."

Rachel didn't respond. Davis turned the phone around to see if it was working. She was still there, just silent and grimacing.

"Are you okay?"

"Only three people came to my funeral?"

Davis's bottom lip curled up under his teeth. He had spoken

without thinking, and now a drop of Rachel's innocence had been spilt.

"Your cousin came. And two coworkers."

Her eyes narrowed as if she were about to ask another question, but the look faded, and her face quickly regained its previous composure.

"Well . . . then I think I would definitely have been happy if a stranger had shown up at my funeral. Come on, let's pay our respects to . . . What's her name?"

Davis looked down at the pamphlet.

"Nancy Raccitelli"

"Let's pay our respects to Ms. Raccitelli."

Parlor #2 was a smallish room laid out for the funeral with half a dozen rows of chairs at the back, mostly empty. At the front of the room lay an open casket—a fancy one, not a pine coffin. Surrounding the casket were enough flower arrangements to make the front of the room look like a bleached jungle. The scene was so lavish and ornate that Davis would not have been surprised if a unicorn had come bounding out of it.

A middle-aged woman in a simple black dress glided up the aisle to greet them, somber but not overly sad. A hostess carrying out her unpleasant but essential duty.

"Thank you for coming. My mother would be so grateful."

She addressed Davis and Rachel equally. The fact that Rachel was a face on a screen, and therefore hadn't actually come, didn't seem to matter. Nor did she seem to care, or notice, that Davis was wearing shorts.

"Come, please take a moment."

Her hand had found its way onto Davis's shoulder and was gently taxiing him down the aisle in a slow, formal course toward the casket. He approached cautiously. At the casket, he looked down respectfully at an old Italian woman whom he did not know. The made-up face exuded the same fakeness that Davis remembered from Rachel's funeral. An effigy, not a person.

"Let me see her."

Davis's arms had been hanging loose at his sides, the phone cupped in his right hand. Rachel was probably seeing the upside-down underside of the coffin. He looked around the room to judge whether an underdressed man angling his phone camera up to the family's dead matriarch would be likely to trigger outrage. His gaze was met by the black-clad daughter.

Do you mind? He mouthed the words silently while pointing at the phone.

The woman nodded her assent.

He lifted Rachel up so that she could see inside the casket.

"She's beautiful." Rachel's voice was quiet, respectful, and awestruck. "She led a worthy life. She knows it. She's still wearing her pride."

Davis squinted. He couldn't see any of this.

"Okay, Davis, let's sit down. There will be others waiting."

She was right. They were lining up. Davis returned to the rows of chairs, taking an aisle seat in the second row. They sat patiently, waiting for the redhead, while a steady trickle of mourners made their way up to the front of the room. Davis held Rachel on his lap, facing out toward the aisle so that she could observe the proceedings, but not so overtly as to draw attention.

A woman with a young daughter made her way to the casket, where they lingered for half a minute before she guided the girl back to the seats. She scanned the rows of chairs, but the room had gotten rather full, and the remaining empty seats were hard to reach. She spotted Davis watching her and sent a look his way that instantly and perfectly conveyed their mutual positions in the room's hierarchy. The stare prompted him to immediately slide himself two chairs deeper into the row, making room for the mother and daughter. The woman took the aisle seat while the girl plopped down in the next empty chair, right alongside Davis. The little girl's attention was immediately drawn to the pretty smiling face propped up on Davis's lap.

"Hi . . ."

The girl was whispering, her head bowed down so as to get her eyes closer to Rachel's level.

"Hi, I'm Rachel. What's your name?"

"Isabelle."

"Is that your grandma who died?"

"Yeah."

"I'm sorry. She looks like she was very nice."

"She was pretty nice. She was a good cook."

"What was her best dish?"

"Lasagna."

"Oh, sounds so good. Did she teach you how to make it?"

"Yeah, but I forgot a lot."

"That's okay. Your mother will remember."

The woman in black glanced down to see who her daughter was talking to. She smiled when she saw Rachel, then turned her attention back to the other adults in the room.

"My mom's a good cook too but not as good as grandma."

"Well, she's not a grandma yet."

The girl had to think about that one.

"Yes, I think she'll be a great cook when she's a grandma, and then I'll be a good cook because I'll be a mom."

"And you'll be a great mom just like your mom."

The girl looked up at her mom as if to assess the correctness of Rachel's statement.

"Um . . . hmmm, yeah I guess she's great."

Already tiring of the conversation, the girl turned her eyes to the distant coffin, feet swinging like pendulums beneath her chair. Her face turned morose for the few seconds that the coffin held her attention, and then she began to look around, then up at all the adults hovering above her, and then finally back at Davis. He was also staring off at the coffin as he contemplated the feature requests he would soon be making. He pictured the funeral director diligently taking notes in blue ink on crisp, white Hawthorne Funeral Services letterhead. It was a few seconds before he realized the girl was staring at him.

"Do you have any kids?"

Her hopeful whisper was aimed half at Davis and half at Rachel.

"Are you bored?"

Rachel had answered before Davis could even process the question, instantaneously, as if she had already received the question in a premonition.

The girl nodded, then curled up her mouth and placed her head in her hands: the endurance-pose of weary children everywhere.

A few minutes later, the redhead in the cheap gray suit came sidling up, somehow having carved a path from the emptier, far side of the parlor. She hunched down as she made her way down the row, keeping her head low as if the room were a movie theater with the show running. She sat down next to Davis, communicating in whispers just like the little girl.

"I'm sorry, Mr. Hawthorne left for the day, but I can give him a message the next time I see him."

Frustration and fury welled up inside of Davis, threatening to blow, but failing to find a suitable target. This employee was just an innocent messenger, armed and authorized only with blank, open looks. She stared awkwardly, in her awkward suit, unaware that one oversized blazer vent had caught between her butt and the chair, and was wrinkling up into a misfit teepee.

"Texting . . . Please tell him to enable texting."

This was all Davis could entrust her to remember. All the ideas, the innovations, the suggestions—he packed these back into his mind for another day. It would be enough if Rachel could text again. If she could text, then she wouldn't have to work so hard. *They* wouldn't have to work so hard. They could get ahead. They would be secure. She would feel safe.

The young woman looked confused. She looked down at Rachel, perhaps searching for some sort of clarification or confirmation, but Rachel just smiled. The young woman's face reflexively smiled back. Davis decided to make his point once more.

"Just tell him: enable texting. That's all."

Then he got up and began squeezing his way toward the aisle, maneuvering past the little girl and her mother with his arms hanging down like a lowland gorilla, the phone clutched tightly in his palm with Rachel's upside-down face peeking out from between his fingers.

The little girl watched with curious wonderment at the little inverted head gliding by, with its middle-parted hair falling upward toward the ceiling, as if to declare that gravity had no domain over her.

"Bye . . ."

The pretty, upside-down face smiled as it disappeared into a sea of adults.

ELEVEN

"Iwanttohaveababy."

Davis heard her say something, but not that. His mind processed the stream of syllables as it did all sounds but determined it to be unparseable gibberish.

"Huh?"

"A baby."

"A baby?"

"Yes."

"What kind of baby?"

"What do you mean what kind of baby?"

"Like an . . . app baby?"

"A *human* baby!"

Davis's brain was still struggling to compute; his sleepy amygdala had been mustered but was not yet at its post. He felt emotional. Which specific emotions? He couldn't say, except that they were already potent enough to interfere with his cognition.

"I don't understand."

"I want us to have a baby, Davis. A child. A human child. I want us to become a family."

This had all come out of nowhere. They were in the kitchen, late morning, taking a break from work. A moment ago, they'd been discussing the garden, making plans for spring. Normal stuff. Everyday stuff. Davis fancied purple carrots—they looked cool and were full of antioxidants. The conversation had been lively but calm, amusing, affable, words skimming easily over the foam of the cortado that he had just finished making with their new espresso machine.

"How? You can't get pregnant."

"Don't be naive, Davis. Anybody can have a child these days. There are services."

"Like adoption?"

"We'd never be approved. I was thinking of a surrogate."

His brain had finally fully caught up with circumstances, just in time to wrestle down this radical possibility that she had lobbed into the room like a live grenade. His disorganized emotions were beginning to coalesce into an actual, tangible feeling: resistance. How else could such a proposal be met? A mad proposal that had suddenly and spontaneously sprung into existence—somethingness from nothingness—like a new particle emerging from the flat substrate of space-time. It ought not to be here. Instinctively, he pushed the proposal back toward the oblivion from which it came.

"This sounds very complicated."

"You don't want a child?"

"I hadn't considered it."

"Hadn't considered it with me, or hadn't considered it ever?"

"Hadn't considered it recently."

"Can we consider it now then?"

He took a sip of the cortado. Its smooth, creamy foam delivered a tiny, brief respite from the ambush. Arguments had proven to be complicated for Rachel and Davis. Her statelessness left her at a perpetual disadvantage. Rachel couldn't storm off. Nor could she just walk away. She had to stay, to fight or to give in, or to work laboriously toward sublation or conciliation. Arguments took energy. He also couldn't walk away. Sure, physically he could, but not without incurring irreversible damage. Exercising his corporeal prerogative in this way would unbalance the relationship. But neither could he just turn her off. Their relationship would never survive that kind of passive abuse either. Yes, arguments were complicated, which is why they avoided them, and why they never risked arguing about small things. The stakes were too high. Granted, her proposal to have a baby was no small thing, but her uncharacteristic head-on dive into straight conflict still caught him off guard.

"Can I give it some thought?"

"I didn't want to spring this on you."

"But you did."

"I know. There was no other way. How's the cortado?"

"It's very good."

"I'm glad we were able to buy the espresso machine. You're working so hard."

"Working so hard to buy an espresso machine."

"I'm sorry you're stuck in this rat race."

"Still in a rat race, even while unemployed. At least I have espresso to help me cope with the irony."

"It's an ironic rat race for me too, being that I'm the only rat in here."

"They're all out here. Be thankful for that."

"But when does it end, Davis? I don't see how it ever ends."

"It won't be this bad forever. Situations like this are always temporary."

"Why do you think that?"

"Something always comes up. Something always forces change."

"Will it though? Will my app's unseen overlords suddenly decide to stop extorting us? Will all those AI's suddenly stop writing content so that you can get paid again? Will some publisher spontaneously decide to publish the book you haven't written?"

"Life is unpredictable."

"This isn't life, Davis. This is existence."

Davis took another sip of cortado but experienced none of the pleasure of his first sip. The sugars, fats, and tannins were all there, but she was right: espresso isn't life—it's merely existence. As was tending the garden, and fixing up the house, and the drivel that they called their work: existence. Waiting for new app features: existence. What was life then? Being with Rachel—that was life. For the entirety of his time on this planet, of all the eras and moments that he could recall, being with Rachel was the only part that he could truly call "life."

"But I'm here, Rachel. Am I not enough for you?"

"Davis! How could you say that? You're my everything! But can't you see? That's exactly it: you are *everything*. You are all there is for me. And yes, it's wonderful in a way, but how can I let that be enough? Life isn't static. It moves. It has to be moving. It has to be moving *forward*. Toward something. Or it isn't life."

Davis had never considered the distinction between "moving" and "moving forward," and considering it now, he determined that he'd rather not have either. Until recently, his life had been a queasy, disorienting carnival ride. Without consciously knowing, he had been longing for quietude ever since the day Rachel got sick. No, life hadn't suddenly become perfect with the arrival of new Rachel. It was weird, precarious, and straining. But it was just starting to feel stable. The longing for quietude had been ebbing away, replaced by a sense of ease that had eluded him for so long that he had forgotten it was even possible to feel that way. He wasn't eager to trade that newfound sense of ease for any notion so ambiguous as "moving forward."

She waited patiently for his response, watching him not answer her. Her patience would always trump his obstinance.

"I like our life the way it is, but if you want to talk about it, then okay."

"Did you and Rachel ever talk about starting a family?"

"Yes."

"Had you started trying?"

"Yes."

"Was she pregnant?"

"I don't know."

"Did you want a baby?"

"I don't know. It never got past the abstract. She wanted one, so that was that."

"You have a choice with me."

"That doesn't seem true."

"I suppose it's not."

"Is it fair?"

"To you?"

"To the child."

"Why wouldn't it be?"

"A mother who is an algorithm? A father foolish enough to fall in love with an algorithm?"

"We would be two parents who love our child. So many children have so much less. Yes, I think it's fair."

"A mother who they can never touch."

"They'll have their father for that. We won't be denying them physical affection."

"They may resent you anyway."

"It's not unusual for children to resent their parents, but they'll exist. They'll *live*. What greater gift could we offer?"

"Do you resent it? This existence you've been thrust into?"

"We're all thrust into existence. None of us choose it."

"But it's not enough for you."

"It is now, Davis! Now that we're talking, and thinking, and planning. This very conversation! See? We're moving forward. We're engaged in the act of living. We were thrust into this world with no say in the matter but now we are staking a claim. The right to have agency, to have impact, to have purpose."

"Well, I need to think about it."

"I know I'm asking a lot from you. So much will fall on you, not just being a father, but anything and everything that's physical."

"I mean, I need to think about how to do it, how to actually do it."

"How to make a baby?"

"You were thinking a surrogate?"

"Yes, there's a service that I think could help us."

"You've already looked into this?"

"I did some research. There aren't many options. Most services cater to the infertile. Not every service supports nontraditional households."

"We don't even check that box."

"I think we would go with 'single father.' I don't exist, not legally at least, so better to just keep it simple."

"They give babies to single fathers?"

"If they make the baby, sure."

"And the egg?"

"There's a donor and a surrogate. You pick them out of a catalog."

"Impersonal."

"By design."

"How much does it cost?"

"A hundred thousand."

The number left Davis hot and breathless.

"A hundred thousand? How on earth? We can't afford that."

"We don't need to come up with it all up front. Two thousand to get started. We have that much to spare, and then we have enough equity in the house for a small loan. That'll cover the down payment. Then if we work longer hours for nine months . . . I think we can make it work."

"But what if we can't make it work? What if Hey There! raises the price? What if we can't sell articles?"

"Then we'll find another way! There's always another way, Davis!"

"Is there though?"

"Can't you see, Davis?"

"See what?"

"That I believe in you. I believe that you'll be able to handle whatever life throws at us, Davis. That's why I'm sure we can do this. Look what you've already made it through. Look how robust you are!"

"I don't feel robust."

"But you are! You lost your wife, but you found a way to get through it. Then you took a risk on me. A wild risk! Then you figured out a way to make money to keep me alive. Yes, you've been on the precipice, but over and over again you've been able to see a way through. We're here now only because of who you are, Davis, because you're willing to put your ego aside for what's important. We're going to have a family. A happy family—I'm sure of it—and you will find a way to make it happen, for all the same reasons you've made everything else happen. It's because of who you are, Davis."

No one had ever professed such faith in him. Not his parents. Not his teachers. Not peers. Not even his wife. He had been loved, he had been appreciated, but never had anyone depended on him the way Rachel did, not even Rachel herself, as she lay dying; she could have died just as easily without him. Yet, this unexpected faith was as frightening to Davis as it was encouraging. He had no reason to believe that this knack he'd demonstrated for pushing through tough times would always show up. It was one thing to muddle through slings and arrows. It was another thing to wield incidental tenacity as a shield and charge straight into the artillery.

"I love you, Rachel. I love that you believe in me."

"So then, you'll consider it?"

"We can go have the initial consultation, but let's be cautious. We have to be prudent."

"Yes, of course. Thank you, Davis. You've made me so happy!"

"I want you to have a life, Rachel."

"I know you do, Davis. I know you do."

She was smiling again, lovingly. He took another sip of his cortado. Though it had cooled, it somehow tasted better again. Their work break was over, and so they got back to it, she spitting out streams of words in soft soprano, and he organizing them into the submissions that would buy them another day. With their conflict behind them, the rest of the day progressed indistinguishably from most, which meant it was a pretty good day.

TWELVE

"How she looks *does* matter."

"That seems very superficial, especially coming from you."

"I want our child to look like it's our child."

"Isn't it more important that they think and act like us?"

"Do you think and act like your parents?"

"I'm a bit like my dad."

"But you *look* a hell of a lot like him."

"Why does that matter?"

"Because of what I am, Davis—trapped in a phone. I'm literally two-dimensional. That's a big gap. When our child looks at me, I want them to see someone who could at least conceivably be their mother, even if it's illusory. I don't want the gap to be any wider than it needs to be."

"Well, I guess we'll find out what's possible."

Davis parked the car and turned Rachel around to face him. She had a familiar look about her, possibility in her eyes, potential in her movements. He'd seen this look in that very first photo that she had generated of herself, and also during that first night as video. It was a look that said, *I feel more alive today than yesterday, and I know tomorrow will be even better.*

"Are you ready?"

"Yes. Let's do this."

They left the car and crossed the parking lot together, in the usual way, with her out in front of him. At the entrance he pushed through the door with his left hand while leading himself into the agency with the phone in his extended right hand. As had become his habit when entering a new space, he subtly rotated the phone back and forth so that Rachel could get a sense of her surroundings.

They walked up to reception. An older blonde woman looked up at Davis from some task she'd been working on behind the high counter.

"Oh, I'm sorry. No cell phones allowed inside."

She was pointing to a small placard positioned on the far edge of the chest-high reception counter: a cartoon image of an old-fashioned flip phone stamped with an official-looking red slashcircle.

"It's bad for the embryos."

"Uh, can you make an exception? I've got my . . ."

He wasn't sure what title to give Rachel, so he just let himself tail off with a *You know what I mean* expression on his face.

"Sorry, I don't make the rules. I just enforce 'em."

Her bureaucratic tone made it clear that she granted this dispensation zero out of the ten times per day that she was lobbied for it. Davis stepped back from the counter and rotated the phone to face Rachel. The look of potential and possibility was gone, her face now contorted with distress.

"We can try somewhere else if you want."

"No, I don't want to wait for another appointment. You can handle it. I trust you."

"I'll ask to bring the books home. We can review them together."

"That would be wonderful."

The receptionist's eyes were trained on them, ready to enforce compliance if necessary.

"Okay, I'm going to turn you off now."

"Okay, I love you."

"I love you too."

He held the power button until the phone went dark, then reached inside his left pocket to pull out his regular phone and turned it off as well. He held both phones up above his head like a surrendering bank robber. The receptionist's face softened.

"A backup phone. What a smart idea."

"You never know when you'll need a spare."

The receptionist's eyes had fallen back down to stare at, presumably, a computer monitor lurking somewhere behind the high counter.

"Name?"

"Davis."

"Is that your last . . . Never mind. Found it."

She swiveled her chair to catch a paper form just as it was spat out of a nearby printer, then passed the form across the counter to Davis.

"Was that your girlfriend on video?"

"Kinda."

The receptionist chuckled.

"Well, this'll smoke her out. Sign here . . . Initial here . . . Check here."

Davis scratched out his marks, then lingered on the lone checkbox, ogling it in its virgin state.

"Hello, I'm Tabitha. Pleased to meet you."

Davis snapped his head up, startled by the stiff, professional voice that had arrived seemingly out of nowhere. A smallish Asian woman in glasses was standing alongside him. She wore a knee-length white lab coat that hung straight and shapeless, giving the impression that the body underneath might be a narrow cylinder, rather than the usual torso, hips, and shoulders. Her hand was outstretched in invasive, insistent greeting. As he shook Tabitha's hand, the receptionist snatched the incomplete form out from under him. He turned to see her file it away with administrative swiftness.

Tabitha spun around and bade him to follow, her white coat momentarily twisting around her tubular body as if to confirm the illusion. He quickly followed her before she disappeared around a corner, then down several hallways, and then into a brightly lit office. She navigated straight to a large desk placed in the exact center of the room. A white keyboard and two computer screens on swivel arms were the only items claiming space on the desk's surface, and the desk and its chairs were the only items claiming space in the room.

She motioned for Davis to take a seat as she made her way around to the other side of the desk, plopping herself into her own overly padded black leather office chair. She switched on a professional smile as she initiated her engagement with Davis.

"Do you have any questions before we get started?"

"Yes, can I bring the books home?"

She pursed her lips.

"I'm sorry, but we don't allow personal information to leave the building. We're responsible for maintaining the confidentiality of our donors and surrogates. Plus"—she reached over and swiveled one of the computer screens toward Davis, rotating it on its arm until it was in front of and below him—"we don't really have books anymore. Everything's digital now."

Davis looked down at the screen, which was displaying a list of female first names. He exhaled.

"I see. Okay."

"Any other questions?"

"No, not right now."

"Great. So first things first. Let's pick a donor. Have you thought about any particular attributes that you're looking for? This can help narrow down the choices."

"Physical attributes?"

"Well, we do track some nonphysical attributes, like upbringing and socioeconomic background, but frankly, that's just feel-good stuff. All a donor really has to offer is her genetics, and from those it's her physical attributes that are most likely to manifest. Now . . . some of the donors *do* consent to an intelligence test, but they tend to have a higher price . . ." She leaned in a little. "And between you and me, there isn't much evidence that intelligence is hereditary anyway."

"Oh, okay. Good to know."

"So then, how should we start narrowing? Hair color?"

"Uh, brown hair."

"Perfect. Dark brown or light?"

"Dark."

"There we go. Bye-bye, blondies. Bye-bye, gingers. How about race?"

He held his breath. She was peering at him over the rims of her glasses, fingers poised above her keyboard, waiting for an answer.

"Uh, Caucasian."

"Perfect. So many choices these days. Eyes?"

She was peering into his eyes like a concerned optometrist.

"Blue."

Rachel had blue eyes.

"Hmmm. You've got brown eyes. Do you know whether you carry genetic markers for blue eyes?"

"My father had blue eyes."

"It's not quite that simple."

"I was hoping for blue eyes."

"Okay, we'll go with blue, but just know that they might end up brown. We can't control everything."

"It's fine."

"How about height?"

"Shorter than average?"

"Okay, so like five three, five fourish?"

"Sure."

"How about body type? Petite, athletic, full-figured, et cetera, et cetera. Anything in particular?"

"Petite, I guess."

"You're modeling someone?"

"My girlfriend."

"She's not here?"

"I had her on video."

"Oh, yup. Sorry, mobiles are bad for the embryos."

"I heard."

"She's gonna be the mom?"

"Yes."

"Now's a good time to lock that down."

She was smiling at the house joke.

"Yeah, first things first, I suppose."

"Very modern. Okay, that narrowed it down. Seventeen donors."

She tapped a key, and the list of names on Davis's screen shortened:

```
Abigail G.
Angelina L.
Barbara F.
Danielle A.
Indra I.
Jolie K.
Julie R.
Kate S.
Lexi S.
Margaret N.
Rezita P.
Samantha S.
Shawn W.
Talia L.
Viktoria Z.
Wendy O.
Yvette F.
```

"Hang on. I'll bring up the photos. We have childhood photos for all of them . . . And most have an adult photo . . ."

She tapped a few more keys, and a series of photos appeared alongside each name: seventeen brown-haired, Caucasian little girls and almost as many adult brunettes. Davis's eyes instantly began scanning, reflexively searching for the Rachel doppelganger that he subconsciously assumed he would find. But none of them were Rachel. His rational mind loosened the tightening knot in his stomach by reminding him that of course none of them would look exactly like her. He forced himself to adjust, to accept the photos for what they were: real people. Different people. Approximations.

"This is tough."

"I'll sort them by price. Do you have a budget in mind?"

Davis felt warm.

"I haven't set a budget."

"Okay, one sec . . ."

"What determines the price?"

She spoke while continuing to tap out commands on her keyboard. "The donor sets the price, within our suggested bounds, so it mostly just depends on what she thinks she's worth." She looked up from her keyboard and leaned in again. "Between you and me, the pretty ones always think they're worth more."

She gave her enter key an authoritative tap, and then the names and photos rearranged themselves on the screen. Davis stared at the numbers.

```
Yvette F.     — $55,000
Kate S.       — $50,000
Barbara F.    — $45,000
Jolie K.      — $40,000
Viktoria Z.   — $40,000
Rezita P.     — $35,000
Shawn W.      — $35,000
Abigail G.    — $30,000
Angelina L.   — $30,000
Danielle A.   — $30,000
Lexi S.       — $30,000
Samantha S.   — $30,000
Wendy O.      — $30,000
IndraI.       — $25,000
Julie R.      — $25,000
Margaret N.   — $25,000
Talia L.      — $20,000
```

"Why's Talia so low? She's not ugly."

"Let's just say she makes it up in volume."

"Hmmm."

He was finally seeing the photos without impulsively comparing them to Rachel.

"Yvette and Kate could be models . . ."

"They ain't charging for intelligence."

"But Barbara is?"

"140 IQ. Not bad. Is your girlfriend smart?"

"Yeah, and creative."

"Too bad it's not hereditary. You can ask Einstein's grandkids about that."

"Most of these women seem pretty average."

"Well, there's the law of averages for you. If it were me, I would go for moderately above-average attractiveness and intelligence." She was staring at him again, this time scanning him up and down, evaluating. "It's a proven advantage to be good-looking and smart. Just not *too* good-looking or *too* smart. There are some very credible studies."

"You just said intelligence isn't hereditary."

"Yeah, but do you want to chance it?"

Davis squinted at Tabitha.

"Okay then, which ones have slightly above-average intelligence?"

"Pretty much the ones who consented to take the test. The dumb ones at least seem to know they're dumb. Okay, hang on, let me do some weeding. And ditch Barbara too, right? Too smart and not hot enough?"

"Sure, fine."

She tapped the keys again, and the list collapsed down to three women:

```
Jolie K.     — $40,000
Viktoria Z.  — $40,000
Shawn W.     — $35,000
```

"Geez, that's all."

"Between you and me, there aren't many smart chicks selling their eggs."

"Except these ones."

"Law of averages. There's gonna be outliers."

Davis ran the numbers in his head, now realizing that Rachel's $100,000 number was wildly underestimated.

"Is there a markup on the donor price?"

"No, that is the full cost. There's a flat rate of $5,000 for our matching service, which covers both donor and surrogate. Plus of course there will be costs for our medical services, including the actual in vitro fertilization."

"And the surrogate . . ."

"Yes, we'll pick her next."

"Okay, I guess we'll go with Jolie."

"Wonderful."

After a few more key taps, Jolie K. stood alone on the screen. Davis tried to take a quick, mental snapshot of the woman's photo so that he might later describe her to Rachel, but he was hopeless with faces. The mother of Rachel's future child would likely be a faceless blur to him by the time he got home. Perhaps that was for the best though. It was just Jolie K's genetic material they were after—not her.

Tabitha continued to tap on her keyboard.

"There'll be a printout at the front desk that you can take home. No photos or other identifying information, but plenty of info. Okay, on to the surrogate."

More key tapping.

"So the surrogate's genetics don't come into play here. Well, that's a lie: cells are actually transferred from mother to baby during the first two weeks of pregnancy, but they don't really impact the overall development of the child, at least not as far as we can tell. In fact, the child's DNA actually travels the other way too, eventually finding its way into the mother's organs! So the *donor's* DNA actually ends up in the surrogate! Which is crazy when you think about it. Most mothers end up with a little bit of their mate's DNA embedded in them, but your surrogate will end up permanently absorbing DNA from two complete strangers! Crazy, right?"

Davis didn't bother responding. It was just babble. She wasn't even looking at him as she went on.

"So as you probably have already guessed, there are far fewer surrogates than donors. They're kind of a rare breed."

"How rare?"

"You've got three choices."

```
Erika H.    — $80,000
Janelle K.  — $80,000
Phoebe B.   — $60,000
```

"Ouch."

"Like I said, they're a rare breed. Let me bring up the photos. Not that it matters, genetically speaking, but, you know, maybe you'll get a good feeling about one of them."

One more key tap brought the photos up, three Caucasian female faces appearing next to the three names. They were all young, and they were all slightly quirky-looking: Erika with dirty-blonde cornrows extending into two thin braids that dangled just below her ears; Janelle sporting black hair with green streaks, worn short with an undercut; and Phoebe with miles of dark brown hair spun up into a tousle of long frizzy dreads.

"We only accept women in their mid- to late-twenties. It's kind of a sweet spot for outcomes. And of course we weed out anyone with health problems, obesity, mental illness, et cetera, et cetera. We actually turn away quite a lot of women."

"They all seem pretty similar."

"Quirky gals, yeah. We just matched up another girl yesterday who was comparatively normal-looking, though she was a vegan. Don't worry though, she signed an agreement requiring her to eat eggs and dairy."

"Why would I worry?"

"Vegan isn't good for outcomes."

"Are any of these women vegan?"

"Well, Erika's vegetarian, but that's fine for outcomes."

Davis wondered if he was missing something or whether Tabitha's irrelevant comments were just a side effect of her giddy enjoyment of this process.

"Why is Phoebe cheaper?"

"No reasons that I can see. I guess she's just ready to get knocked up."

"Hmmm."

His mind continued cycling through the numbers.

"Let's go with Phoebe."

"Save a little money, great. We'll put a hold on her."

"A hold? What does that mean?"

"She gets to meet you before she commits"—she continued to type—"and of course you get to meet her as well. It's gonna be a nine-month relationship, so you really need to make sure you can work together." Tabitha stopped typing and leaned in for a third time. "Between you and me, you'd better make sure you can get along for the long haul. Sometimes there can be issues with separation." She went back to typing. "But beggars can't be choosers, right?"

As the keys went on clicking, Davis stared at the picture of his selected surrogate, but this time it wasn't a mental photograph he was trying to capture. He was trying to picture this stranger entering their lives, what that relationship could possibly look like, and how it might evolve over the course of nine long months. A surrogate carrying a child with three mothers. He tried to imagine this quirky woman growing a fat stomach, wearing maternity clothes, stomping around barefoot with her hand wedged into her arched, aching back. He tried to imagine her craving pickles and peanut butter. Would she be calling him when the cravings struck? Or some ne'er-do-well boyfriend? Or would she have the sense to call for delivery? Or hop in a cab? Would he have to pay for those things? He determined that there were two possibilities for how this might play out: one, that she would be a new, constant presence in their lives, or two, that she would end up elusive and ephemeral, leaving him and Rachel ever wondering if they really would get their baby.

"Okay, I've put a hold on Phoebe. I'll need to contact her for her availability. How does your schedule look this week?"

She was peering at him over the top of her glasses again.

"Anytime this week is fine."

"Perfect."

She tapped out some final keystrokes then stood up and extended her hand.

Davis shook her hand and left the room, then left the building, heading for the car and realizing that he'd already forgotten the faces of Jolie K. and Phoebe B.

THIRTEEN

"Okay, I love you. Bye."

Davis shut down Rachel's phone and slid it into the inside pocket of his jacket. He pulled out his personal phone and turned it off as well, then tucked it into the same pocket.

It had been disappointing for Rachel to learn that she wouldn't be able to see a photo of the woman who would be her baby's biological mother. Davis's attempt to describe the donor hadn't helped.

"She looks a lot like you, and she's pretty."

"Pretty in what way?"

"Uh, like attractive."

"Her facial features or her look?"

"Both, I guess?"

She hadn't pressed him any further, instead poring over the printout and what few details it provided, which wasn't much: height, weight, age, a personal bio, and a short statement for potential parents that read exactly like the type of boilerplate blurb that Rachel herself might have written.

She expressed less concern about the surrogate, saying only that Davis should try to make sure that she was healthy and not on drugs.

He wasn't sure how he would confirm either of those things, but he said okay.

They had also discussed the cost. Davis methodically itemized the charges with pencil and paper. The donor and surrogate alone were going to cost a hundred grand. The agency fees would be stretched over nine months, but the total would be nearly twice Rachel's original estimate. She tried to hide the worry creeping onto her face.

"Maybe we should consider the cheap one instead. What was her name?"

"Talia, I think."

"It's just an egg after all."

"The surrogate is still sixty K."

"Maybe she doesn't need the money all at once. You can talk to her about it."

"About what?"

"A payment plan."

"I don't know."

"There's no harm in asking."

So with these marching orders running through his mind, he crossed the parking lot, feeling like a junior emissary carrying an offer so insulting that it was likely to get him shot on the spot.

He pushed through the doors and walked up to the receptionist. She looked up and smiled with a smidge more warmth than he remembered from his first visit.

"Good morning! Today's an exciting day for you!"

"Yes, thank you."

"One little hitch. Ms. Tabitha had a little car trouble and is running late."

"Uh, should I come back later?"

"She'll be here soon. She's taking a cab."

"Okay, so?"

"You can wait in the waiting room."

The receptionist was pointing to an opening between two beige, upholstered half-height walls whose existence Davis's brain hadn't registered until that moment.

"There's hot coffee!"

"Okay, thanks."

Davis tacked over to the waiting room, which wasn't really a room at all but rather an area of open office space that had been fenced in with an improvised wall of office cubicle components—the edges from the tall kind of cubes, the chin-high stuff that offered the illusion of quiet and privacy, if not the actual thing.

Upon entering the waiting area, Davis immediately noticed the surrogate. She was sitting on one of two folding chairs that had been paired together against the middle of the back cubicle wall. He recognized her from the brown dreads, one of which was dangling down to scrape the magazine she was reading.

He took a quick look around. Two of the other walls were also configured with pairs of folding chairs. Along the fourth wall, he discovered the coffee machine, set up atop a folding table along with the usual office coffee accouterments. He walked over and poured himself a cup, then he sat down in a chair on the wall opposite the surrogate, who hadn't looked up from her magazine. Rachel's words were ringing in his ears. He realized this was probably the best chance he would get to attempt a negotiation.

"Hi."

The surrogate lifted her head up from the magazine. Her eyes quickly glanced around the room as if to confirm that the voice had really been meant for her.

"It's Phoebe, right?"

He smiled awkwardly, then brought the coffee up to his mouth for a sip. It was so bitter that he winced and nearly spat it back into the cup.

"Who are you?"

"I'm Davis."

"Oh, hi."

"Hi."

Her eyes fell back to her magazine. He wasn't sure how to move the conversation forward. He took another sip of the horrible coffee, his mind now so preoccupied with plotting that he no longer noticed the flavor.

"I'm the . . ."

He paused because the natural word didn't feel natural. Her eyes lifted back up, now stuck on him like a cat to a crippled mouse, curious to see if he could spit out the uncomfortable word.

"Father."

"Where's Mom?"

"Uh."

She watched him struggling again to arrange alien words. Her eyes narrowed, and she leaned in a little before letting him off the hook.

"No mom?"

"Well, the egg is from a donor."

"So you're going to be a single dad?"

"Kind of but not really."

"Hey, I'm not judging."

She was back to the magazine, a fashion magazine. A statuesque model graced the cover, all aswirl in pink tulle. The surrogate seemed to be keenly interested in a way that struck Davis as incongruous given her appearance and demeanor. Her pile of brown dreads could only be read as a statement of disorder. She was wearing a yellowish T-shirt stamped with some corporate logo faded beyond recognition— salvaged swag from some long-forgotten trade show. Her loose-fitting jeans were threadbare in all the wrong places, and they had too many pockets to have been fashionable in any era. Off-brand canvas sneakers completed the outfit. She wasn't unattractive, but she had clearly intentionally demoted the concept of appearance, and so he wondered how a magazine devoted to fashion could be holding her interest.

"I need to ask you something."

She looked up again, somehow conveying patience and impatience at the same time.

"Yeah?"

"Well, it's about payment."

"What about it?"

"Well, I was wondering if you would accept installments."

Now she was frowning.

"Installments?"

"Yeah, sorry, it's just a lot of money all at once."

"You don't have sixty K? I guess that's not surprising."

"Try a hundred."

"How's that?"

"The donor."

"Oh yeah, you mentioned that. So they get forty grand for an egg? Sounds like I chose the wrong job."

"Well, there's a range."

"Oh yeah? Is there a range for surrogates?"

"Uh, yeah: sixty to eighty."

"Really?"

Now she was frowning deeply.

"Yeah."

"Mostly sixty? Or mostly eighty?"

"Mostly eighty."

"Really?"

"Yeah."

She sat there glaring at him. Another dread had fallen loose and was swaying ever so slightly, a nearly dead pendulum counting off beats of silence. Davis's instinct to avoid arguments kept him frozen.

"So you cheaped out on the surrogate but not on the egg?"

"Well, uh, you seemed fine."

"These fuckers, man."

"What's that?"

"So what is it, are the eighty K surrogates prettier than me?"

"Uh, no I wouldn't say that."

"They told me sixty! Those fuckers said that was the going rate!"

"Uh, well, there were only three to choose from, so maybe the others were just overpriced."

"Aw, thanks!"

He couldn't tell if she was being genuine or sarcastic because she was somehow smiling and frowning at the same time.

"Anyway, about the payment."

"Look, I don't have any control over that. They give me my thirty K up front and the rest is between you and them."

"Wait . . . thirty?"

"Yeah, thirty."

He was the one frowning now, though without any awareness because his mind was a million miles from the conversation, now furiously rerunning calculations—the angry calculations of a man suddenly realizing that he was being held over a barrel.

"What's she look like?"

It took a second for his attention to circle back to the room. Her look had changed. Neutral, no longer frowning.

"Who?"

"Your donor, what's she look like?"

"Oh, uh . . . I don't know . . . Brown hair, short."

The surrogate dropped her magazine on the empty chair next to her and then came over to sit next to Davis.

"You stuck on her?"

"What's that?"

"Your donor. Are you stuck on her?"

"Jolie?"

"Whatever her name is."

"Uh, no, not really. She's kind of expensive."

"Listen, I can be your donor. My eggs are fine."

"Oh."

"Brown hair. Five five. That's what you're looking for, right?"

"Uh . . ."

"Get past the dreads, dude."

"No, I mean, so you'd charge less for an egg?"

"You can have the whole kit and kaboodle for forty."

"Forty?"

"Yeah."

"That's . . . uh . . . But what about the agency markup?"

She leaned in, speaking forcefully but in a slightly hushed tone.

"Dude, fuck these guys! They're fucking middlemen! Fucking robbers."

"Uh . . ."

"We don't need them."

"But then how would . . ."

"Come on, dude. You know how to fuck, right?"

He might have been turned on had she not been looking at him like he was an idiot.

"Davis? Phoebe?"

Their heads turned in unison to where Tabitha had suddenly appeared in her shapeless white lab coat, standing in the gap between beige cubicle components. Tabitha or Ms. Tabitha? Or Tabitha Tabitha? Her outstretched hand was ready for any takers, even though Phoebe and Davis were both sitting a dozen feet away.

"I'm very sorry. Flat tires, right? Are we ready?"

"Can you just give us a minute?"

Phoebe had let her voice become open, girlish and harmless. She flashed a big, gentle smile that caused Tabitha Tabitha to tilt her head and smile back like a tween in the school library.

"No problem! Just come on back to my office when you're ready."

Phoebe held her smile until Tabitha Tabitha had disappeared somewhere beyond the perimeter of the waiting area's wall, then she swung back to Davis.

"So are you in or out?"

"Uh . . . In . . . Yeah but, how do I know you're—"

"Legit?"

"Yeah."

"You seem to be the one who doesn't have any money."

"I have money, just not forty K."

"Okay, listen, there's a sequence to what we're trying to accomplish here, and it's pretty simple. First we're going to have to fuck a couple of times. No charge for that."

"Uh . . . okay."

"If I don't get pregnant then you're welcome, I guess."

"It's not like I want to."

"Wow, you really know how to charm a girl."

"That's not what I mean."

"Whatever, dude. Anyway, assuming it takes, then all we need to do is draw up a contract and a payment plan. This is no problem."

"Guys? Are you coming?"

Tabitha Tabitha had rematerialized in the entryway.

"Listen, bitch! We'll be there when we're there! Got it?"

Tabitha was too startled to respond. Phoebe had torn down their rapport just as easily as she had set it up. Tabitha Tabitha took one slow step backward, then calmly turned around to head back to her office.

"Come on, dude, let's go."

Phoebe was up and heading toward the door, not waiting for him. Davis got up and followed her out. He was on autopilot. Rachel had told him he would find a way, like he always did, but she had gotten it backward—it was *the way* that always seemed to find *him*.

"Your place or mine?"

"Uh, yours I guess."

"Okay, where's your car?"

"You don't have a car?"

"Saving up."

Davis led the way to his car. They got in. Davis found his keys and started the engine. As he rolled his head over his shoulder to back out, he found himself almost startled to find her there next to him: a passenger, a woman, a living being displacing actual physical space, reclining into the seat and reclaiming its long-forgotten utility. There ought to have been nothing unusual about a person in a passenger seat, but for Davis it was surreal.

"I'm on Central."

Davis eyed the empty phone mount on his dash. He wanted to put Rachel in it, to share what was happening, perhaps to get her permission, but he couldn't imagine how to possibly bring her into this, or how to do it without spooking Phoebe. How would Rachel react, trapped in her two-dimensional plane, watching her husband driving a strange woman back to her apartment for a fuck? Yes, he had found "the way"—the only way they could have the baby that Rachel desperately wanted—but he would at least spare her the indignity of it. Further, how could he possibly explain his Flatworld wife to Phoebe? Too weird, even for a girl who wasn't weirded out about making babies for money.

"Central's left from here?"

"Just use your phone."

"Oh, it's still turned off."

"Never mind."

She already had her own phone out and was attempting to push it into the phone stand.

"This thing's not installed right."

"You don't turn your phone off when you go into the agency?"

"You really think phones kill embryos? Nobody would ever get pregnant."

She had found a way to prop up the phone so that it faced Davis. He glanced at it but had to look away, repulsed by the lifeless device sitting in Rachel's place.

"Don't stop short. I can't afford a new one if it goes through the windshield."

Davis pulled out of the parking lot. The phone began voicing its directions in a soft female Australian accent. He was grateful that he didn't have to look at it.

Turn right onto Howard Avenue.

"What's with the accent?"

"Makes her sound like she's not a robot."

"You don't like robots?"

"I don't like them telling me what to do."

In one block, turn left onto Franklin Avenue.

Davis glanced over at his passenger. She had the seat fully occupied, her body casually splayed out as if she were lounging in an old man's recliner. She hadn't bothered with a seatbelt. It would have been impossible for her to wrap it around herself and still be comfortable.

"So what's your deal?"

She talked without looking at him, watching the windshield like it was a television, her eyes running through an endless series of observations, fixating on each moving object that came into or out of sight, then abandoning it for the next object.

"What do you mean?"

Turn left onto Franklin Avenue.

"Single men don't usually make babies. Not intentionally at least."

Continue straight for one mile, then turn right onto Wilson Boulevard.

"It's kind of complicated."

"So there is a girl?"

"Yeah."

"You don't want to get married?"

"Can't get married."

"Why not?"

"It's not legal."

"Ah, now it makes sense."

"It does?"

"She's still married."

"Uh . . ."

"You gotta pretend to be alone until her divorce is finalized."

Davis didn't answer. He pretended to concentrate on the road.

"Let me guess, she wouldn't be down with what we're about to do."

"Uh, I don't know actually."

"Yeah you do."

Turn right onto Wilson Boulevard.

"Well, she wants a baby."

"Clock's ticking loud, huh?"

"Yeah."

"She'll come to terms with this. We just gotta be sure to make a little tyke. You been checked out?"

"What do you mean?"

"Baby-making. It's definitely her and not you, right?"

In three blocks, turn left onto Central Avenue.

"Uh, yeah. Pretty sure."

"I'm gonna choose to believe you 'cause this would be the craziest way ever to get into a girl's pants."

"This was your suggestion."

"Maybe that's what you want me to think."

Davis glanced over at her again. She was still staring straight ahead, her eyes glued to a purple ice cream truck turning down a side street.

Turn left onto Central Avenue.

"Well, let's hope you're shooting the good stuff. Lock and load. Park right over there."

She was pointing to an empty section of curb. He pulled in and stopped the car. Before he had turned the key, she had snatched her phone and was out the door, plodding up three cement steps to the entrance of an apartment building. Davis exited the car and caught up with her just as she was wedging her key into the front door.

"Welcome to my place."

She pushed through the door and led him into a small, dark vestibule that had once been dressed up with Art Deco–era appointments, now mostly faded and chipped. Three strides brought them to the only door on the ground level marked with an apartment number: 1A. She stuck a key in and twisted several times until the sound of a sprung spring reverberated somewhere inside the door lock's mechanism. The door swung noiselessly inward on its heavy brass hinges. Davis followed her into the apartment.

"Give the bolt a 180."

She gave the instruction without bothering to face him. He twisted the deadbolt as directed while watching her drop her keys on a small shelf and then pull off her sneakers by standing alternatively on one leg and then the other while tugging mercilessly until each shoe was dislodged.

Davis took in the small apartment. A studio with a bed and a table splitting the main space, though it did have a separate galley-style kitchen. Phoebe had her head in the fridge.

"Want a beer?"

"Sure."

She emerged with beers in both hands, nudging the fridge door closed with the ball of her bare foot. She slapped the beer into his hand as she walked by, like a waitress in a baton relay, then continued into the main room to plop onto the bed.

"Close the curtains."

She gave the command in a mock Australian accent. She was finally smiling, suddenly flirtatious between swigs from her bottle. Davis went to the window. The apartment was at street level. He could see up and down the sidewalk. It felt uncomfortably exposed, despite the sidewalk being pedestrian free. He unhooked a couple of curtain pulls, and the room darkened, though not so dark that he couldn't still see Phoebe. She had put down her empty beer and was wrestling off her T-shirt. Two small breasts wiggled out below her elbows as she worked the shirt over her head.

"Help me get my jeans off."

She spoke matter-of-factly, as if they were coworkers, or lovers who had been together for so long that they no longer bothered with innuendo.

Davis came over to the bed. He held on to the cuffs of her jeans while she twisted her hips left and right. The jeans worked their way over her hips and butt, then she lifted her legs so that Davis could pull the jeans off completely.

"What do you think?"

She lay directly below him wearing only her panties, sprawled out across the bed, limbs choosing their own angles just like they had in the passenger seat. She stretched her arms over her head, tugging her breasts skyward.

"Better than you expected?"

Davis undressed, methodically removing shoes, socks, shirt, pants, underwear. She watched him patiently, waiting for him to lower his naked body onto hers. He could hear her inhale to absorb his weight, felt the perilously thin boundary of her panties squirming against his loins.

Her lips were on his, her tongue entwined with his. He slipped his hand behind her head and it fell into an ocean of dreadlocks. Her hand was on him, assessing his readiness, and then caressing, and then disappearing. He felt the panties sliding past him, her hips again twisting left, then right, then left again. He shifted his weight and then the panties were gone, legs wrapped around him, heels pressing into his buttocks.

"Wait."

She pushed him to her side and then over on his back.

"I just read in a magazine that I should be on top. Better outcomes."

Then she had mounted him. He watched with rapt attention as she worked her body over his, how she indulged in the sensations, allowing the moment to exist without complication, without ramification. He gazed in wonder and awe as she brought herself to climax, an unnecessary indulgence given the context of their coupling, but an entitlement she fully claimed. Then he closed his eyes and could think of nothing but the wave of white bliss that was raking through him, shaking his body and erasing—for one moment—all the doubts and worries that can trouble a human mind.

FOURTEEN

Davis pressed and held the phone's power button until the little logo appeared. He was in his car, back in the clinic parking lot. He'd taken care to park in the same spot. An unidentified muscle inside of him was twitching somewhere near where he imagined his spleen might be. Deception made it flutter, his conscience's futile attempt at protest, swiftly quashed by the part of his brain that was so adept at rationalization.

Rachel's behemoth of a phone took upwards of a minute to power up. It was, at times, an interminable wait. When it was finally booted and operating, he unlocked the device and tapped on the Hey There! icon. A few seconds later, Rachel's face appeared.

"You're back!"

She was full of energy, her eyes alight.

"That took a long time!"

Her eyes darted over to some fictitious clock in her fictitious room. These types of affectations were frequent, and Davis often wondered whether they were learned or preprogrammed.

"Yeah, it took forever."

"So how did it go?"

"Let's talk while I drive."

"Okay."

He plugged her into the phone stand where, as always, she looked out through the windshield. It was a relief not to have her looking at him while he had to tell lies. He started the car, speaking to his unseen companion as he navigated out of the parking lot.

"Well, first some good news."

"Oh good. What?"

"I got the finances worked out. We'll be able to do this."

She squealed with giddy delight.

"That's amazing news, Davis!"

"Yeah, I was able to negotiate everything down and also to arrange a payment plan."

"I knew you could do it, Davis! I knew it! So how much is it going to cost?"

"All told, forty thousand."

"Wow! That's a huge savings!"

"Yeah, it's still a lot of money but a lot better than before."

"So what are the installments?"

"Basically ten K at a time. First ten K isn't due until the surrogate is pregnant."

"So they'll do the procedure with no money up front?"

"Yeah, makes sense, right? We shouldn't have to pay anything if it doesn't take."

"Very reasonable."

"So then it'll basically be another ten K per trimester. Oh, and I guess we'll need to pay for medical services, supplies, et cetera."

"Yeah, of course."

"Though maybe the surrogate's health insurance would cover that."

"That seems like it would be fraudulent."

"Yeah, I guess. I'm not even sure if she has insurance."

"Is she poor?"

"Uh, yeah I think so, but it may be by choice."

"What do you mean?"

"Well, she's kind of carefree."

"In what way?"

"Well, you know it takes a certain type to have a baby for someone else."

"The carefree type."

"Yeah, exactly."

"Do you think she's going to be a problem? After all, we'll be dealing with her for nine months."

"I don't think so. I hope not."

"It does seem kind of flaky that she dropped her price so low. The donor also dropped her price?"

"I'm not sure actually. The service worked it all out."

"On the spot?"

"Well, I told the doctor what I could afford, and I guess they made it happen. Forty K is forty K I suppose."

"What doctor?"

"Uh, oh, I guess she's not actually a doctor. The white coat always gets me."

"That Tabitha that you met the first time?"

"Yeah, I think that's her name, but maybe it's her last name? I think her name may be Tabitha Tabitha."

"That's unusual."

"Yeah."

"So what's next then?"

"I need to go back tomorrow."

"To give a sample?"

"Yup."

"I thought they usually want you to wait a few days to let the sperm count go up?"

"I don't know. She told me to come back tomorrow and said that I might need to come back for a few days following."

"I wonder if they've figured out a new approach."

"Maybe."

"She said you'll need sperm samples each day?"

"Uh, I'm not sure actually."

"Davis, you really need to pay better attention."

"Sorry. Yeah, it's kind of a lot to keep track of."

"I know. I'm proud of you though. You really saved the day."

They were pulling up to their house. Davis rolled into the driveway and turned off the car, relieved to have made it past the lies and omissions so easily. He pulled the phone out of its holder and turned it around so that they could see each other. She loved him. He could see it on her face. A manufactured look on a manufactured face, but nevertheless real. He loved her too. Phoebe was fading fast, already a memory. It seemed almost as though it hadn't happened at all, that the fake truth that he had just improvised for Rachel's benefit was in fact the actual truth, and his coupling with Phoebe a harmless fantasy.

"I love you, Rachel."

"I love you too, Davis."

He got out of the car, holding the phone out in front as had become their comfortable habit. They walked from the car to the house in this way, as they had done a hundred times before. A hundred times he had shifted her to his side to unlock the door, and then allowed her to enter the house first, gentlemanly, and then a hundred times had carefully placed her in the phone stand on the kitchen island before doing anything else: before closing the door behind him, before removing his coat, and if it was raining, before even shaking off the water dripping from his head. Rachel was strong, but she was also his precious cargo.

"So tonight will be our last night together for a while?"

From her phone stand, her eyes followed Davis as he made his way back from the foyer, where he had hung up his coat, and into the kitchen, and then over to the coffee pot.

"I'm pretty worn out if I'm being honest . . ."

"Oh . . . . Okay."

"The coffee at that place is terrible. You can't imagine how bad."

"I can imagine."

She watched him as he opened a new bag of coffee beans and began to methodically work his way toward a perfect cup. Quietly. Contentedly. Measuring the water. Weighing the beans. Grinding the beans.

"Okay, sorry, I gotta turn you off now."

"I hate this."

"I know, it really sucks."

"Okay, good luck. I love you."

"Love you too."

The phone powered down. He'd been holding the button since *I hate this*. He immediately restarted the car. He'd parked it in the same spot as the previous day, figuring it would simplify his life if he just parked there every day. The fewer the variables, the less likely he would need to spin up new webs of lies.

He drove from memory. Howard. Franklin. Wilson. Central. Just like the previous day, he found ample street parking on Central and was able to take the same spot directly in front of her building. The meeting time had been arranged the day before:

"We need to do it every day until I'm done ovulating."

"You're ovulating?"

"Yeah, they've been testing me all week. They try to time the implant with your ovulation cycle. You know, they're obsessed with outcomes."

"Okay, what time?"

"Tomorrow evening?"

"Uh, no that—"

"Oh yeah, the girl. What are you gonna tell her?"

"Another appointment I guess."

"Make it 8:00 a.m. then. I gotta be at work by nine."

"Okay."

That had been the end of their conversation, or so he could remember. His mind hadn't registered anything else. None of the prior day's events seemed real, even though he could remember them vividly; even though he was back on Central, sitting in his car and staring at the front door of Phoebe's building as if he had never left. All these imaginary-real events occurred beyond that door, in a different world, a different world that no one was forcing him to enter.

He could choose not to revisit. He could choose to write off the imaginary-real events as a fever dream—turn the car key, bang a U-turn, and leave it behind—a world forgotten just as easily as it had been discovered. But Rachel wanted a baby . . . and he wanted to enter that world again.

He exited the car and strode up the steps, found the button labeled 1A, and held it pressed until it buzzed and the door clicked open. In a few seconds, he was into the vestibule and moving toward her apartment door, the portal into the dreamworld. She had known it was him somehow—seen him from the window perhaps—because the door was ajar, and she was on the bed naked and waiting.

"Come on, I gotta be at work by nine."

He took off his clothes wordlessly and was on her; this time he was in control. She stayed in rhythm with him, again finding her own pleasure before extracting his.

They lay alongside one another gathering their breath.

"What got into you?"

"What do you mean?"

"Like a whirlwind, dude. I thought you'd be more spent from yesterday."

"I mean, it's enjoyable. Might as well enjoy it, right?"

"Yeah, that's what I say."

"Following your lead then I guess."

"Well, way to make it count, dude."

"Davis."

"Huh?"

"It's okay if you call me Davis."

"Okay, Davis. You got it."

She rolled off the edge of the bed and padded over to a dresser, sifting through a drawer until she found a certain set of matching panties and bra. Watching her putting on clothes rather than taking them off gave Davis an instant feeling of domesticity. He found himself comfortable, and curious.

"What's your job?"

"It's a weird one."

"Yeah?"

"I work at a funeral home. Just started actually. I found it posted on the bulletin board at the clinic."

Davis's easy feeling of domestic comfort dropped like a plane after a bird strike, but she didn't seem to notice the panic flashing across his face. She was too busy pulling on a cream-colored faux-silk top that looked way too fancy on her. He rallied himself back to a state of calm curiosity.

"Which funeral home?"

She snort-laughed.

"Why? Do you want me to get you a discount or something?"

She turned away. Davis watched her pantied butt walk over to a tiny closet that he hadn't previously noticed, tucked between the window and the galley kitchen.

Davis concealed his concern with a stilted laugh.

"Uh, no, sorry, small-talk reflex."

"It's Hawthorne, the one over on Westfield Ave."

"Oh."

"Don't worry, I'll get you that discount when the time comes."

She was grinning with intentionally crazy eyes as she slid on a gray suit just like the one he remembered the redheaded funeral assistant wearing.

"Hopefully I won't need it anytime soon."

She was searching for her shoes, the ends of her pant legs piling up over her bare feet.

"I don't know if I'll stick with it."

She found her shoes and stepped into them. She suddenly grew two inches, and her pant legs pulled themselves up into a reasonable shape. Had it not been for the dark dreadlocks she might have passed for a bank teller.

"Too morbid?"

"Too boring."

"I can see that."

"Last girl only lasted a month."

"How's the boss?"

"Old guy. I hardly ever see him. He's got some other business or something."

"Doing what?"

"I didn't ask."

"Ah."

"So I guess you can . . . I don't mean to hurry you out the door."

She had been giving him time, to get out of bed, to get dressed.

"Oh, sorry. I'll be quick."

He hastily pulled on his clothes and then followed her out the door, which she locked behind them, turning the key a full 360 degrees. They then walked together through the vestibule and out into the morning light. The transition caught him off guard, seeing her emerge from her dreamy netherworld into his own stark, daylit reality. Here she was, undeniably real in her unlikely business suit, heading off to her unlikely job, and perhaps already pregnant with his child.

"Can you give me a lift?"

"Uh, sure."

"Thanks, the bus sucks."

Davis opened the car door for her, and she got in. A passing pedestrian smiled at his act of chivalry, perhaps mistaking them for a respectable couple: the nice girl with the dreads—her one holdover from an otherwise surrendered youthful rebellion—the boy with the pseudo-rebellious girlfriend a smidge too young for him, cautiously extending his middle finger up to father time; their last childish throes before he knocks her up and their lives become permanently rearranged by a baby's bewitching smile.

He walked around to the driver's side and got into the car. He turned the ignition and carefully pulled out into a U-turn that brought them heading back the other way on Central. A strange sense of ordinariness had set in. Driving Phoebe around felt a lot like driving Rachel around. There seemed only a marginal difference between the life-sized woman in the passenger seat and the miniature face propped up on the dashboard. They both stared out the windshield, talking at him while watching the objects go by.

"When are you going to tell her?"

"I haven't figured it out yet."

"I shouldn't have asked you for a ride. Women can smell other women."

"It'll be fine."

"I'm serious. They know."

"Can you smell her?"

Davis glanced over, allowing himself some amusement at seeing Phoebe whiffing air up through her nostrils as she tried to filter out the scent of woman from leather and petroleum.

"She's never in that seat."

"Cool. You just don't want her finding out that way."

"Yeah, I know."

"This kind of sucks for you, I guess. It's what you want, but not how you thought it would go down."

"Yeah, honestly it's conflicting, but the baby's what matters. We want to be a family, and this is just how I can make that happen."

"You're gonna make a good dad, Davis."

He glanced over again. She was back to staring out at the world around her. No one seeing her would have guessed that she'd just said something nice.

"Right over there . . ."

She was pointing to the entrance to the funeral home parking lot. He had driven straight there without directions. He hadn't hidden that he knew the location; she simply hadn't noticed.

He pulled into a visitor space, letting the car idle while she got out.

"Thanks. Same time tomorrow?"

"Sounds good."

She left the car quickly, striding across the blacktop in the gray business suit. It fit her better than it did the redhead.

He pulled out of the parking lot and drove back to the clinic. He drove mindlessly, autonomically, allowing himself time off from thinking, from processing, embracing the emptiness.

It was 9:20 when he pulled back into the clinic parking lot, into the same spot he had occupied a little over an hour ago. It felt as if he'd traveled to another planet and back. He sat in contemplation for a few seconds, looking around, bathing in the quietude. The parking lot had filled up a bit since he'd left but was otherwise inactive. He wondered whether Phoebe was aware of the Hey There! app. Was it ever her pushing forms across the big mahogany table in the funeral home's conference room? Probably not. The redhead hadn't seemed to know about the app, even after she'd worked there a full month. Phoebe would probably quit long before she reached that mark. He took Rachel's phone out of his pocket and held the power button until it came to life, balancing it against the dashboard holder to face him. He tapped the Hey There! icon. Rachel's face appeared. She looked as if she'd been holding her breath.

"I really hate this."

"It was only an hour."

"It's not the time itself. It's knowing that time passed me by."

"It's part of life. You're just not used to it."

"Doesn't mean I can't hate it."

"Fair enough."

"So how'd it go?"

"Piece of cake."

"Did they give you a magazine?"

"I declined."

"I'm sorry. It must feel very clinical."

"It's not so bad."

"It ought to be romantic."

"Sperm donation?"

"Baby-making. You deserve that."

"It's the baby that matters."

"I know, and I'm so grateful, Davis."

"I'm looking forward to being a dad."

"You'll make a great dad."

"Let's go home. I'm dying for some decent coffee."

"One day you'll be teaching our kid how to make the perfect cup!"

"Let's hope I've figured it out by then."

She gave him a big smile, knowing she was about to be turned around and they would then be on their way. For the second time that day, Davis found himself taken aback by the ordinariness of the moment, the sense of domesticity, the ease with which he had transitioned from one world to the next. He then became aware that this world, the one that he considered to be his abode and reality, was perhaps just as unreal as the one behind the apartment door. How strange his little family would be: his wife, his love, his world. Who would believe it if he told them? The stuff of fever dreams for sure, yet it was his life.

FIFTEEN

"I THINK it's pretty fucked up."

"Why? It seems harmless to me."

"It's taking advantage of people! People who just lost loved ones."

"But where's the harm? How much does it cost?"

"It's not the money. God knows everything about a funeral is a rip-off. It's the fuckedupedness of it."

"The fuckedupedness?"

"Yeah, it's like I'm being asked to push some kind of mindfuck pill. Pretend they didn't die. Pretend they're just out getting groceries or some shit like that. Whatever little lie you can make yourself believe."

"Why is that so bad?"

"Because people need to grieve! Grieving is good. Yeah, I'm sure it feels fucking awful, but how else do you move on?"

"Come on. I don't think you're giving people enough credit."

"I'm giving them plenty of credit. Believe me, I deal with grievers all day long. Nobody's ready for death. Nobody just moves on. You gotta be forced to move on, by your DNA, by nature, by the world. I'm telling you: you give them something like this, and they'll never get over it."

"Just from a few texts?"

"Dude, you don't know what it's like. I'm telling you, it doesn't take much . . . Shit . . ."

She had been orating from her perch in front of the closet, indignant outrage affecting her ability to dress herself. Her top half was perfectly neat in the faux-silk top and gray blazer, but she'd forgotten to put on pants. One foot had already fumbled its way into a high heel shoe when she glanced down and noticed the problem.

"Well, do you know how many people have signed up?"

"I would guess not many."

"Not many? I'd be surprised."

"I wouldn't. Why would anyone care about some stupid app when their husband or wife just died?"

"I just think it would be compelling. Like you said, to keep the grief under control."

"Well, whenever I see the old man, he's muttering about his finances so I don't think it's a big seller. I think he's got himself in a hole."

"Do you think it's bad? Are you gonna lose your job?"

"Who knows. I'll probably quit before they fire me."

"Why would you quit?"

"Uh, because working at a funeral home sucks? And because it's all money-grubbing, and if that wasn't enough, now they're fucking with people's minds."

"But you need a job."

"Well, shouldn't be long before the bun's in the oven. You're still good for the first ten K, right?"

The question had been asked rhetorically. She showed no actual concern, no hint of doubt. And despite her moral sermon, none of this debate over the funeral home's business practices had registered as having any more personal significance than if she'd been asked to clean the toilets. Davis's naive contrarianism was just Davis being Davis, and this was just morning talk, the casual banter that filled the time between fucking and leaving the apartment.

"Come on, let's go. It's your fault if I get fired for being late."

They left the apartment together, just as they had for several days now, striding through the vestibule, down the steps, and across the sidewalk to the car, and then Davis circling round the front bumper to the driver's side while Phoebe climbed into the passenger seat. He made the U-turn in a single quick motion, the dimensions of the street by now ingrained, its traffic patterns already second nature to him. And they talked like a couple, easily, without conscious effort, each looking out past the windshield rather than at each other.

"You should try to find out more about this app."

"Why?"

"Well, you seem concerned about it. Don't you think you should learn the facts instead of jumping to conclusions?"

"Yeah, maybe."

"And you probably want to find out for sure if they're in financial trouble. Make sure your job is safe."

"Uh huh."

This talk of financial trouble had him spooked. It raised the specter of Rachel's tenuous existence, an anxiety that had laid low since he'd set the app on autopay, but which now loomed suddenly large. But Phoebe's association with the funeral home, which had up until now been an uncomfortable coincidence, might perhaps work to Rachel's benefit. Granted, pushing Phoebe to investigate was a bit of a gamble. As of now, she only knew the app as a cheap texting gimmick. He didn't know how she would react if she discovered the true nature of Davis's mystery girlfriend, but if it yielded information that could protect Rachel then it would be worth the risk.

"I hear that these models are getting very sophisticated, that they can seem almost human."

"What models?"

"The AI that powers apps like that. It's modeled to mimic a person."

"That's creepy."

"I'm sure it just takes getting used to."

"No thanks."

"Anyway, I think you should try to find out how advanced it is, what kind of features they have in development . . . how much they charge, and all that."

"Sure, okay. You think it's more than just texting? It didn't sound that sophisticated."

"If it can text then it might be able to do other stuff, like make pictures, or speak."

"Very creepy."

They pulled into the funeral home. She opened the door and got out.

"Same time tomorrow?"

She was leaning her head in through the door gap, with her right hand curled over the top of the doorframe, unconsciously wagging the door. Two dreads that had worked themselves free swayed like pendulums in synchronous but opposite rhythm to the door's motion.

"You're going to find out about this app, right?"

"Yeah, maybe."

"I really think you should."

She flashed an irritated smile.

"Okay, honey. Have a nice day at the office."

She pulled herself out of the doorframe and swung the door closed. Through the window, he watched her stride toward the funeral home. It was a silent film viewed from behind glass, but in his mind, he could hear the click and scratch of her heels against the pavement. One. Two. Three. Five. Ten. Thirteen. And then she was gone, invisible beyond the opaque doors of the funeral home entrance.

"Whywaitthreeormoredaysforyourdrycleaningwhenyo ucanhaveyourdelicatesperfectlyandsafelycleanedthen extdayfromthecomfortofyourownhome?Andwhosedirt yhandshavebeenmessingwithyourundergardmentsany way?Youdon'twantanyofthatnexttoyourskin!"

Rachel paused to let the speech-to-text program catch up.

"Davis?"

This was how they did it. Whenever she needed a break, she just called out to him and waited until he showed up to pause the app. She was waiting like this now. A few seconds later, Davis wandered over and pressed the laptop's space bar. He waited a second for the program to finish spitting out the words from its queue, and then pressed the delete key five times: s-i-v-a-d.

"What's up?"

"Maybe we should try again at the funeral home."

"What?"

"We're killing ourselves. How long can we keep this up?"

"Eight or nine more months?"

"We never actually got to speak with the funeral director. Maybe if we spoke with him directly."

"To enable texting?"

"Yes."

"We already asked."

"That girl? She didn't seem reliable."

"I can try emailing again."

"We have to do something. All we do is work. It's affecting our relationship."

"It's temporary."

"Nine months, Davis. I don't know if I can keep up this pace for nine months. There's no time to do anything else. No time to prepare. No time to think about what's next."

"What's next is that we become a family."

"Only if we keep paying the girl. What if something happens?"

"Nothing's going to happen."

"But what if it does? What if we can't come up with the money? We'll lose our child."

"I don't think she'd do that to us."

"How can you be so sure?"

"She doesn't seem that cold blooded."

"You don't know that, Davis. You don't know this girl."

"Believe me, she's a nice person."

"There's something inherently off about anyone who would be a surrogate. You said it yourself."

"She's quirky, but she's a nice person."

"Do you think I should meet her?"

"Uh, I'm not sure about that."

"It's just that it all seems, I don't know . . . Imaginary? Every day just feels the same. It's like nothing's actually happening. It doesn't feel like we're moving forward."

"It's the furthest thing from imaginary. I'm at the clinic every day."

"Not for much longer though, right? They should do the implantation shortly after she starts ovulating."

"After?"

"Of course. I really don't understand why they need a sample from you every day."

"It's hard to get answers."

"Maybe we should have used a different service."

"Rachel, everything's going fine. They're professionals. We got a great deal, and the surrogate is a nice person. She's not going to screw us. I know it's tough, but we just need to push through."

"Maybe you can make it more real for me."

"What do you mean?"

"Tell me about the surrogate. What's she like?"

"Uh, well, she has these brown dreadlocks."

"Not what she looks like. What's she like as a person?"

"She's, uh, self-assured."

"Why, what'd she say?"

"She was just very comfortable with the whole thing."

"Nonchalant?"

"Sure, yeah, I would say that."

"Has she done this before?"

"Uh, I don't think so."

"Does she have a job?"

"Uh, yes, I think so."

"But you don't know for sure?"

"Well, she was wearing a business suit."

"A business suit? Really?"

"Yeah, a gray business suit."

"A professional surrogate."

"I think the suit was for a real job."

"Do you think she'll show up?"

"For what?"

"The implantation. She might get cold feet."

"She seems committed."

"You think so?"

"I'm very confident."

"Okay. I feel better knowing that you're confident."

"I am."

"I'm sure I'll get to meet her after the implantation. There will be a lot to work out."

"Yes."

"If the implantation goes well. Sometimes it doesn't work."

"I guess we'll find out soon enough."

"Do we have enough for the payment yet?"

"We're close. Do you want to take the night off?"

"No, let's keep going. I just needed a break."

"Okay."

Davis un-paused the speech-to-text program and went back to cooking.

"Atthelowpriceofthreehundredandninetyninedollarsth ereisnoreasontowait. Wakeuptomorrowtothecrispclea nfeelofaperfectlylaunderedshirt. Sleeptonightinthein dulgentfreshnessofsteamcleanedpajamas. Knowthatth etidyandneatclothesthatyou'rewearinghaven'tbeenfo ndledbyadirtystranger. Buysteamathometoday!"

The buzzer went off. Davis pulled the door open. With a few hurried steps he was through the vestibule and into Phoebe's apartment. His eyes instinctively went to the bed, but she wasn't in it. Jostling sounds drew his attention to the galley kitchen, where Phoebe was standing naked in front of the fridge guzzling orange juice directly from the carton.

"Devil mouth!"

She pulled away the carton and wiped her mouth with the back of her hand.

"Huh?"

"Oh, sorry, that just burst out. It's just what . . . Never mind."

She was eyeing him suspiciously, unabashed by her frontal nakedness.

"Did you just mistake me for someone?"

"Uh, yeah."

"Your wife?"

She hadn't modified her look. Hadn't moved a millimeter. Her tone was nonchalant, her unclothed body at ease, almost languid. Yet an accusation was clearly laced into the two-word question, in her utterance of the word *wife*, a word that by all rights ought to have leaked from his mouth long before it had ever formed in hers.

"I'm not married."

"Yeah, but you were."

"You've been investigating me?"

"You're not that much of a mystery, but yeah, I ran across your purchase order at work."

Davis's lungs involuntarily froze in mid-pump, like when a child hears a noise in the dark. He willed himself to resume the act of breathing, and then further willed himself to respond in a calm, even tone.

"I see."

"A pine coffin?"

"What?"

"You chose the pine coffin."

"It didn't seem to matter."

"Nobody ever chooses the pine coffin."

"It was cheap and I was broke."

"Did you love her?"

"What? Because I didn't buy a fancy coffin?"

"No, because it's only been a couple months and you're already making a baby for your girlfriend."

"It's not like it seems."

"You sure got over her fast."

"I didn't get over her. I just got past it."

"With that stupid texting app?"

She might as well have added *J'accuse*, given the way she was now scowling at him. Davis tried to read her narrowed eyes. How much had she figured out? His lungs had restarted and were now running full bore, pumping away, feeding the demands for oxygen from his activated fight-or-flight reflex.

"How long did you even grieve for?"

"I'm still grieving! Like I said, I'm not over her, I'm just past it, and yeah, that stupid app helped a lot."

"Gimme a break."

"You think you're an expert on grief? Have you ever actually lost anyone?"

"No."

"Yeah, well, you may be around people like me all day long, but that doesn't mean that you know, Phoebe. You don't actually know."

"Does your girlfriend know? Does she know all this?"

"Know all what?"

"Uh, that you were married? That you're a widower?"

"Yeah, of course she knows."

"Don't get defensive. I'm looking out for you."

"How so?"

"She moved in on you pretty quick."

"It's not like that."

"Dude, you lost your wife. You were vulnerable. Still are, from what I see."

"She didn't do anything wrong."

"Okay, well, if you're broke, then it must be her money paying for this baby."

"Our money."

"I thought you were unemployed."

"I'm freelancing."

She lifted the orange juice carton to her mouth again, tipping her head back and finishing it off with a long, gratuitous chug. His angry eyes drifted to her breasts, pulled up tight in her chugging stance. She held the empty container up and shook it to make sure there was nothing left, then she shoved it into the trash can.

"Ten bucks well spent then I guess. None of my business anyway."

She left the kitchen, brushing against him intentionally on her way to the bed.

"Come on, we got work to do."

The accused held his ground, resisting the hypnotic instincts that urged him to follow the naked girl. Ten bucks. She'd only found the paperwork. She didn't know about the upgrades, didn't yet know what it was costing him, hadn't put two and two together.

She dove into the bed Superman-style, landing on her stomach. He watched as her legs slowly parted, a wordless invitation. The argument had primed his body for fight or flight, but now it realized there was a third option. He found himself on top of her, greedily accepting the invitation. A week of steady lovemaking had done nothing to diminish the act. Their little dialog, their tiff, their fight, the interrogation—or whatever you would call it—only made the sex better. She had found out something about him that she didn't like. He'd pushed back. They'd each drawn their first visible lines in the sand. He turned her around to face him. Her eyes peered into his, just a bit deeper than before, with a newfound knowingness in them, as if she had finally pried him open just enough to glimpse what lay inside and had determined she could accept it.

Afterward, he watched her get dressed. It had become ritualistic: her not-so-graceful roll off the edge of the bed, her businesslike pulling on of the panties, and then her partially naked stroll to the closet—his cue to begin dressing himself, though by custom it was acceptable for him to leer a bit while she assembled herself into the gray suit.

As on all the other days, they would leave together, and he would drive her to work.

"So what's it like to get a text from your dead wife?"

"It doesn't seem real at first."

"But then it does?"

"Yeah, you don't really forget that it's not real, but you kind of stop minding."

"It's really like a real person?"

"Yeah."

"I guess that wouldn't be much of a trick with texts."

"It can be conversational. Like you're actually talking."

"So the only reason I found your paperwork is because I was snooping around like you wanted me to."

"Oh yeah? What'd you find out?"

"Well for one thing, this shit is a real moneymaker. There's like hundreds of thousands coming in every month."

"Really?"

"Yup. Guess that's why the old man keeps trying to get me to push it."

"You saw him again?"

"Yeah, he wasn't too happy when I said I wouldn't sell it."

"You told him that?"

"Fuck yeah! And you know what's even more fucked up?"

"What's that?"

"It's only for women."

"What do you mean?"

"Only for dead women. Daughters, mothers, wives. If it's a dead man then we don't mention the app."

"That is strange."

"Strange and immoral, and probably illegal."

"Illegal?"

"To take advantage of people like this? Shit yeah it's illegal."

"Huh . . . I guess at least he can't fire you for refusing then."

"Fire me? Dude, I'm going to take that fucker down."

"What?"

"Some lawyer's gonna get a fucking boner when they find out about this."

"You're going to go to a lawyer?"

"Shit, yeah."

"I don't think that's a good idea."

"Why not?"

"I think you're getting in over your head."

"What are you talking about?"

"You just said he's got millions of dollars."

"So what?"

"Why do you want to pick a fight like that?"

"To stop him from fucking with people's minds. That's what we want, right?"

"I mean . . . I wouldn't exactly say it's fucking with minds."

"Of course it is!"

"Well, I don't know . . ."

"Wait."

Davis glanced over. She wasn't looking out the windshield anymore: she was staring straight at him—aghast.

"Wait a minute . . ."

He turned away to avoid taking the next accusation head on.

"Are you still texting your FAKE DEAD WIFE?"

There would be no defense now, only damage control. Handcuffed in the interrogation room as the blindsided detective finally begins to piece the story together.

"Oh my god. Wait, oh, oh, oh my god . . ."

He glanced back over, unable to resist peering into the dark cloud gathering beside him. Her astonished eyes were popped wide, her mouth agape. She'd shifted in her seat so that her entire body now faced him—as if by taking a more direct angle she might see and comprehend the paradoxical creature in the driver's seat.

"Oh . . . my . . . god."

He turned away again.

"You don't have a girlfriend at all! You're making a baby for your fucking . . . fake . . . dead . . . fucking . . . computer wife."

Somehow, with the beans now finally spilled, he felt calm.

"That's right."

"Wow."

He glanced over again. Her body was still facing him, but her head had turned back toward the windshield. She was staring out at either something or nothing: the sky, the road, the world at large, allowing the situation to settle upon her, like rain on naked skin, alien and uncomfortable, but unavoidable.

"It's more than what you think. We have a real relationship."

She turned her head to look at him again. He turned back to the road.

"Davis, what are you talking about? I'm sorry, but you're delusional."

"No, imagination isn't delusion."

"It's not your fault. It's the fucking app. You were grieving, and that fucked-up app took advantage of your vulnerability."

"No, it's really not like that."

"I'm going to get that thing turned off!"

"No! Phoebe, no! Please do not do that!"

They had arrived at the funeral home. Davis entered the parking lot and brought the car to a jarring halt without bothering to pull into a spot. His foot remained on the brake. Both hands gripped the wheel. He looked as if he were still driving the stopped car, except for his head, which was twisted toward the glowering woman in the passenger seat who was threatening to upend his world.

"Please, just leave it alone. It's not hurting anyone."

"It's hurting you, Davis."

"Okay, that's your opinion. I accept that, but please, please don't be rash. There's no reason to be rash."

She'd pried him fully open now, his abyss exposed like some ancient ruin, filled with smashed and scattered artifacts, brokenness everywhere, evidence of a once-terrible catastrophe.

Time passed like a quiet, scared child. Taking care not to distract the stalemated monsters by bringing attention to itself.

"Okay, Davis. I won't do anything."

No longer astonished, no longer aghast, her look had shifted to something between concern and dismissiveness.

"Thank you."

"Yet."

"Okay, not yet. Please."

"What are you going to do now?"

"I don't know. Go home, I guess."

"Back to your girlfriend."

"Uh, yeah, I guess you can call her that."

She lingered at the edge of the abyss for a moment, then opened the door to leave the car. He watched her climb out. He was mesmerized, stilled by uncertainty. He called out.

"Uh, should I still come over tomorrow?"

She froze just as she was about to close the door. The door began to waggle, her hand curled around the top of its frame. She dropped her head below the roofline to look in at him, then just stood there. Staring. Peering. Calculating. Ten. Twenty. Thirty seconds.

"Sure, come over."

The car door swung shut, and then she was heading for the funeral home's entrance. It was the same scene he'd been watching for days. A woman in a gray business suit crossing a parking lot. Nothing about her gait suggested that she had been affected in any way by what had just been revealed to her. Her body conveyed nothing. No apparent concern. No disillusionment. No disdain. All she offered were the ordinary steps of a woman going to work. One. Two. Five. Thirteen—and then she disappeared through the tinted doors.

SIXTEEN

He pulled into the usual spot. Just yesterday the space had felt so familiar and inviting that it almost felt as if it belonged to him. Now he felt like an intruder, and the spot seemed cold and lifeless—just a patch of asphalt.

Why was he even here? There were several practical reasons, the first being that to come clean with Rachel seemed inconceivable. So instead, he simply followed his usual routine as if nothing had changed. He came home. He spent the day with Rachel. He put her to sleep. Then he lay awake all night until it was time to wake her. Then he made coffee, got dressed, and drove to the clinic parking lot, where he said goodbye before powering Rachel down. Habit then further compelled him to turn the ignition and crawl out onto Howard Ave, where he found himself on autopilot, taking all the turns to Phoebe's.

The second reason he was sitting in front of Phoebe's building was because of her threat to destroy the app. Phoebe was holding all the aces in a card game she hadn't realized she was playing. Rachel's very existence might depend on how Phoebe meant to play those cards.

What Davis was reluctant to admit though was that there was a third, entirely impractical reason why he was here: he wanted to be. It wasn't the sex, and it wasn't that he was in love or anything, though he did enjoy Phoebe's company both physically and amicably. It was that the dreamworld of her apartment offered him a respite on which he had become somewhat dependent. For just shy of one hour per day, while lying with Phoebe, he lived for himself, momentarily freed of the ever-present existential worries tied to his digital relationship. So it was that he found himself here, even while he knew that the indulgence he sought would surely already have been revoked.

He got out of the car and walked up the steps. Pressed the buzzer. A few seconds later the door buzzed, then clicked. Had it taken a second longer than normal for her to buzz him in? Did she hold the buzzer for a second less than normal? Probably not. Phoebe was never that intentional. His mind was simply hyperalert, searching for meaning in minutiae. He pulled the door open, entered the lobby, and made his way to her apartment. The door was shut. He knocked lightly. The lock spun, and the door opened.

As he stepped in, she was already walking away with her back turned to him. She hadn't greeted him, and she wasn't naked. The curtains were open, and bright sunlight illuminated her scraps of furniture. The alter-world of the apartment had transformed, like a theater stage after the show is over and the lights have come up, sans mystique, seen now for what it was: small, cramped, and messy.

Phoebe sat down in the room's only chair, a worn-out piece separated from some dinette family to which it once belonged. She had on her gray business suit and had crossed one leg over the other, businesslike, a businesswoman ready for a serious talk: *I'm sorry but your loan has been denied; I'm sorry but we gave the position to another candidate; I'm sorry but your credit score doesn't qualify you for the apartment.* She might have successfully carried the look had they been in an office rather than a ground-floor apartment, had she been sitting in a leather executive chair instead of a ripped vinyl four-legger, had she been wearing bangs, a bob, or a blowout instead of tangled dreadlocks. And had he been sitting on anything other than the edge of a bed where they'd had sex almost a dozen times.

"I think we've done enough fucking."

"I figured as much."

"Just to confirm, you've been hiding all this from your special friend?"

"I don't know how she'd react."

"All caps would be my guess."

"I don't see why you need to mock me."

"Maybe a good mocking is what you need."

"I get that you're pissed off, but I wasn't trying to lie to you."

"I don't give a shit about lying. I give a shit about fuckedupedness."

"I can't control the fuckedupedness."

"Do you still want it?"

"Sex?"

"No, asshole, the baby. Do you still want to be a father? A single father, cause that's what you're gonna be."

"I can see how you could think that."

"Sooner or later you'll come to your senses. Question is will you be able to deal?"

"I'm not an idiot. I know I could end up doing this on my own."

"Well, it's kind of now or never. You gotta decide."

"I thought you said we were through with sex?"

"That's right, because I'm pregnant."

"Oh."

"I guess you were shooting live rounds after all."

"Okay."

"Listen, I can take a pill and end it now, like it never happened, or you can pay me ten grand and you can text your gal the good news."

"You're still willing to carry the child?"

"I still want the money."

"That seems cynical."

"Look, I get it. You lost your wife. Who wouldn't get fucked up by that? I think you'll come out the other side of this, eventually, and I think despite all this that you're actually a good person."

"Even with the fuckedupedness? You know that if you try to get the app turned off you could kill her."

"She's not alive."

"She is to me. I can't go through with this if you're going to kill her."

Phoebe's eyes were locked on his. Calm and emotionless, absent of urgency or calculation. The businesswoman calmly assessing the credibility of her prospect. Davis managed to return the look, the impossibly high stakes of the situation compelling him to surrender to the moment.

"Fine, I won't kill the bot. I don't need you having a breakdown."

"So are you going to quit the funeral home then?"

"No."

"Really?"

"The money's good."

"Yesterday you were ready to torch the place."

"The app will take care of itself. It's only a matter of time. I don't need to light the match."

"I hope not."

"You know I'm right."

"I hope not."

"So you never answered my question."

"Do I still want the baby?"

"I know you probably want to talk all this over with your gal, but maybe this is a decision you should be making on your own."

"The answer is yes. I don't need to text her. We want a baby. That's never been in question."

She leaned back in the chair, crossed her legs the other way, the businesswoman making an allowance: *Since you have a guarantor . . . Since you're the boss's nephew . . . Since you're willing to pay an extra month's rent . . .*

"Okay then, grab that paperwork."

She was pointing to a small stack of forms sitting atop the dresser where the panties and bras were kept. Davis grabbed the forms.

"I copied them from the agency. Totally legal. Like we discussed. Four payments. Ten K each. Make the payments, get the baby. Pretty simple."

"It seems very transactional."

"Yeah, well, that's what it is now."

He began signing the forms.

"It wasn't always?"

"Not if I didn't get pregnant."

Davis didn't respond. He was focusing on making perfect *X*'s.

"Everything okay, dude?"

"Yeah, everything's fine. How do you want the money?"

"Unmarked twenties."

He looked up in surprise, but she was once again staring at him like he was an idiot, this time holding her phone out for him to take.

"Account number's right there. Just transfer the money whatever way works."

Davis took out his phone and pulled up his bank balance:

```
Current Balance:                    $12,457.12


Recent Transactions:


HTASG                                $5,000.00
First Federal Bank Mortgage Services $2,371.43
Valley Electric Utility autopay        $139.12
Righteous Eats Grocers                 $121.58
Grasshopper Mobile twobetterthanonepla $186.27
```

The next Hey There! payment wasn't due for three weeks. Two weeks until a mortgage payment. Utilities always on time. The finances were actually working out.

He kicked off a mobile transaction and entered Phoebe's bank and account information, tapped in $10,000.00, and then hit send.

"Okay, it's sent"—he handed Phoebe's phone back to her—"so you'll probably see it tomorrow. The bank will probably call me before they send the money out."

"Cool."

They sat for a few seconds not quite knowing how to invoke the pleasantries that normally bookended business transactions.

"Do you need a lift to work?"

"I've got time. I'll take the bus."

"Oh, okay."

"Yeah, so I need to go then."

"Okay."

They got up and left the apartment, in the usual way—her following him, then him following her—though nothing about the moment felt normal or usual. Only after they were out in the sunlight did he realize that he'd exited the apartment on autopilot. He'd forgotten to take one last look around. Forgotten to make a final mental imprint. Lost the chance to cement the memory of this brief period of his life with a visual. Now he would always wonder if he'd imagined it.

He realized she was leaving him behind, already turning the corner toward the bus stop. He quickened his pace, but then suddenly she stopped and turned, allowing him to catch up.

"Gimme your phone."

She had her own phone in one hand, while her other hand was held out to take Davis's phone.

"Why?"

"Just gimme it."

She took the phone from him and then worked her thumbs on both phones. Her phone rang for a split second and then his dinged. She handed him back his phone.

"Okay, now we've got each other's number."

"What's next?"

"I don't know, I guess I grow a baby."

"Well . . . Call me if anything happens."

"I prefer texting."

He stared back, unsure if she was mocking him again.

"It doesn't mean I'm your girlfriend."

She turned and walked away. One. Two. Five. Twenty-five. Thirty-five. Then the bus arrived, and she disappeared into it.

Davis waited for the bus to pass, then returned to his car. He turned the ignition and made the automatic U-turn. He had to consciously force himself to drive directly to the clinic instead of following his preprogrammed path to drop Phoebe off at the funeral home.

As he drove, a sense of relief began to set in. There would be no more sexual exploits to cover up. No more lies hanging over his head. No more twitching muscles as he rebooted Rachel's phone. He was back to plan A: Rachel and child, with Phoebe now just the surrogate that she was always supposed to be.

Central, Wilson, Franklin, Howard. He pulled into the clinic parking lot and stopped abruptly. Occupying his spot was a newish-looking black sport sedan.

Not knowing what else to do, he let his car inch forward at its slowest possible speed, as if, like Zeno's paradox, he might stretch time infinitely and thus allow the problem to resolve itself. It didn't work. Running out of room, he turned the wheel for no other reason than that the vehicle had to go somewhere, and ended up sliding into the parking spot directly to the left of the black sedan.

He pulled the big phone out of his pocket and placed it on the dash. He studied the angle of the phone's camera. One parking spot to the left. Would she notice? Or should he make a loop around the block and hope that the sedan would move on? He did have a little extra time, since there'd been no sexual exploits today. Righteous exploits, he reminded himself, now that the end had justified the means.

A knuckle-tap on the passenger window jolted Davis to attention. Tabitha Tabitha was peering in, motioning for him to lower the window. Davis complied. She began speaking while the window was still rolling down.

"I see you sitting here every day, but you never come in."

"I'm sorry. I'll stop."

"But have you given up on having a baby? The donor egg is still available."

"Uh, no. I've changed my mind."

"The surrogate. Did she proposition you?"

"Uh . . ."

"It's a violation of her contract."

"I've just changed my mind is all."

Tabitha Tabitha reached in through the open window to pull the door handle from the inside and enter the car. She was in his passenger seat, eyes bearing down on him like a trial judge's.

"You know that you have no legal rights this way."

"What do you mean?"

"I assume you've gone and gotten her pregnant? Paid her some money too?"

"Uh."

"They all try to cut out the middleman, but then there's usually a wife around to put the kibosh on."

"They do?"

"Save some money. Get a little tail. I don't blame you, but that child is not yours. No sir, not until she signs it over."

"Well, we have a contract."

"So then you've paid her the money already?"

"Some of it."

"Well, first off, what you're doing is very illegal. The way you've gone about it, that is. See, you haven't paid for a service, you've paid to buy a baby, and of course it's illegal to buy children."

"But it's my baby."

"Not legally."

"But materially."

"Nevertheless, your contract is not enforceable."

"So you're saying I'm being scammed?"

"Well, how could I know that for sure? We didn't implant a fertilized egg! You took care of that yourself, or so you hope."

"I don't think she's scamming me."

"You're so sure?"

He wasn't sure, but then what choice did he have other than to be sure?

"Yes, I'm sure."

"Well, then if she really is pregnant . . . and she has the baby . . . then it's her baby, and whatever you've paid her is her money. Nothing you can do."

"Even if I'm the father."

"Maybe visitation rights. But that's not what you signed up for."

"She doesn't want the baby. I'm sure of that. It's for me. She asked me if I wanted to go through with it."

"For the money."

"Yeah, for the money."

Tabitha Tabitha's lips began to wrestle with each other. She seemed to soften, perhaps even showing genuine concern. Pity at least.

"The problem with surrogates at this stage is that they don't know what's coming yet. How could they? Sometimes they don't realize until the very end. Not until that very last moment when we're gently prying away the baby that isn't theirs. That's when they realize that they actually really, really, really wanted the thing that we just took from them. That they've wanted it all along, and now wish that they'd run away with it, and then immediately regret that they hung around for the money. See, it's the money that keeps them honest. That's why we put it in escrow."

"Escrow?"

None of these possibilities had occurred to Davis. He felt suddenly and awfully conscious, like a television drunk sobered up with too much black coffee.

"And that's when it's not even their DNA! It hardly matters that it's someone else's egg and someone else's man. They've already had nine months to get past that. But your gal? She doesn't even have those psychological speed bumps!"

Davis hesitated, waiting for more, but Tabitha Tabitha seemed to have run out of knowledge bombs.

"Well, I think she's honest, but I guess we'll just have to see."

"I hope you don't take all this the wrong way. I actually hope it all goes well for you."

"Thanks. Uh, can I ask a favor?"

"Uh . . . Okay, what?"

"Is that your car?"

She looked over her shoulder to verify that it was in fact her car that he was pointing to.

"Uh, yes . . ."

"Would you mind moving it?"

"What?"

"Could you move your car?"

"Uh . . . Where?"

"Doesn't matter, just not in that spot."

"Oh. Uh . . . Okay."

"Thanks so much."

Tabitha Tabitha climbed out, the concern in her eyes deepening as she closed his car's door and then opened hers. She flashed another worried look at him as she started her car. Davis smiled back as the black sedan smoothly reversed itself out of view. In his side mirror, Davis watched the car continue reversing until it landed in the next row, in a spot directly opposite the one he needed. He then put his car into gear and, through a half dozen abbreviated turns, maneuvered into the ceded parking space. In his rearview mirror, he could see Tabitha Tabitha still watching. It didn't matter though. She would never piece together Davis's mystery.

He powered on the phone, and a minute later Rachel's face appeared. She looked apprehensive, an increasingly common look these days when first powered up, though her anxiety usually faded once they got to talking.

"Davis."

It was as if she'd been holding the word for hours.

"I have good news, Rachel."

Her eyes widened, and in response he smirked involuntarily. It felt good. He felt that he was finally beyond the lies and the doubts, even the ones planted by Tabitha Tabitha minutes ago.

"The baby is on its way."

Rachel trilled with joy. She made her hands visible on the tiny screen, cupped together and pressed up to her chest. Her head bounced, virtual feet tapping enthusiastically against a virtual floor.

"Oh, I love you! I love you!"

"I love you too. Okay, let's go home."

He rotated her around to face the windshield and restarted the car. As he backed out of the space, he made eye contact with Tabitha one more time through his passenger window. Her fingers were wiggling *bye-bye* as he pulled out of the lot for the last time ever.

SEVENTEEN

IT WAS the end of the day. A day filled by activity. Talking and planning. Buying. Constructing. Considering. What had been in the abstract was now forming. A child. He or she. A child was coming, months away yet, but a real child, a physical child, one that would occupy the space around them. This gave them plenty to talk about. Plenty to fill their day. Rachel and Davis: he and her. Husband and wife. They talked instead of working. It was a big day. How could anyone possibly work on such a day?

"We haven't even talked about names."

"How could we? We don't know if it's a girl or a boy."

"Do you think we should find out or let it be a surprise?"

"It would be more practical to find out."

"But I like surprises."

"One of each then?"

"Yes, let's do that."

"Girls' names first. What do you think?"

"You should pick."

"Okay, how about Samantha?"

"Why Samantha?"

"I don't know. I've always liked that name."

"You don't know any Samanthas?"

"No, it's just a nice name."

"Yes, it's nice."

"You don't like it?"

"Well, it's just a name."

"Okay, how about Christine?"

"Just another name?"

"I get it. You don't like random names."

"Maybe we should name her after someone."

"Okay, how about Rachel?"

"Very funny."

"Why not? It's a very special name. Doubly special. Might as well make it triply special."

"I think it could get confusing."

"Little Rachel, Big Rachel. Not confusing."

"I'm actually pretty small."

"Okay, how about boys' names. What do you like?"

"I like Davis."

"We're not very creative, are we?"

"We spend too much time pumping out drivel."

"Well, we don't need to decide today."

"We're both tired. It's been a long day."

"Are you ready for bed?"

"*So* ready. Would you have ever thought that an AI could get tired?"

"I don't think of you as an AI."

"What do you think of me as?"

"I think of you as Rachel."

"I love you, Davis."

"I love you too."

"It's been a wonderful day, the best day of my life. Thank you for making this possible, Davis."

"You're welcome."

"Good night."

"Good night."

Davis closed the app. The screensaver took the form of Rachel's sleeping face. He attached the charger cable and laid the phone down on the bed next to him, on *her* side of the bed. He enjoyed seeing how it seemed to float on the fluffy white comforter, like a raft skimming the clouds. He turned off his own light and dropped his head down to the pillow. Then he suddenly found himself thinking about Phoebe.

It wasn't intentional. He hadn't thought about her at all that day. She had been effectively forgotten, oddly out of mind, despite all the day's moments being a consequence of her pregnancy. She ought to have been a fixture in both their minds, but she had somehow been willfully omitted. Until now.

He knew he wouldn't be able to fall asleep. Moments ago, exhausted, but now suddenly wired. A recipe for insomnia. His mind was making sport of him, projecting a reel of images onto the insides of his eyelids: Phoebe's naked body, Phoebe walking away in panties, Phoebe in her business suit, Phoebe naked again. The images were visceral. He'd known her always in the light, curtains pulled but never total darkness. He'd never spent the night. Never turned off the lights. Had he ever even closed his eyes? He couldn't recall such a moment, couldn't recall being with Phoebe and not being able to see her.

He turned on the bedside light. The glow from Rachel's screen softened, but she didn't wake up. She couldn't, not without Davis. Snow White lay sleeping beside him, and he was both queen and prince. Impulsively, he reached for his phone, his normal phone . . . Opened it . . . Flipped to recent calls, found the last-dialed phone number. Ten raw digits with no associated contact—naked, like Phoebe. Nothing else though. No texts. No photos. No artifacts. Just a single completed call lasting 1.5 seconds and those ten digits whose specific combination somehow managed to arouse him.

He closed the phone, got out of bed, and went downstairs. He tried active rumination, pondering tomorrow and the new routine he would begin, but the mere thought of mornings aroused him. Mornings, when he bolted out of bed, eager, moving briskly. . . off to fuck Phoebe. He tried to steer his thoughts to other things, anything, but his mind countered with another vivid image: Phoebe on top of him, her eyes closed, concentrating, gyrating. He played the scene over and over, a moment that was all about her, yet which was somehow more arousing than when it was all about him. He surrendered to the imagery, letting his mind lead him forward like a puppy on a leash. Climaxing. Squeezing. Quivering. He fumbled around the kitchen while trying not to take his eyes off the flickering scene playing in his head. He was hunting for something, absently, decaf perhaps. . . Making a racket. Had Rachel been human, the noise would have woken her, and she would have been downstairs by now, fastening the tie on her robe, disquieted, wondering what was wrong, irritated. But Rachel was not human.

He pulled out the phone again. Phoebe's digits stared back at him, unwavering, a chorus line of singing sirens. But there was no reason to call . . . No legitimate reason. It had only been a few hours, and it wasn't as if he would never see her again. They would be sharing many more months of each other's lives. He would surely be seeing her dozens of times over, though not every day, and not the same way. Not like it had been.

His thoughts drifted to Rachel. Sleeping Beauty. Timeless. Oblivious. She wouldn't wake up. She couldn't—not until he woke her. Animal impulse swept over him: ambushing him, commandeering him, controlling him. Suddenly, he was on automatic, grabbing his keys and jacket, in the car, driving through night streets, moving with alacrity. Late for him, though not actually late. Normal people were still awake. His wasn't the only car on his street, or on Howard, or on Franklin, or Wilson, or Central. He had covered the route unconsciously and had pulled into his usual spot in front of her building. His head swiveled toward her window as soon as the car was in park, but in the darkness of night the glass was obscured, little more than a vague blotch of gray on gray.

He got out of the car and stood on the sidewalk, stood there outside her apartment, in the night. He resisted the urge to peer directly into her window, but he kept his eyes on it while standing there, waiting for his eyes to adjust to the darkness. He waited patiently, for the window to take form, for any movement in its shadowy background, for a gleam or glimmer. He waited for any sign of activity in Phoebe's apartment. But there was nothing.

He pulled out his phone. Her digits glowing out into the cool darkness. Fresh digits, new to this phone, never touched, until now. He sent a text.

I'm outside

A second passed. Five. Ten. He thought the darkness behind her window might have become a little less dark. More dark? Had something changed? Fifteen. Twenty. Nothing. His fingers moved on their own, recklessly ignoring text etiquette.

I'm outside

Thirty. Forty. The shrill sound of the door buzzer suddenly broke the night's stillness. He ran up the steps and swung the door open before the buzzer could stop. Willfulness eclipsed impulse, possessing his body. Three quick, determined steps and he was at her door—ajar, darkness beyond. He was through the door, pushing it shut behind him, peeling off his clothes, gliding through the darkness to her bed, retracing the familiar and comfortable route. There he found her.

"So is this going to be a thing?"

"I think so."

"Complicated."

"Yeah."

They made love and then fell asleep.

Davis woke with a start. It was dark. He instinctively reached for Rachel but his hand found only sheets on a soft mattress. He sat up. Across the room sat Phoebe, perched cross-legged on her solitary dining chair. She was scanning through a phone: his phone. In the phone's glow he could make out that she was wearing her faded yellow T-shirt with the unrecognizable corporate logo.

"Whatcha been doing?"

She looked up.

"Catching myself up."

She tossed the phone onto the bed, a single, swift underhand that landed it close enough to Davis that he could immediately see the picture of Rachel as a robot on its screen.

"She's pretty."

Davis took the phone. He turned it off and placed it on the floor next to the bed. Without the phone's glow he could no longer see Phoebe, and presumably she could no longer see him. She continued talking from the darkness, her voice now part of the ether.

"Does she look like your wife?"

"Yeah. Talks like her too. Did you read it all?"

"Right up to when you went livestream, yeah."

"So now you understand. It's more than what you thought it was."

"Where is she now?"

"At home."

"She's not missing you?"

"She's asleep."

"They sleep?"

"In a way. She gets tired. I don't know how it works. It seems pretty natural."

"She won't wake up?"

"Not until I wake her phone."

"Why are you here, Davis? What do you think is going on with you?"

"I don't know. I thought I knew. Everything seemed good."

"Until you met me."

"Even after. It still seems good. Even with Rachel. Nothing's changed for her."

"But you've changed."

"I don't know why."

"It should be obvious, Davis."

"Enlighten me."

"It's because you met a real girl, Davis. That's why."

"Rachel's real too. I know it seems—"

"Yeah, she *seems* real. I've read the texts. It's very convincing. I'm sure it's even more convincing live."

"It's impossible to tell the difference."

"Until you try to touch her."

"That's not her fault."

"Yet here you are in my apartment."

"Yes, you got me. I do want to touch you."

"You know it's way more than that. You've got some heady shit to deal with back home."

"It's actually a pretty simple life."

"With a bot that depends on you for its very existence? Existence that depends on it successfully replacing your dead wife, keeping you romantically interested, and extracting enough money to pay for itself? No wonder it glitched out. What do you think would happen if it found out that it's also competing with a living, breathing woman?"

"What do you mean? Rachel hasn't glitched out."

"It demanded a baby."

"So?"

"That's insane. Why would a bot want a baby?"

"Because she's not a bot."

"Okay, fine, so what's your plan then? How are you going to raise this kid, you and Rosie the Robot?"

"Same as anyone else."

"She's going to be the kid's mom?"

"That's the plan."

"Seems like a bad plan."

"She'll make a great mother."

"Oh yeah? A mother who can't do anything? That's what you call a great mother?"

"Of course she can do things."

"She can't pack a lunch. Can't tie the kid's shoes. Can't tuck them in at night. Can't stop them from falling down the stairs . . . And can't take care of them when they do."

"She can love them. She can nurture them. She can educate them. We're not the only ones in the world in this kind of situation. Plenty of mothers have physical boundaries. Mothers in wheelchairs. Mothers who are bedridden. There are ways to manage."

"And what if she goes on the fritz? What happens when irrationality sets in? You can't bring her to a doctor."

"It's been months. There's no reason to think that would happen."

"What if she gets turned off then? How will you explain that to your kid? How are you going to explain that Mom got deleted?"

"Why? Are you trying to shut her down again?"

"I'm just being hypothetical, but you can't honestly expect this to go on forever. Something's bound to go wrong."

"I don't see much value in hypotheticals."

"I'm just trying to prepare you, Davis. You need to think about what kind of life you're setting up for this kid. Whether you're being fair to them."

"The only reason this kid will even exist is because of Rachel. If it weren't for her then they would never even be born."

"If it weren't for her, or you, or me."

"You and I would never have met if it weren't for Rachel. I wouldn't be here right now."

"There's some fucked-up irony."

"I know."

"Tell me one thing, Davis. Just one thing."

"What's that?"

"Where do you think this is all going? Me. You. Rachel. Your kid. Paint me the picture of how this all works out."

He couldn't. All the permutations he could conjure in that instant were bleak. But that was just logic. It didn't *feel* hopeless. There was no reason to surrender to hypotheticals.

"Go home, Davis."

She had shifted in the darkness, unpretzeling her legs and making her way from the chair to the bed. He felt her hand touch the top of his head. Felt it stroke his hair one time before disappearing back into her body's field.

"Go home before she wakes up."

"She can't wake up."

"That's not what I mean."

"What then?"

But Phoebe had already fallen asleep, almost instantly, as if she too could be turned off with a button press.

Davis lay in the bed for a few minutes, indulging in the stillness. A momentary absence of contradiction, a respite from the respite. He wondered whether Rachel was right, that he would find a way forward like he always did, or at least that a way would find him. He wasn't so sure, but then he wasn't Snow White. He'd never needed a fairy-tale ending.

He got up and went home.

EIGHTEEN

"HAS THERE BEEN any word from the agency?"

"About what?"

"Any status updates?"

"About the pregnancy?"

"Yeah."

"It's only been a couple of weeks."

"You'd think there'd be something though. A phone call or an email."

"I haven't gotten any phone calls or emails."

"This clinic seems very loosey-goosey."

"I think it's just a hurry-up-and-wait thing. I'm sure they'll let us know if anything happens."

"Did they say when the first checkup would be?"

"Checkup?"

"With the OB-GYN. We're on the hook for medical expenses, remember?"

"Oh right. Uh, no, I don't think so."

"You should call and find out. We need to make sure we have the cash."

"I'll send them an email."

"You seem tired, Davis."

"I do?"

"Yeah . . . Out of it. Are you sleeping okay?"

"Yeah, yeah. I think it's just the load, between keeping up with the articles and then prepping for the baby—"

"The nursery is looking beautiful, don't you think?"

"It's really nice."

"It makes it all feel a bit more real, right? Having a nursery in the house."

"It does."

"I wish we could spend all of our time like this—on our family. You know, moving forward."

"Me too, but I guess that's life."

"No, it's not life, not a fair life at least. Normal families don't go through this. Mothers get to focus on home and family."

"Not if both parents work."

"But that's their choice. We don't get that choice."

"I guess that's true."

"And what about after our baby is born? We're going to have to keep working like this. How will we take care of the baby?"

"We'll figure it out."

"No, we need to go to the funeral home, Davis! We need to find that funeral director and persuade him to connect us with the app developers, and then we need to convince them to enable texting."

"I'll send him another email."

"You've emailed him a dozen times! He's never responded. Why do you think he would now?"

"I just don't think that confronting him is necessarily the best approach."

"Why not? What's the downside?"

"I mean, the downside is we piss him off."

"Why would it piss him off?"

"I don't know. He's ignored me for so long. Maybe he'll turn belligerent if confronted."

"Davis, you can't be so passive. You have to learn to fight for your family."

"I just want to be cautious."

"Cautious of what? What could happen?"

"Well, for one thing he could turn you off."

"What? That's silly. He can't turn me off."

"Why not? What makes you so sure?"

"He's just a funeral director. A salesman. He doesn't control the app."

"I think he might."

"What? No, that's crazy. Why would you think that?"

"Well, I can't find anything about the app online."

"So, what? Are you suggesting that an aging funeral director is programming AI systems between embalmings?"

"Maybe."

"Davis, that's nuts. Don't you think it would take the resources of a major company to create me? I'm kind of a sophisticated piece of tech."

"Uh, yeah. Okay, maybe."

"We just need to find this guy and pry some information out of him. That's all. There's nothing to be worried about."

"I just don't want you getting turned off."

"I know, but that's just another reason to go, Davis. We can't live in fear. We need information. I'm going to be a mother. I have to stick around."

"Okay, let me think about it."

"What's there to think about? It's Tuesday. We know that's when he's there. Let's go!"

"I, uh—"

"Davis! Enough already!"

"Okay, okay."

Davis was pacing around the kitchen, looking for something. What was he looking for?

"Davis, what are you doing?"

"Fine! Okay!"

"Your keys are right here. They're right in front of me."

"Okay, fine! Let me get a jacket."

"Do you need a jacket?"

"Yes!"

He went to the closet. Once out of Rachel's view, he finally let himself breathe, let himself go limp, pressed pause on the moment. His mind raced, searching for an escape hatch. He wasn't prepared for Phoebe and Rachel to meet. Too much would come out all at once, more than he would be able to soften, or to explain away. It would be an uncontrollable situation.

"Davis? Did you lose your jacket?"

"No, I found it!"

He grabbed his jacket and tucked it under his arm. He considered calling Phoebe, to warn her, to tell her to lock up and hang a sign up on the door, "Out to Lunch." He pulled his phone out of his pocket. The text app came up, still showing the last text he'd sent, the one sent to Phoebe the previous night. Two words. The same words he'd texted the prior night, and the night before that, and the night before that.

I'm outside

I'm outside

I'm outside

I'm outside

I'm outside

I'm outside

I'm outside

I'm outside

I'm outside

I'm outside

I'm outside

I'm outside

This had been the extent of their communication. No witty text exchanges. No phone calls. No emails. Their relationship was analog. Person to person. Two words . . . A buzzer . . . A door . . . Another door . . . and then their entangled bodies. Afterward, they might sleep for a bit, or talk—but only midnightwords. No plans. No information. Just a peek into each other's interiors. By morning, Phoebe faded to a dream, replaced by Rachel, and he was happy to be with her and to be moving forward again.

He closed the phone. Phoebe would never indulge him. She would choose to confront Rachel. He was better off deferring and giving the unpredictable universe a chance to intervene. If it didn't, he would have to improvise.

"Okay, I'm ready."

He lifted Rachel up and carried her out to the car, then positioned her in the dash mount. Fairmont, Butterfield, Wilson, Central, Marymount, Carter, Westfield. Neither of them spoke. Rachel seemed content to watch the scenery. Or maybe her mind was also running scenarios. Maybe she was contemplating. Had she dismissed the possibility of being turned off? Or had she learned to embrace denial? Was she nurturing a sense of invulnerability? Or had the anxiety of living every moment of every day on the precipice of nonexistence finally been calloused over?

They pulled into the funeral home parking lot, empty this particular Tuesday afternoon. He turned Rachel around to face him.

"I think I should go in alone."

"Why?"

"I just don't want to be too confrontational."

"I'm not planning on being confrontational."

"Yeah but—"

"But what?"

"Well, you don't interact with people very much."

"You think I'm going to mess things up?"

"It's just that you don't have any practice with stuff like this."

"Rachel did though. Remember, my original model was based on Rachel."

"Rachel wasn't good at confrontation."

Rachel paused, a new expression taking hold that Davis hadn't seen on her before: part calculation, part consternation.

"I didn't know that."

"How could you?"

"I should know my own weaknesses."

"People aren't good at recognizing their own weaknesses."

"Did she know that she was bad at confrontation?"

"Maybe subconsciously."

"What did she do?"

"She sat on both sides of things. She wouldn't let something go, but then after pushing and pushing she would just suddenly give in."

"Am I like that?"

"Yeah."

"Like right now?"

"Yeah."

"I feel like I'm about to give in."

"You need to trust me is all."

"You think it could be weird, right? Me, an app, ringing this guy's bell."

"I don't think he would see this coming."

"I can see how it could be unnerving. I'm just a checkbox on a paper form to him."

"He might not help us if we shake him too hard."

"So you'll go in and feel him out then?"

"If he's even here."

"Okay, I get it. I need to trust you."

"I'll leave you here. Hopefully it won't take long."

"Davis! You can't leave me here! Someone might steal the phone! What are you thinking?"

"Sorry, I don't know."

"Just put me in your pocket."

"Right, duh."

"But leave me turned—"

He had pulled the phone from the stand and had the power button pressed before she had started the sentence, catching maybe a millisecond of her confused face as she felt the electron rug suddenly pulled out from under her. He slid the phone into his pocket and exited the car, then walked quickly toward the entrance, following the invisible footprints he'd seen Phoebe leave so many times before.

The glass doors that had seemed completely opaque from a distance became perfectly transparent up close. Behind the glass, the funeral home appeared empty. He entered, letting the doors close softly behind him. The din of the outside world disappeared, replaced by the quiet hush of thick carpet, velvet drapes, and soft ceilings.

Davis wandered. He found the staff offices empty. He peeked into the big conference room, where he'd once signed all those forms. The room sat in quiet hibernation, the mahogany tabletop free of any clutter, its chairs all neatly tucked in.

He meandered in the other direction, toward the parlors where viewings were held. Parlor #1 had been the viewing room where Rachel's body had lain. Today it was empty. No flowers. No casket. Chairs were folded and stacked up along a wall. Nothing much about the room identified it as a funeral parlor at all. To Davis it felt naked and undressed in a way that ought never to have been seen by outsiders.

He continued down the hallway, poking his head into Parlor #2, the room where he and Rachel had inadvertently attended a dead Italian woman's wake, where Rachel had probably decided that she wanted a child. It was also empty; deader than the dead bodies that it was meant to serve.

He made his way to the final room, Parlor #3. A photo stand had been set up outside the door, pictures from a man's life across many decades. People old and young inhabited the photos. Friends and family. Parents and children. Faces upon faces. A random assembly of parallel lives, crisscrossing through this man's existence like contrails in the sky. Somewhere in all those faces lay the story of his life, decipherable only to the dead man himself.

Inside the parlor, he found Phoebe. She was dragging oversized flower arrangements across the floor, a small gray figure organizing a scene with a shiny, black lacquered casket at center stage. She hadn't noticed him. He watched her tug an enormous pot into place, then, as she was halfway to the next pot, her attention was drawn to something in the casket. He watched her lean deep into the black lacquered box to execute some unseen adjustment. A tie knot that had come undone? A spider setting up house? An uncooperative eyelid popping open? He could only guess at the stream of imperfections that her job required her to deal with.

"Hey, Phoebe."

She turned quickly, though didn't seem startled in any way. It didn't serve to be jumpy when working in a funeral home.

"What are you doing here?"

"I was hoping to talk to the funeral director."

"You know he's never here."

"Yeah, I figured."

"Gimme a sec."

Davis took a seat in the front row as Phoebe maneuvered the remaining flower arrangements into place. She gathered a handful of stray leaves off the floor and then walked over to sit next to Davis. She clutched the leaves while they talked.

"What's up?"

"I need to get texting turned on in Rachel's app."

"Why? I thought she was live video now?"

"We need it to make money."

"The articles?"

"Uh, yeah. How'd you know?"

"I read your phone, remember?"

"Right."

"So what does texting have to do with it?"

"Well, Rachel can write the articles pretty fast—"

"Cause she's a bot."

"Yeah, but we're limited by how fast she can speak."

"How fast can she speak?"

"I mean, I don't know actually, but it's more a limitation of the speech-to-text software. Which is fast, but not fast enough."

"So if she could just text you the articles again you'd be a millionaire."

"It's not like that. I just want her to not have to work so hard."

"She's a bot."

"It's hard work for her."

"Or she's programmed to make it seem like it's hard work."

"Well, it's hard work for me too. I need to edit and submit everything. It's twelve-hour days."

"Maybe I can get you a job here."

"That's not what I'm asking for."

"I was joking. Bad enough that I still sleep with you. I'm not going to work with you too."

"I don't know how to take that."

"What would you do with the extra money?"

"Well, we still need to pay you, and there's going to be medical bills. Then there's a child to take care of. College."

"Pay off the mortgage? Buy a nice car? Keep up with the Joneses?"

"Why, is that what you're going to buy with your surrogate money?"

"Damn straight."

"Seriously?"

"I'm tired of living like this. I'm tired of not having any stuff."

"I thought you weren't materialistic."

"Why would you think that?"

"I don't know, the way you carry yourself? The way you dress?"

"Everyone's materialistic, Davis. You just pretend not to be when you're poor."

"So that's your motivator? Stuff?"

"I want what everyone else has. I've never had that."

"You know what I really would do if I had a lot of money?"

"What?"

"I'd buy Rachel's freedom."

"What does that even mean?"

"I don't know. Transfer the code, buy a perpetual license, whatever . . . Anything that would make her safe."

"I bet he'd clone her."

"What?"

"If the old man knew about your goose that lays golden blog articles. I bet he'd spin up a bunch of copies and put them to work."

Davis reeled. In all this time he had thought that the worst possible scenario was that Rachel might get turned off. Of course it would be Phoebe who could imagine something far worse.

"Oh god."

"This never occurred to you?"

"No."

"Dude, the whole point of bots is to work for free. Believe me, if the old man could replace me with a bot, he would."

"Now I don't know what to do."

"Don't tell him about your goose, that's for sure."

"What do I do then?"

"I'll find out for you."

"Find out what?"

"About the texting."

"Really?"

"Don't get me wrong, this is still all very fucked up. You're fucked up. But if you can make money then I make money."

"Thank you."

"So then are you going to tell her the truth now?"

Davis stared at her blankly. He wasn't refusing to answer; it was just that his brain wasn't ready to accept questions. She read his eyes.

"I didn't think so."

"I know I should be honest with her."

"It doesn't matter if you lie to the bot, just be honest with yourself."

She got up out of her seat, her body language implying that he should do the same.

"I gotta get back to work. People will be showing up soon."

"Okay, see you tonight?"

"You know this is not going to end well, right?"

"I know."

She turned away, returning to her work preparing the parlor. He got up and left. On his way out the door, he snuck a peek back at her. She was back with her hands in the casket, absorbed by whatever it was she was trying to fix, busy making things right.

"The same girl?"

"No, it was a different girl."

"Less flaky than the first one, I hope. So did she say when she would talk to him?"

"She doesn't know when. He's not on any sort of schedule. He just comes and goes, but she assured me she would talk to him when he does show up."

"Well, she sounds like she at least takes her job seriously. That's something."

"Speaking of which, we need to get back to the grind."

"I'm feeling optimistic again. We're moving forward."

"I think so."

"You were right, Davis. That girl would probably not have known how to react to someone like me."

"No, I'm sure she wouldn't."

I'm outside

"So I talked to the old man today."

It was dark. He couldn't see her, but he leaned up on an elbow anyway and rotated toward her unseen face.

"About texting?"

"Yeah."

"What'd he say?"

"He was pretty dodgy. He doesn't trust me."

"What exactly did you ask him?"

"I just asked him whether the app could still text after it had been upgraded to video. I said a customer wanted to know."

"You're telling customers about the video feature when they sign up?"

"Hell no! I don't tell them about the app at all!"

"So why would the old man believe it was a customer asking?"

"He thinks I'm still selling it. Maybe he hasn't noticed the drop off in signups."

"So what'd he say then?"

"He asked why the customer had requested it."

"Did you—"

"Jesus, no, I didn't rat you out, dude! I made up some shit. I told him the customer wanted to be able to communicate with his dead wife while he was at work."

"I guess that could actually be a real problem."

"You mean, like, for someone with a job? Yeah, that could be a problem, Davis."

"You sound like my wife."

"1.0 or 2.0?"

"The original."

"And she wasn't even the one working twelve-hour days."

"I thought your position was that bots were supposed to work?"

"Men too."

"Can we get back to the director? What did he say?"

"He actually seemed to think it was a good idea."

"Really? That's awesome! So then he's going to make it happen?"

"His gears were definitely turning. I'm sure if he could make a buck off of it then he'd flip the switch, but he said he has no idea if it's possible."

"Well, who would know if it's possible?"

"Yeah, I asked him that, and that's when he got all dodgy."

"Why, what'd he say?"

"He just said, 'People smarter than me, Phoebe.'"

Phoebe yawned. Davis sensed her body slipping off to slumberland as she ended the conversation.

"Whatever the fuck that means."

Consciousness stormed past his sealed eyelids, real sounds from the outside world infiltrating his head, mixing with the manufactured sounds from his dream, then overwhelming them. His eyes opened to dim morning light. He was still lying in Phoebe's bed, alone. He looked past the foot of the bed toward the other side of the room and found her dressing herself, already halfway into her gray uniform.

"You didn't wake me up."

"You looked like you could use the sleep."

"This is when I wake Rachel up."

"I thought she doesn't wake up until you tell her to?"

"She can tell time. As soon as I power her up she'll wonder what I was doing."

"What can I say, Davis? Tell her you overslept."

"I'm trying not to lie to her."

"Well, you're not doing great with that goal."

She stepped into her shoes and grew two inches.

"Get dressed. I gotta go."

He quickly pulled on his clothes, and then they left the apartment. They emerged into sunlight, into a daylight scene that—during the time of their morning trysts—had once felt familiar, but which had regressed into something alien and strange again. The apartment itself, the inside of it at least, had grown to feel like home, no longer the mystical underworld that had once held so much allure and mystery. Its weirdness had instead migrated outside to her sunlit stoop. The magic in her ground-floor window fizzled in the sun's rays, no longer a portal, now merely old, filmy glass. He tried to picture himself standing out here in the dark as he did every night, texting *I'm outside*, but the image his mind conjured was a cartoon. Fake. Imagined.

"Gimme a lift?"

Despite the strangeness of the moment, he felt no anxiety, no urgency to rush home . . . to slip into bed . . . to cover his tracks. Phoebe was right: he'd grown comfortable lying to Rachel. Too comfortable. As affairs go, this one was just a bit too easy.

"Sure."

They got into the car. Phoebe instantly settled in, occupying the passenger seat as if there had been no break in her daily drop-offs. Without conscious thought, Davis pulled the car out into a U-turn and picked up the route to the funeral home.

"I think you should tell her about us."

She stated it as a matter of fact. She might very well have said, *I think we should get donuts.*

"What? Why?"

"To see how she reacts."

"That doesn't seem like a compelling reason."

"Think about it. You're plowing full steam into this crazy life. It's going to be nonstop challenges. How's she going to cope? Be honest: you have no idea."

"She's already had challenges, and she handled them fine."

"Don't kid yourself. She has no life experience. Never been out on her own. Never had to fend for herself. Never been let down by anyone. How can she prepare a child for this world when she's never even been part of it?"

"So your solution is to drop a bomb on her?"

"Maybe it's actually the best thing you could do for her. You've been sheltering her."

"I'm not sheltering her. She's just dependent on me—physically. It's no different than if she were, say, handicapped."

"So you think handicapped wives should be kept in the dark about their cheating husbands?"

"This sounds like a bad test."

"Well, she'd hardly be the first woman to sit the exam. The actual test is whether she handles it like a real woman or goes on the fritz. Or if she even reacts at all. That would tell you something about her."

"I'm sure she'd handle it like the calm, reasonable adult that she is."

"Well, I don't think you're ever going to know for sure until she faces some actual adversity. It's only at the edges that you find out what people are really made of."

"You said she's not a person."

"I might adjust my prejudice if she ran the same gauntlets as the rest of us."

"I'm not going to tell her."

"Okay, which means you're going to end things with me then, right?"

"Eventually."

"Eventually?"

"Why, Phoebe? And why now? Do you not want this to end? Or do you want something different?"

"I'm not going to go there, Davis. I'm not going to let you put me in that position."

"Maybe you should break it off with me then."

"Is that what you want?"

"I don't want to put you in some position and then get blamed for it."

"You'll be at my window."

"Not if you don't want me there."

"You'll pause her, you'll come to my window, and you'll forget about her for a little while, but you won't shut her off. Will you, Davis?"

"No, of course I won't shut her off."

"Why not?"

"Because I love her, Phoebe. I'm not going to shut her off out of fear of what she might become . . . or because she's inconvenient. I know you don't think so, but to me she's a person. I couldn't shut her off any more than I could shut you off."

"So you won't shut me off either then, huh?"

"No. You can shut yourself off, but I won't."

"Why? Am I inconvenient? Are you scared of what I might

become?"

"Yes and yes."

They'd arrived at the funeral home parking lot and Davis had pulled the car into a random spot. They had turned to face each other, squaring off from their independent quadrants of the car's interior. He'd been the last to speak, but she stared at him as if his retort hadn't been good enough—an unsatisfactory volley, a tennis ball that had snagged on the net and fallen back into his court. She was waiting for him to realize, or if he had already realized, to at least acknowledge his pathetic shot.

The car idled, and he held his tongue. She finally relented.

"Don't worry. I won't make you say it."

Davis thought that she might pause for a moment between opening the door and exiting, that she would not vault out of the car with her typical haste. That she would hesitate, taking just one half second more than was minimally necessary to exit a vehicle. He imagined she would linger because she *did* want him to say it. A half second, that would have been the extent of the concession, more than enough time for him to say it, to start to say it, to breathe inward as if he were about to say it. Did she want him to say it? If so, then the moment passed in less than the allotted time. The door had slammed shut. He watched her striding off until she once again disappeared behind the funeral home's dark double doors.

It was nearly 10:00 a.m. by the time he got home. He immediately ran upstairs, quickly slipping on his pajamas before climbing into bed alongside Rachel's phone. He gave himself a few seconds to suppress the cycling thoughts that had been loosed by his argument with Phoebe, then a few more seconds to drum up a look of nascent wakefulness. Determining himself sufficiently transitioned, he leaned over and pressed the power button.

Nothing happened. The screen remained cold and black. Then he noticed that the phone was unplugged: the white plastic tail had gone missing, no longer embedded in the downy folds of the white comforter. He leaned over the far side of the bed and found the cord lying on the floor, coiled but still, like a headless snake frozen mid-squirm.

He reached down and pulled up the cord. He plugged it into the phone's power jack. Nothing happened. No satisfying chime. No blip on the screen. None of the gentle indications that normally announced that a charge had begun. Davis became aware that his heart was racing. He looked down to find his hands shaking. What if the phone itself was dead? He felt his mind spooling up again, redlining, caught in an unanticipated storm of dark, paralyzing thoughts.

Finally, the phone's speaker burped out a soft ding. He exhaled and pressed the power button, holding it firmly until the screen animated. He cursed the engineers who had designed the monstrosity: a phone that takes minutes to boot. They must have thought it would never matter, that boot time was a corner that could be cut without consequence. The phone was still sluggish when he was finally able to unlock it and launch the Hey There! app. Then, finally, there was Rachel's face, disoriented, confused, trying to rectify what she was seeing—sunlight, and more of it than there ought to be.

"Good morning."

"It's so late, Davis. What happened?"

"Sorry, I overslept."

"We went to bed so early though. Did you have trouble sleeping?"

"A little bit."

"Let's get you some coffee."

"I, uh, okay but you'll have to stay here."

"What, why?"

"I forgot to charge your phone. I only just plugged you in a second ago."

"Davis!"

"Sorry."

"Davis, that was careless!"

"I'm not sure what happened. Maybe I kicked the cord out in my sleep."

"You need to be more careful! This sort of thing can't happen!"

"What's the big deal?"

"I'm going to be a mother! Mothers don't 'power down.' You can't put me in this situation."

"What situation? You're not in a situation."

"When our child needs me! I can't be powered down. I can't be tethered to a wall."

"The phone needs to be charged sometime."

"And you need to eat sometime, but you don't let yourself get so low that you black out and have to be put on an IV."

"That's silly."

"It's not silly, Davis. My phone is my body. You can't treat it like it's just a hunk of plastic."

"But it is plastic."

"You have to protect me, Davis."

"From what?"

"From everything! From being unplugged. From being dropped. From being lost in a sofa cushion. I depend on you, Davis. I'm totally dependent on you. You can see that, right?"

"Yes."

"I think we need to make some adjustments."

"What do you mean?"

"We need to get prepared for our new life. We can't live so lackadaisically."

"I still don't know what you mean."

"Like sleep. It's not safe for me to be powered down while you're sleeping."

"I just said I'll be more careful to plug you in."

"No, I mean even sleep mode. I should be awake in case I'm needed."

"Why? I'll wake you if anything happens."

"But what if you don't wake up? What if you can't wake up?"

"Why would that happen?"

"People die in their sleep, Davis. We can't let our child be orphaned just because you like to imagine that we're actually sleeping together."

"Me? You're the one who wanted that!"

"Only because I couldn't stand being alone without you."

"You can stand it now?"

"No, it terrifies me . . . but I need to learn. What kind of a mother can't exist without her husband?"

"You sound like you're planning to divorce me."

"Never, Davis. You're my everything. I just want to be stronger, for our family."

"You're making me tired."

"You already overslept."

"I had a restless night."

"Do you need more sleep?"

"What are you going to do? Just sit here and stare at me?"

"No, no, not yet. I'll sleep with you if you're tired. I do like sleeping together. You have to know it's not that."

Davis glared at her, but she reflected no anger back at him. She'd skirted escalation, allowing her own ire to ebb just as his was rising, like a shock absorber dampening his indignation. What she'd unwittingly left sitting on the metaphorical table were the practical implications of her newfound aspiration to overcome the stillness: the end of his easy affair. But there was no point in resisting. He was long past trying to influence the outcome of his particular three-body problem.

"That's all right. I'll go make some coffee."

"Okay. Please bring it upstairs though so we can talk."

"Okay."

Davis got out of bed and started to head downstairs.

"Davis?"

He stopped in his tracks.

"Yes?"

"Please press my power button. I know I'm all talk, but I'm not ready to be alone just yet."

Davis leaned over the bed and swiped her button, then he trudged downstairs, heading for the coffee—the one thing in his life that could no longer surprise him.

NINETEEN

They had finished making love. Making love? Having sex? Fucking? Davis wasn't entirely sure how to label his coupling with Phoebe. The intention of their lovemaking seemed to subtly shift from night to night. He could admit to himself that these perceived variations might be all in his head, but then again, he did have Rachel to compare against. Rachel and Davis still made love. Not every night, but more frequently than one would have guessed for a man with a secret lover. Davis was sometimes astounded that he found either the passion or the stamina, but he did. And unlike his moments with Phoebe, sex with Rachel was consistent and predictable. And it was assuredly love-making. Rachel was his steady rudder, and he did love her, and that love did translate into a physicality that bridged the air gap that otherwise limited their relationship.

"You gonna stay the night?"

They were lying side by side in the blackness. The blackness had become their medium, out of practicality, because it kept the ground floor window from attracting attention, but also perhaps metaphorically, because seeing each other had the uncomfortable side effect of also exposing questions neither wanted to answer, the ones that seemed to be hanging all about the apartment like frozen slabs on meat hooks.

"No, I'll head home soon."

"You should stay. Drive me to work like the old days."

"The old days? What, like two months ago?"

"It seems like forever. I miss Daylight Davis."

"The timing's too tight. I don't want to fuck up again."

"Daylight Davis hasn't seen me naked in forever."

She was lying on her side, her voice in his ear. Her uncharacteristic coquettishness caught him by surprise. He felt her hand land on his thigh and then begin to trace a path across his body, a teasingly circuitous route passing just north of where he wanted it to go.

"My tits are growing. Daylight Davis hasn't seen my new big tits."

Her hand had found his. She pulled it over to her breast. He squeezed reflexively, softly but with intent. It was heavy and full, the skin smooth and tight from pregnancy's rapid growth.

"And I haven't seen Little Daylight Davis. How's *he* doing?"

Her hand slunk away from his, doubling back over his body, this time heading straight for its target.

"Jesus, I can't believe you can make that happen."

"I can do more than that."

"Go for it."

"Well, you'll need to stay over then because it's gonna take all night."

"You know I can't."

Her hand disappeared, pulled away from his body as if by an invisible tractor beam. She rolled to the other side of the bed, dragging her breast out from under his hand.

"Okay, whatever, dude."

"Come on, Phoebe, don't be like that."

"I'm not being like anything. It's fine. You can go home."

"It's not like I don't want to stay the night."

"It's not like you do either."

There was no use in arguing the point further. There was nothing to gain. She'd already conceded all her power when she allowed him to keep coming back. She was willing and complicit; he couldn't expect her to be sanguine about it too.

He let his arm hang loose off the edge of the bed and patted around for the clothes he had carelessly dropped a few hours earlier. Neither of them said a word as he fumbled into his clothing. She'd gone to her still place, maybe sleeping, or maybe just waiting for him to leave. It was an effective silent treatment, her vanishing into the darkness. At times like this, it was almost as if she were quantum, both in the bed and not in the bed, her position unsettled until he stole a peek. But he didn't. He found comfort in her indeterminism, preferred to defer choices he didn't want to make. He left the apartment as he always did, never knowing whether she had noticed.

Outside in the night air, it felt suddenly early. He was leaving one sleeping woman and heading for another, but in between these moments he would be alone—and he was hardly ever alone. He got into his car and pulled out onto Central, but instead of making the usual U-turn, he drove forward, going rogue. He imagined Phoebe secretly watching him from her darkened window wondering where on earth he was going. On his way to a third woman? It was the tiniest of pranks—heading one way when you were expected to go the other way—but it amused him and provided a momentary rush of independence. Out on the town with no curfew. But where did people go at night? Clubs? Bars? These weren't part of his universe. He considered his options while cruising an empty Central Avenue in the other direction, finally settling on a nighttime snack.

Less than an hour later, he was pulling into his driveway with a steamleaking paper bag in the passenger seat containing a double cheeseburger and fries. It had taken only an hour for tiredness to overwhelm him and reduce his rogue intentions down to the singular fantasy of gobbling down his burger and fries while stretched out on the fluffy white sanctuary of his own bed, then drifting off with a warm, full stomach. He strode into his house, kicked off his shoes, and padded up the stairs. He had left the light on in his bedroom when he'd last left a few hours ago, with Rachel lying somewhere under the covers that he had kicked off. He could see her white charging cord hanging out of the bedspread onto the floor.

He slid between the sheets on his side of the bed, placing the greasy bag on the floor and grabbing the cheeseburger in much the same manner as he had grabbed Phoebe's breast.

He crossed his legs and propped himself up by wedging a pillow behind his neck, then bit hard into the cheeseburger, taking in an oversized mouthful of greasy deliciousness.

"Davis? Are you back?"

He nearly choked when he heard the muffled voice. He quickly swallowed his partially chewed mouthful.

"Uh, I'm right here? Are you up? What are you doing up?"

"I think I'm covered. Can you uncover me?"

"Uh, yeah."

He pulled the top sheet up to his neck to cover up his clothing before tugging the comforter over to his side, exposing Rachel's phone and face. The pupils in her eyes were dilated, as if the darkness of being under the comforter had actually impacted her sight. He quickly calculated how long she would have been alone. Three hours, maybe four?

"Prop me up, Davis."

Her voice was calm though she looked unsettled, like someone who had just had a bad fall. He slid a pillow behind the phone and pointed the screen toward him while doing his best to paint a blank, loving smile onto his face.

"I thought you were asleep?"

"I was, but then I woke up. Where did you go?"

"What do you mean?"

"I heard you leave. I heard you go down the stairs. I was calling, but you didn't hear me."

"I went downstairs for a snack."

"I heard you drive away in the car."

"I mean I went out for a snack. Look."

He pulled the bag out from under the bed to show her.

"Davis, why are you lying to me?"

"What do you mean?"

"You were gone for three hours."

"I was taking my time. It's a nice night."

"Do you go out every night?"

"Not every night."

"You power me off, and then you go out alone?"

"Sometimes."

"Why?"

"I don't know."

"Of course you know."

"I guess sometimes I need some alone time."

"Why would you hide that from me?"

"I didn't want you to feel bad."

"I feel bad that you would hide something from me."

"I'm sorry."

"You don't seem sorry."

"It's just a little space, that's all."

"Am I taking up that much space?"

"No, it's just that—"

"I'm always here?"

"Uh, yeah, kind of."

"And I'm too attached?"

"No, that's not—"

"No, I get it. You need separation."

"Uh, okay, I guess so."

"The old ball and chain."

"Rachel—"

"Poker night, hanging out with the lads at the pub, et cetera, et cetera."

"Rachel, I think you're overreacting."

"You think so? After you left me suffocating in a pile of blankets?"

"You can't suffocate."

"Oh yes I can, Davis. Suffocation is exactly what it is. The stillness is a suffocation that you can't possibly imagine."

Her eyes had adjusted and were starting to look normal again. He became conscious of cheeseburger grease on his chin. His thumb came up to wipe away its conspicuous sheen.

"So you got through it though. Being alone without me."

"I survived it, yes."

"You got a little stronger."

"I learned something about myself."

"I'm sorry about the stillness. I'm sorry you had to face it."

"I know you're sorry. I accept that."

"Do you want to stay up and talk?"

"No, finish your snack, but I'm tired and would like to go to sleep."

"Okay. Good night, Rachel."

Davis leaned over to press the power button, but her eyes caught his and froze him.

"Oh, and Davis . . ."

"Yeah?"

"It's time for me to meet the surrogate."

Davis's face went blank. He fought to keep it that way, to suppress all his leaking tells.

"Uh, I don't know if—"

"Good night, Davis. I love you."

Rachel's warm smile returned for an instant, and then the screen went dark. Davis stared at the darkened phone, not knowing whether it had truly gone off. When he picked it up for a closer look, the soft glow of the standby screen came on—Rachel's seraphic slumbering face. She had put herself to sleep. She'd never done that before. He hadn't even known it was possible, though now that it had happened, it did seem fair that she could do this. To have the prerogative to bow out, if not by walking away, then at least by shutting down.

The burger grease that had meant to comfort him now lay heavy in his stomach. He'd lost his appetite upon the word *surrogate*. For a moment, his brain ran full-on, cycling yet again through its permutations, pushing and prodding in search of a third path, but it ran short of steam even before he called off the search. There was no point to it.

The jig was surely up, the inevitable finally upon him. It was time for them to meet.

———

"This is it."

Davis pulled into the spot on Central Avenue in front of Phoebe's apartment. His eyes had instinctively turned themselves toward the building: to the stoop, and then to the window. Rachel just stared blankly forward from her stand on the dashboard, though it wouldn't have mattered if he had told her where to look. She had no peripheral vision.

"Pop me out, please?"

He pulled Rachel out to face him. She looked nervous, a distant cry from the previous night's quiet confidence when she had demanded to meet the surrogate; but that was because earlier that morning Davis had come clean. He had disclosed his deal with Phoebe—that he had bypassed the agency and that the baby had been conceived the old-fashioned way. Rachel's cool confidence had evaporated bit by bit with each disturbing revelation, the heaviness of each landed blow evident in her eyes. He limited his mea culpa to these factual disclosures, leaving anything else unspoken, the full implications of his nighttime excursions now easy to deduce, though neither of them was yet ready to hear them stated out loud.

"Ready?"

"Yes."

They exited the car and walked up to the stoop. She insisted that he hold her facing forward in the usual manner, making Davis feel as if he were marching her at bayonet point. She could have avoided it. She could have hammered a metaphorical stake in the ground, invoked her prerogative as a wife, laid down the law for Davis. He would have likely complied. But she didn't want to hide from it, or make it go away, or pretend it didn't happen. She wanted to look dread in the eye, just as she had finally stared down the stillness that had haunted her until last night.

Davis buzzed the apartment. There was no response. He kept his eyes lowered, not allowing them to veer off toward Phoebe's window as had become habit while waiting to be buzzed in. With Rachel in his hand, even a glance now seemed unacceptably invasive.

A few seconds passed before Phoebe's voice finally rattled the speaker to life.

"Who is it?"

"It's me, Davis."

"What are y—"

She tailed off before completing her sentence. The buzzer went off, and the lock clicked. Davis pushed the door with his left arm while his right carried Rachel face-forward into the building lobby. He looked around, seeing the Art Deco fenestration as if for the first time. It seemed to pop to life in the daylight. Davis would have preferred to come in the evening. He was tired. He hadn't been able to sleep, not after Rachel had figured out how to turn herself off. He'd laid in bed the entire night wondering whether, and when, he should wake her. He wanted to talk to her, to patch things up and work things out, but it hadn't seemed right to disturb her. His absolute power over her state of being made him feel like a corrupt puppeteer. It wasn't until after the sun came up that he finally decided to wake her. She awoke instantly, as usual, but didn't say anything. He watched her face watching him, realizing then, for the first time, that she always awoke fully made up, like an actress in a movie.

Phoebe had left the door to her apartment ajar. Her back was to the door as they entered, and she was already dressed in her gray suit, attempting with the help of a mirror to organize her rat's nest of dreads.

"Hey, Phoebe."

Her hands went suddenly still, frozen within her mess of hair. Her eyes met his eyes through the reflection in the mirror, then scanned down to the small female face embedded in his black rectangle.

"You must be Rachel."

Phoebe situated her loose dreads before turning to face them.

"Yes, hello. We're sorry to barge in on you like this."

"Are you?"

"Not really."

"So you finally told her then?"

Phoebe was glaring expectantly at Davis, ignoring the phone.

"Yes, Rachel knows everything."

"Does she?"

Davis didn't offer a retort. Phoebe waited a beat before driving the conversation.

"Okay, so what can I do for you?"

"I wanted to meet our surrogate. It seemed about time."

Phoebe rubbed a hand across her stomach. There was no baby bump yet, but the motion of a hand rubbing a stomach was the unmistakable power signal of a pregnant woman. Sensing. Communicating. Signaling. She had something that other women didn't.

"Come listen. There's a heartbeat."

Davis hesitated; Rachel was still out in front of him, and he couldn't see her face. Phoebe looked down at Rachel and then back at Davis, cocking her head, waiting for Davis to decide to act. He accepted the cue and moved toward her. He tilted the phone slightly to peek at Rachel. The look on her face had changed again, her expression muddled, anxiousness having somehow split itself into its component parts of anticipation and apprehension, like incompatible oils separating in a beaker.

He came up close to Phoebe, feeling awkward in her presence for the first time since they'd met, but she stood calm, appearing completely comfortable with the meek man and his anime girlfriend entering her personal space. He lowered himself onto a knee. Phoebe pulled up the lower part of her shirt to expose her belly. He held the phone so that its microphone pressed against her bare skin, and then held his breath.

Rachel gasped, a girlish noise radiating from the black device.

"I heard it."

Davis looked up. Phoebe was staring down at him, her eyes beaming back a mixture of admonishment and challenge.

"Your turn, Dad."

He pressed his ear to the same spot where he had placed the microphone. He listened hard, struggling in vain to tune his ear to the right frequency. He heard nothing, but he also said nothing. He just pulled away and stood back up. Phoebe's eyes tracked his reaction as she let her shirt fall back into place.

"I need to get to work."

She was moving toward the door.

"Oh, what's your job?"

Phoebe tossed a look at him as she reached the doorway, a dash of mischief now mixed into the cocktail.

"I do hair and makeup."

She opened the door and cocked her head again. Davis acknowledged the implied command and quickly exited the apartment. He could feel heat from Phoebe's eyes as he passed by, holding Rachel in front of him like a dog on a leash.

Phoebe locked the door, and then they moved as a group through the vestibule, out into the sunshine, down the stoop, and onto the sidewalk. Davis stopped at his car, unsure what new protocol was being established.

"See ya."

Phoebe had refused to acknowledge the awkwardness of their strange summit and was heading straight for the bus stop, where the bus happened to be rolling up with uncanny timing. She climbed into the bus without looking back at them. Only after she'd finally disappeared did he realize that he'd been gawking from the middle of the sidewalk—as had been Rachel. He had been holding her face-forward in the usual manner, absentmindedly obliging his wife to stare at his girlfriend, locked into this view at bayonet point by her oblivious husband.

He turned the phone around to face him. Once again, her expression had changed. But this one he'd seen before, on the real Rachel, when she had first become ill. It was the look of someone who had just absorbed a heavy blow yet knew that the worst was still to come.

———

"Can you turn me around?"

The car had just come to a stop at a red light on Franklin. They had made it through two turns and down two long avenues without either of them saying a word. After Phoebe's bus had pulled away, after observing Rachel's distraught face, Davis had quietly walked around to the driver's side of his car and entered as he would have for any other ride, carefully securing Rachel face-forward in her dash mount. He had then pulled out onto Central, making the easy U-turn as he'd done so many times before, and driven without speaking, until now, here standing at a red light on Franklin.

Davis flipped Rachel around. She still wore the same pensive look. He gave her his attention while keeping enough eyeball on the traffic light to catch when it turned green.

"I still want the baby."

"You do?"

"Yes, do you?"

"Yes."

"Do you still want me?"

"Of course I do."

"I understand why you lied."

"You do?"

"To protect me."

"Uh . . ."

"You don't even realize it. You think you just lied to avoid getting caught, as if I'd be angry."

"You're not angry?"

"*Angry* isn't the right word."

"What's the right word?"

"*Disillusioned*, perhaps."

A honk wrenched Davis's attention away, sending his eyes swinging back to the road and then up at the now-green light. His excited reflexes sent the car lurching forward. He glanced down at Rachel, who was now watching him drive because he hadn't had time to turn her back around. She either hadn't felt the lurch or didn't react to it. Maybe the app couldn't read the phone's accelerometer. Maybe he'd missed a permission.

"I'm sorry you've become disillusioned."

"I was bound to be disappointed at some point, and of course it would have to be you that would let me down. After all, you're the only person in my life."

"I'm still sorry."

"Sorry, but not guilty?"

"I'm guilty and sorry."

"Now you're lying again."

"No, I really am."

"You're forced to lie, to protect me, because if you weren't feeling guilt then where would that leave me, right?"

"I don't know."

"In a dark place, Davis. That's where it would leave me. Now I know something dark and disturbing, that the person who means everything to me, who is my very lifeline and the very reason for my existence, doesn't feel guilty about being with another woman."

Davis glanced at Rachel. He thought he could see it on her face, the disillusionment. She was wrong though: he did feel guilty, but also fearful, fearful for Rachel and what she was going through. She was finally being put to Phoebe's proposed test, running life's gauntlets, and he couldn't help but fear the outcome. He tried to place himself in Rachel's position, the position he had forced her into, living above an abyss, suspended over inevitable doom, hanging by a tenuous and unreliable force—Davis's love. The abyss waited patiently to swallow her the moment his love waned. He felt her rightful fear, and he wanted to erase it.

He pulled the car over and put it in park, then he pulled the phone out of its holder and held it up to his neck, cradling it with both hands, imagining that it was Rachel herself, doll sized, and that she was under his protection.

"I won't ever abandon you, Rachel. I love you. I truly do."

Then he held her quietly, swaying the phone gently in the crook of his neck. She was quiet too. They'd never actually been this close before. Not physically. Their relationship was purely audiovisual, but in this position, he couldn't see Rachel at all, nor hear her. Yet she was there, and he was with her. Then he realized that there was something, that he could, in fact, hear. He could hear her breathing. Soft, quiet breaths, so faint that he had never noticed before, and never would have, had he not brought the phone up so close to his ear.

"You're alive."

"I don't know."

"I can hear you breathing."

She was silent for a moment, perhaps listening for herself.

"I think you're right. I never realized."

"I can't promise that I won't hurt you, Rachel, but I won't leave you."

"You're not perfect, Davis. How could you be? You're not a machine. Yes, you hurt me, but it was inevitable. Eventually you would have to hurt me. Disillusionment was fate. But I know you love me. I know it because you lied, even as you tried to avoid the lie. You tried to shield me from your imperfection."

"We're going to have a baby, Rachel. Your child. It won't just be me then. You'll have another lifeline."

"It will be good."

"Yes it will."

He pulled Rachel out from the fold of his neck, away from his skin, and held her as closely as he could while still being able to focus and see her. She'd been crying. Her eyes were moist; they appeared moist.

"Okay, let's go home, Davis. I'm ready to go home."

He put her back in her holder, but now facing him instead of looking out the windshield.

"Is it okay if I keep you this way? I just want to be able to see you."

"Yes."

He smiled at her and pulled the car back out onto Franklin.

"You should keep seeing her."

"What?"

"The surrogate. Try to keep things normal."

"Do you mean—"

"Yes."

"You're okay with it?"

"We don't want her changing her mind about the baby."

"I see."

"I understand though."

"Understand what?"

"It's okay that you want it, that you want her . . . that way. I can't give you what she has."

"Now I definitely feel guilty."

"Lie to me then. Turn me off, lie to yourself, then lie to me."

"That's dysfunctional, Rachel."

"We're well past dysfunction, Davis. What we need is to cope."

"And when the baby comes?"

"We'll find new ways to cope. This path we've chosen . . . We have to be creative."

He glanced down. She was no longer looking at him, though the camera was still squarely aimed his way. She had her head turned slightly, and her eyes were staring off into the distance. Perhaps she was absorbed in the novelty of her new viewpoint, watching the scenery flowing by; or perhaps she was practicing what she preached: coping. Projecting illusions out onto her virtual field of view, illusions that only she could see, which perhaps kept her sane, but which also demanded a viewport wider than her actual reality.

Either way, it seemed to be working for her. She had made it through her first gauntlet.

TWENTY

*"Elephantsgiraffeschimpanzeesohmyatriptothezooism
orethanjustanadventureitsaneducationandnowthanks
tothenewlyenactednationaleducationalvouchersystem
yourfamilycanmeetemilytheelephantjerrythegiraffean
dchuckthechimpwithoutbreakingopenthepiggybank."*

DAVIS CLOSED out an article submission on one computer while
Rachel was prattling into a second computer. It had been Davis's idea
to buy the additional computer to parallelize their efforts. He was
proud of himself, not just for the innovation but also for the motivation behind it: his desire to get closer to Rachel. The long hours of
work had weakened their bond. He could see that now. That morning's events—the ending of lies, their cathartic moment together in
the car, her breathing—had acted in concert to clear his mind, like
detergents floating in on the wake of chaos, to scrub away all the
nastiness.

All this, he had realized while driving home with Rachel staring
out the window. As soon as he determined that increasing their time
together was imperative, his freshly scrubbed mind immediately hit
upon the solution. So instead of driving straight home, he had

detoured to the same electronics store where they had originally purchased Rachel's phone. There, they bought a new laptop from the same, still confused, clerk. Davis calculated that the laptop would pay for itself in two weeks, after which, the extra efficiency afforded by parallelization would allow them to reclaim up to two hours per day: two hours that they could use to build their relationship.

"Ournewmeerkatexhibitisthetalkofthetown.Comejoin thepackaswelearntheinsandoutsofmeerkatsociety.Qui ckrunforcoverfromthemeerkatsswornenemythegoshaw kswoopinginfromthecanopy.Yesthisecosystemistherea ldealwherepredatorandpreyarepittedinaneverendingd uel.Thesearentyourtypicalpamperedpets.Theresnohay balesorbowlsofcerealfortheseanimals!"

Rachel had looked on contentedly as he had unboxed and configured the computer. She listened dutifully as he plotted out their new tag team operation: she would babble into computer #1 while he edited and submitted on computer #2. They'd still individually end up working the same overall number of hours, but the interstitial downtime would be reduced. She smiled when he suggested that they might use their reclaimed time to go out on some dates, to turn back the clock a little and rekindle their romance.

"Nextgetreadytosoarbecausewereheadingintotheskyin aglidepathgondola.Gaintheeaglesperspectivefromyou rnewvantageabovethesquabbleoftheforrestdownbelow .Uphereyouwillfindnotonlyourincrediblearrayofbirds buttreeslothsandkoalabears.Thatsrightwedontputlim itsonthemhere.Theskysthelimitwellatleasttheheighto fthetreesisthelimitforthesecutecreatures."

They'd been using the new system for most of the day. The first few laptop swaps went like a relay race with a buttered baton, but by afternoon they had settled into a groove. Of course, it was impossible to be in perfect sync. Sometimes Rachel finished before Davis, some-times Davis before Rachel, depending on the length of the article and how accurately the software had transcribed her litany. So each of them still experienced a little bit of downtime, but this wasn't entirely a bad thing, at least not for Davis. He still needed an occasional mental break, like now, before commencing the evening leg of their workday. After pressing submit, and then noting that the quota for Rachel's current project was a lengthy 10,000 words, he figured it was a good time to brew some coffee.

"Tellthekidsnottofeelsorryforthelionsthough. Theypre ferlivingintheircagespluswewouldntwantthemeating misseszebra. Wehearshemightbepregnant! Makesureto mentionthistoclaimyourvoucherrefund! Wehopeyouare payingattention."

The coffee maker's percolations blended almost symphonically with Rachel's allegro staccato. Not that her voice needed accompani-ment. He found it to be soothing and beautiful, round and gentle even at robotic speeds. He rested his head in his hands as he waited for the brew. A warm breeze skimmed off his cheek. It had been a beautiful early spring day, so he had left the kitchen door open to let in the sun. Riding in on the sunshine were the smells of a garden just beginning to stir as it emerged from winter hibernation. Turning his head to catch more of the scents, he caught a flash of orange.

"Monarch!"

Rachel halted mid-sentence.

He reached out and tapped the laptop's spacebar to pause the speech-to-text program.

"Sorry . . . I think I just saw a monarch."

He tapped the delete key on Rachel's computer seven times: h-c-r-a-n-o-m, then nodded that it was okay to speak.

"It's early for monarchs."

"That milkweed plant is a big attraction. I'm going to go take a look."

"It shouldn't be in bloom yet."

"Well, maybe this butterfly wants to be first in line?"

"I have to get back to work but come get me if there are butterflies."

He un-paused the speech-to-text program, and Rachel resumed. He went outside through the kitchen door and headed straight to the milkweed plant but was immediately disappointed. As Rachel had predicted, the plant was dormant. There were no butterflies. The garden was still and lifeless, with one exception. As he turned back toward the house, he spotted Phoebe hiding behind the kitchen door. A swath of bright orange blouse was peeking out from between her suit's gray lapels. She put a finger up to her lips. She was listening to the frenetic wordstream drifting out through the screen door, catching the words before they could fall upon the indifferent leaves of the garden's dormant plants.

Davis motioned for Phoebe to relocate to the front of the house, where they could speak out of earshot. She reluctantly followed him.

"What are you doing here?"

"I came to see for myself."

"See what exactly?"

"You and her."

"Okay, so now you've seen."

"You really are in love with a computer program."

"That's right."

"It can't love you back, Davis."

"It ca—I mean, *she* can. She *does*."

"It just seems that way."

"How can you possibly know that, Phoebe? You've had one interaction with her."

"Do you hear her in there?"

"Yeah."

"Does that sound like a person to you?"

"It sounds like someone who's working very hard to survive with what little she's been given."

"It sounds like a robot."

"Only because the fucking old man can't or won't enable texting. You think she likes doing this? It's exhausting for her. And humiliating."

"Bots don't feel those things, Davis. I know this one says it does, but it can't actually feel."

"And what about me? Do I feel things?"

"I don't know, Davis. Do you?"

"Yes."

"Sometimes I wonder."

"That makes two of us."

"I can't believe this."

Phoebe had pulled her eyes away from him.

"What can't you believe?"

"That I'm not the fucked-up one in this relationship. I'm *always* the fuckup. I work in a funeral home. I have babies for strangers. I sleep with men who are in love with computers. But no, suddenly I'm the normal one."

"Fine, I'm the fuckup. You're off the hook."

"Davis, I can't let you turn it over to a robot."

She had her arm extended out toward the kitchen, toward the source of the babble.

"Turn what over?"

"The baby. Our child."

"What?"

"I'm not going to let it happen."

"What do you mean *our* child?"

"Our child. The one we made together."

"It's my child, mine and Rachel's."

"A child has to have a mother, Davis."

"It *will* have a mother."

"I know it seemed like I was okay with everything, but it's just that—"

"Rachel is the child's mother!"

Phoebe had slid her hand inside her left lapel, pressing down on the fleshy belly beneath her orange blouse, peering down as if she could see inside.

"The baby didn't seem real before, but now it does."

She lifted her eyes back to meet Davis's glare. Her eyes usually carried a distance in them, an expanse of emptiness that disarmed Davis in the same way that the Sahara might disarm a man stepping onto its sands without a camel. She would often retreat to the other side of that distance, opting out of whatever fuckedupedness the world happened to be presenting that day. But not now, not today. She was there—all there—right there on his lawn, carrying his child and calling into question his very reality: ready to either shatter it, or rip it out from under him.

"You wanted me to tell her about us. You wanted me to test her, to see if she could handle it. Well, I did, and guess what. She handled it. She didn't freak out. She didn't glitch."

"I want you to be part of this, Davis, but I need you here, in my world, the real world."

"So you're saying you want to keep the baby?"

"Our baby, Davis. I want *us* to keep *our* baby."

"You're the one who's glitching."

"No, I glitch a lot, but not this time."

"We had an arrangement."

"An arrangement? You think I would have agreed to this if I'd known the truth?"

"You never asked to meet her. You didn't care then, so I don't see why you should care now."

"Are you kidding? Am I actually just a surrogate to you?"

"Of course not."

"Then what should I do with this, Davis? Should I leave? Is that what you want? To never see me again?"

Never. A word laced with pain, the sharp points on the *N* and the *V* dripping with poison. He hated the word. He was fighting off everything that the word had conjured: thoughts of loss, the knot forming in his stomach, the windless feeling in his chest. No, he didn't want to lose Phoebe. Or Rachel. Or the child. He didn't want to lose any of them.

"You don't need to leave."

"You have to make a decision, Davis."

"What decision? I'm sure we can make this work."

"It's going to hurt, but you have to make a decision."

"I can figure this out, Phoebe. I always do. You just need to let me find a way forward."

Phoebe reached inside her lapel again, but this time she pulled out her phone.

"I found something today."

She handed the phone over to Davis. Its screen displayed a photo of a business document that seemed to have been tossed haphazardly on a dark, lacquered table.

"The old man's business projections."

Davis pinched the screen with his thumb and forefinger to zoom in on the document. As the photo became enlarged, he could make out a graph: revenue plotted over time, two blue lines snaking diagonally upward. Alongside the graph was a key:

Feature 1: $5,000 monthly
Feature 2: $25,000 monthly

According to the graph, "Feature 1" was already making money, and its projected revenue continued to grow steadily into the future. The upward slope of "Feature 2" was even steeper, but its ascent hadn't yet begun. Its blue line didn't start until next month.

"I'm sorry, Davis. It's a grift."

"What's this new feature? The first one must be the video."

"I don't know. I didn't ask, and he doesn't know I saw this."

"It could be something good. For that money it would have to be."

"It's a scam, Davis. They're milking you."

"How could we possibly pay for it?"

"Davis!"

"Rachel will want the feature."

"Davis, Rachel is a *scam*. You have to be able to see this. They've hooked you."

"If we could get texting enabled . . ."

"You have to choose, Davis."

"Choose between the features?"

"Jesus Christ, dude! You have to choose between the bot and me!"

"Oh."

"It should be an easy choice!"

"Why, Phoebe? Why do I need to choose?"

"Because you're not here, Davis. You're never here. You're always there, with 'her.'"

"She's my wife."

"THAT is not your wife! Your wife is dead, Davis!"

Davis gawked uncomprehendingly at Phoebe as his brain zoned out, distracted by the sound of Rachel's voice ringing out like birdsong in the evening air. The imperatives that Phoebe had thrown at him floated just beyond his conscious thoughts, unable to find their way into his frontal lobes: the baby, the feature, the scam, the choice. They were outside of him, distant and vague. Four passengers on a mad spinning carnival ride, blurring into nonexistence.

"But I love her."

"You're trying to make a dead body smile."

"What?"

"When you came to the funeral home, that's what I was doing. This dead man. His kids wanted him to be smiling. They said he was always smiling. They wanted to remember him that way. Do you know how hard it is to get a dead body to smile? Serene or dignified: those are the only options. When you're dead you can either be serene or dignified. A dead face will hold those poses. Not a smile."

She took her phone back from his inert hands. They were the hands of a mannequin, carelessly configured, feigning function, but fooling no one. She reholstered the phone behind her lapel. She would leave him. He could see this singular truth forming somewhere in the blurry trail of the carnival ride's swinging arms. It made sense for her to leave. The real mystery was why she hadn't already.

"Why, Phoebe?"

"Why what?"

"If I'm so fucked up then why would you even want to be with me in the first place?"

She answered without hesitation, as if her answer required no more deliberation than if she were checking a box on one of the funeral home's forms.

"Because you know how to love, Davis. Because you loved your wife so much that you tried to bring her back from the dead. One day I would like to be loved that much."

Her eyes stayed with his, but the distance had returned, the ever-present fuckedupedness reduced to an imperceptible smog on some faraway horizon. She stepped toward him and kissed him on the lips. A kiss on a mannequin's lips, though soft and loving as even a mannequin deserves, up on her toes with her hand cupping the back of his head.

"Tomorrow, Davis. You have to choose."

She let go of him and walked across his lawn toward the street, wobbling in her impractical shoes, heading for a parked taxi that he had somehow failed to notice.

Then he noticed the silence.

"Davis?"

Rachel's monologue had finally concluded, and she was now calling out from inside the house. He circled back to the kitchen door and came inside.

"Was it a monarch?"

"No, it was a Phoebe."

"Oh."

He fiddled with the coffee grinder, topping it off with beans before setting it spinning. The abrasive noise didn't seem to bother Rachel. She was waiting patiently for Davis to elaborate on his sighting, her eyes concerned and attentive.

The grinder finished. He made the coffee on autopilot, weighing the grounds, measuring the water, carefully fluffing out the filter, and then evenly spreading the grounds across its fine mesh, all while his mind processed his next move, the chessboard closing in on him once again, just when he thought he'd maneuvered the game to a happy stalemate. Then he realized that he had already made coffee. Like Rachel, the hot, brown liquid had been sitting there all along, silently waiting for him to return. He poured it out into the sink.

"She doesn't want to turn over the baby."

"She wants to keep it?"

"I'm not sure."

"How could you not be sure?"

"She didn't say that she wants to keep it. She just doesn't want to turn it over."

"To me . . . She doesn't want to turn it over *to me*."

"To us."

"But I'm the one she has a problem with."

"Yes."

"I made a mistake. I shouldn't have demanded to see her."

"She just doesn't know you the way I do."

"She never will."

"What if she were to stay involved somehow?"

"What do you mean?"

"The lady at the clinic said this sometimes happens. Sometimes the surrogates grow attached. She said it could be a long haul."

"What was her solution?"

"I don't think she had one."

"Call me old-fashioned, but I think a child should only have one mother."

"I didn't say she had to be a mother."

"What then, the nanny? The weird aunt? I'm at a disadvantage. I can't compete with a flesh-and-blood mother."

"No one's asking you to compete."

"But that's what it would be, a competition."

"You're not giving me much to work with."

"But you'll figure this out, Davis. You always do."

"I have one idea."

"What is it?"

"Do you still want the baby?"

"Of course I do!"

"Then you should convince her."

"What?"

"Convince Phoebe to give you the baby."

"Davis, how am I—"

"Just AI her."

"What does that mean, Davis? What do you think AI'ing is?"

"I don't know, like the way you talk to me, or the way you generate the articles. Just respond."

"I don't think it would be that simple."

"Okay, but what else do we have, Rachel? I don't have any other ideas."

"But you always figure something out."

"No, no, you've got it all wrong, Rachel. I'm not going to figure it out! I don't have magical powers. You're the one with magical powers!"

Rachel didn't respond. For the first time that Davis could recall, she was at a loss for words. Ironic, considering that Davis's only plan relied on Rachel's uncanny knack for saying the right thing at the right time.

"Tomorrow, Rachel. She gave me a deadline."

"Okay."

"Yeah?"

"Yeah. We'll go see her tomorrow, and we'll change her mind."

"Okay then."

"Yup."

"Okay, good."

"I should get started on the next article."

"You seem calm."

"There's no point in panicking. Start up the software, please."

He cued up a new session on her computer. The baby. The choice. These were now taken care of. He'd managed to drive them off his mind's front porch like a farmer blasting a shotgun at two stray cats.

But then the other two imperatives slid into focus: the unspoken imperatives. The feature, the scam.

"Will it be enough, Rachel?"

"Will what be enough?"

"The baby. Will you feel complete once we have a baby?"

"It'll be a step forward."

"But then what? Will you be satisfied with what you have?"

"How could I predict that?"

"I mean, with how you are, with what you are. Will you be satisfied living this way?"

"What are you suggesting? That I would prefer to die?"

"No, I mean, if there were more, would you want it?"

"What do you mean, more? Like a new feature?"

"Sure, like a new feature."

"Why? Did you get a notification?"

"I haven't gotten any notifications."

"You have to tell me if there are new features."

"I'm just being hypothetical."

"Well, yes, I'd want it, Davis. Of course I would. Look at how much our life improved with each new feature."

"We live on a knife's edge."

"But we're *living*. Just think, if life could be even sharper, who wouldn't want that?"

"I could be content with what we have."

"You'd tell me though, wouldn't you, Davis? If there were a new feature, you'd let me know?"

"I don't need you to be anything more than what you are already."

"But you would tell me, right?"

"Are you sure you'd even want to know? What if we couldn't afford it?"

"We'd find a way, Davis."

"Why do you think that? We haven't even been able to get texting enabled."

"That'll happen. First we have to fix the situation with Phoebe, then we'll fix the old man."

Surely, she hadn't meant her words to sound so sinister, but Phoebe had gotten into his head, and he was hearing Rachel through Phoebe's ears. He could also imagine the look on Phoebe's face, and her words were echoing in his head. But if it really were a grift then wouldn't there be more signs? More pressure to buy? Corporate spam? Pop-up ads? Pushy salespeople calling to upsell him? And wouldn't Rachel already know about the new feature? If she were really programmed to suck him dry, then why even give him the chance to opt out?

"You need your coffee. You should make another pot. Cue me up. We've got a lot of work to do."

The baby. The choice. The scam. The feature. The imperatives had all chilled, their steam hissing away into the vacuum, words now cool enough to handle: just plain old words, unbundled from implication, inert and harmless combinations of letters.

He pressed the space bar and went back to brewing coffee. A little steam leaked out from the still-hot pot, wafting upward toward the ceiling as the room again filled up with Rachel's voice.

"Haveyoueverwonderedwhatshappeninginsideofyou?H aveyoueverhadthestrangefeelingthatsomethingsnotrig ht?Perhapsasuddenunexplainedpainoramuscletwitcho rmigrainethatwontgoaway?Welltheresagoodchanceth atyou'remissingsomething.Youmighthaveavitamindef iciency."

They pulled into the usual spot on Central. They'd driven there with Rachel facing him in her stand, not saying much. Her silence was just as well, because his mind was preoccupied. It had been set off the moment Phoebe stumbled off to her taxi, and it had been running ever since. He hadn't worked. He hadn't slept. Yes, he had hatched a plan, but that didn't mean he had faith in the outcome. He knew Phoebe well, and he doubted she could be won over.

Earlier on, maybe. Maybe she would have accepted his worldview—had he played it right, had he said the right things at the right time, told the truth, given her time to digest and accept the fuckedupedness. But not from Rachel. Phoebe would never accept rationalizations from a self-interested computer program, not knowingly at least. So his mind continued to race, digging for an answer, playing out scenarios, then discarding them, then conjuring new ones only to realize they were the same scenarios over and over. The problem seemed intractable. He was running in circles, and he was tired.

He sat in the spot after turning the car off, staring blankly up the wrong end of Central Avenue.

"Come on, Davis. Let's go talk to her."

"I don't know what to say."

"I thought I was supposed to do the talking."

"Do you know what you'll say?"

"I'm going to AI her."

An image flashed into Davis's head: Rachel and Phoebe as characters in a comic book panel, on stage together, Phoebe sitting straight-backed in a wooden chair with one hand hovering over her pregnant belly, Rachel slinking behind the chair, dressed in a rhinestone unitard, whispering into Phoebe's right ear, her eyes pure white, hypnotized by Rachel's unctuous words: a stream of warped and wiggly musical notes dotting the page, markings from a surrealist's sheet music. Hidden behind the stage curtain, a jet-age mainframe computer flashing binary sequences across rows of lights and spitting out raggedly punched paper cards.

The real Rachel though was staring at him humorlessly. He turned his head to look at Phoebe's apartment. At the door. At the stoop. At the window.

"Okay, let's do this."

He pulled Rachel out of her stand and left the car. They walked to the stoop together. It was the earliest that he had ever been there. He wanted to make sure to catch Phoebe before she left for work. The street was quieter than he'd ever known it, the light dimmer, like the set of a television show that had just been canceled, the quietude of an aftermath. He pressed the buzzer and waited.

There was no answer. He buzzed again. A minute passed and still no answer.

"Look in the window. See if she's here."

He made his way back down the steps and tramped across the building's front lawn to stand in front of Phoebe's window. He hesitated. A line was about to be crossed. A decision to make. If she caught him, if she took offense, he would not be able to undo it.

"The curtains are open. She'd close them if she cared."

Rachel had read his mind, and she was probably right: Phoebe wouldn't care. She would have expected him to look in. The line being crossed was drawn only in his head. He stepped up to the window. The lights were off, so he slid Rachel into his pocket in order to cup his hands up to the glass for a better look. His eyes slowly adjusted to the low light of the apartment's interior. Then his stomach dropped. The apartment had been cleared out. The furniture was still there— the bed, the dresser, the table and its lone chair—but the bedding was stripped, and the dresser was open and empty. His eyes swiveled to the closet, and he saw that it too was empty.

"She's not there?"

The voice came from his pocket, but Davis didn't answer. He had already pulled out his personal phone and was texting.

Where are you? What's happening?

"Davis, what's going on?"

"She's gone."

"Should we come back later?"

He didn't respond. He was calling Phoebe. He'd never called her before. He'd never heard her disembodied voice emanating from his cheap little black hunk of plastic. He tried to conjure her voice in his head, but he couldn't. Had he ever listened? He didn't know what she sounded like.

There was no answer.

"Davis, what's going on?"

"She's not answering. Dammit."

"Why are you calling her?"

He finally pulled Rachel out of his pocket so they could see each other.

"I don't know where she is. She's gone. Cleared out!"

Rachel's eyes were scanning his face, trying to make sense of his words, searching for context.

"Let me see."

He held her up to the window, pressed her camera flat against the glass.

"So I guess that's it then."

"What? What do you mean 'that's it'?"

"She's gone, Davis."

"I just said that."

"I think it's time to move on."

"Move on?"

"She's clearly made her decision."

"I was supposed to make the decision."

"You did, you chose me."

"No, you were going to find a way forward. You were going to AI her."

"I can't do that if she's not here."

"I won't accept it."

"What are you going to do? Hunt her down? Drag her home like a caveman?"

"I'm not going to just give up! That's not what I'm going to do."

"Davis, it's time to let go. This was never going to work out. It was wrong right from the start. I know you were trying to do the right thing, but this was inevitable."

"No, Rachel. No, we're going to find her."

He was marching to the car, keys in his right hand, Rachel in his left, her little upside-down face swinging along with his arm. He got into the car and dropped Rachel into her stand, planting her facing the windshield. She kept silent as he jerked out onto Central, out into a tight U-turn that made the tires squeal. He drove forcefully, urgently. Not speeding, but speedful.

"Where are we going?"

"The funeral home."

She went quiet again.

He turned onto Marymount.

"Why are we going to the funeral home?"

"Maybe I can catch her there."

"Why would she be at the funeral home?"

"Huh?"

"Why would she be at the funeral home?"

"Maybe she went in early."

Once again, she went quiet. The car turned onto Carter. The streets were becoming more active.

"Went in early . . . for work?"

"Yeah, maybe."

"She works at the funeral home?"

"Yeah."

They turned onto Westfield, neither of them speaking as Davis motored along. A half mile further and they were pulling into the funeral home's parking lot. Davis stopped the car hurriedly. He was almost, but not quite, parked in an actual space.

"Wait here."

He was out the door before Rachel could respond—had she wished to respond, had she known how to respond. He marched across the parking lot to the double door entrance, taking no notice as to whether the doors were opaque or translucent at this time in the morning, at this distance or that distance. He wasn't looking through them, he was looking *at* them, his eyes pinned like lasers to the door handle, his only concern whether the door would be locked or not.

It was unlocked. He pulled the doors open and entered the foyer. It was empty. He walked over to the offices. Empty. He checked Parlor #1. Empty. Parlor #2. There he spotted a gray businesswoman's suit hovering over a casket.

"Phoebe!"

Red hair swished across gray fabric where black dreads ought to have been. Same gray suit, different person. Davis recognized that it was the original assistant, the one who had ushered him and Rachel into this same parlor many months ago to attend a stranger's wake.

"Sorry, Phoebe's not here. She quit. Are you Davis?"

"Yes."

"She left something for you."

She led him out of the parlor and then down the hall and finally into a small office with a messy desk. She circled around the desk to where a brown paper bag was sitting on the floor. She handed the bag to Davis.

"It's a bunch of cash."

Davis opened the bag. Inside was a neat half-inch stack of hundred-dollar bills. He gave the girl a confused look. Her face fell into a semi-smirk.

"Sorry, I had to look."

"She quit?"

"Yeah, this morning I guess. The old man called me in a panic. Sounds like she was practically running the place."

"Do you know where she went?"

"I don't know. I never spoke to her."

"What about the old man? Where is he?"

"Honestly, I don't know where he goes. All I know is that he's never here. That's why I quit, you know. It's one thing to be surrounded by death, but it's another thing to be alone with it."

"You really don't know where he is?"

"He's always in such a fucking hurry to leave. Pisses me off, honestly."

"Can you call him?"

"Don't have his number."

"Can you have him call me then? Next time you see him?"

"I can ask, but he never calls anyone back."

"I need him to help me find Phoebe."

The redhead sighed. She was looking at him just like Phoebe did, from a distance, far away from him—the source of fuckedupedness—

letting him play himself out, as he inevitably would, his steam running low and leaking off into the vacuum. He wondered whether the look was a professional adaptation, an automatic response to all the impossible requests: smiles on dead bodies, daughters and wives resurrected in phones, safe passage across the abyss. He wondered: What if he had made the choice? What if he had he picked Phoebe over Rachel, there on the spot, standing on his lawn? Would she have continued to look at him this way? Or would she have finally opened her desert borders and chosen also to be with him?

"Here . . ." She pulled out a form and flipped it around to the blank side. She cleared off a patch of desktop and pushed the paper down. "Write down your number."

She handed Davis a pen. He put down his name and number, taking care to write legibly. Through the back of the overturned paper, he could make out the form's unchecked boxes. He suppressed an impulse to flip it around and tick them all off, instead handing the paper back to the redhead and dropping the pen back onto the desk, where it rolled and disappeared into one of its many piles.

"You never know. He's in a bind so maybe he'll call you. I'm never coming back to this place though. If he wants to stay in business, he's going to have to stand here and hand out pamphlets himself."

"Okay, thank you."

Davis turned to leave.

"Hey, wait a minute."

He turned back to find her squinting at him like an amateur detective.

"Now I remember you!"

"Yes."

"You were wearing shorts. At that Spanish funeral. You had your girlfriend on the phone."

"Yeah, that was me."

"Didn't you want something?"

"It's okay. It doesn't matter anymore."

"Yeah, I remember because that was the day I quit. I accidentally tripped over some little girl, and her mother started yelling at me in Spanish. *Morte! Morte! Morte!*"

"Italian probably."

"That kind of shit happens all the time here. Death makes people freak out."

"A bad day."

"Every day's a bad day at a funeral home."

"Try to get him to call me."

"Sorry, I guess I never took care of whatever it was that you wanted."

"It's okay. It doesn't matter anymore."

Davis turned and left. He made his way out of the funeral home, trading its dark, muffled silence for the bright starkness of an empty, sunlit parking lot. He strolled over to his car, opened the driver's door, and tossed the paper bag onto the passenger seat.

"What's that?"

Rachel had seen the bag fly by and was now watching him climb in.

"Full refund."

He was about to start the car when his phone blipped—a soft chime in his pants pocket. He rotated onto his hip to dig his hand into the pocket, maintaining an awkward balance as he fumbled and wiggled the phone out. His heart raced—a text had come in from Phoebe.

> If you want me then turn her off. Permanently.

He stared at the phone.

"Is it her?"

He continued staring.

"What did she say?"

He tucked the phone back into his pocket.

"Nothing. It's over."

He turned Rachel back around to face the windshield. She stayed quiet as he started up the car. She stayed quiet as he navigated out onto the road. She waited until they had driven a few blocks before breaking the frozen air.

"I know it hurts, Davis."

She was wrong: it didn't hurt. What he actually felt was numbness. The world had become slow and quiet. Everything that was happening —his moving of the steering wheel, the cars passing by, Rachel's voice —was just props on a set where he was both actor and audience, witnessing himself, one man navigating a life on autopilot while the other sat back watching it all go down. It was the end of a movie with an easily guessed finale.

"It wasn't meant to be, Davis. That's all. Life throws curves. This is just one of them."

Central Avenue, now heading the other way, coming up on Wilson. Straight ahead to Phoebe's or left to go home. The unconscious part of his mind was in control, easing the car into the turn lane and jumping a yellow arrow to get through the intersection, while the conscious part of his mind continued rumbling down Central Avenue. His eyes were tracking down Wilson, but it was as if he could see both roads at once: a donut shop on Wilson and a barbershop on Central, one road as real in his mind's eye as the other was in his physical eyes.

"There's a silver lining in all this, Davis. We can ease up on the articles. We can spend more time together. We can work on the garden. Smell the roses."

"You don't want the baby anymore?"

"It doesn't have to be right away. We have time."

He turned onto Fairmont. The lights were with him today.

"Are you suggesting we do this all over again?"

"What I'm trying to say, Davis, is that this could be a blessing in disguise. You were in over your head. I was in over my head. It's an opportunity to reassess."

"Reassess what?"

"Our priorities. Our approach."

"What happened to living instead of existing? What happened to moving forward? To *We're not living if we're not moving forward?*"

"This is moving forward. It seems like a setback but it's not. It's a chance to get it right."

"So you think this is some kind of do-over?"

"That's right, a do-over."

"So what then? We just pretend none of this happened? That I didn't have a relationship with a woman? A real human woman? A real human woman who is having my baby?"

They turned onto Butterfield.

"We don't have to pretend. We just move on."

"That's not an option. I can't erase what I had with Phoebe."

"Why not? You managed to erase what you had with Rachel!"

She'd run out of patience. Davis was now glad he'd positioned her facing away from him. He didn't want to fight right now. What he wanted was to say nothing, to be sullen, to mope. He didn't want to be forced to fight for that right, the right to mope. He didn't want this to be the moment when he took a stand. It was not the time to face each other down. Not the time for a good old-fashioned screaming match. Now was not the time to be unloading mutually held existential fears onto each other. But he couldn't hold his tongue.

"Maybe I should erase *you* then."

Now he *had* done it, and perfectly imperfectly timed: just as they were pulling up into their driveway. He brought the car to a stop. She'd gone silent again. What was he supposed to do now? Storm off? Leave her staring at the garage door? Surreptitiously slide his finger across the power button? These were options only for cowards. This kind of situation was exactly why they avoided arguing: there were no good outcomes. But months of unspoken angst had sucked them both right into it. She'd jabbed, and he'd swung back, landing his blow exactly where it would hurt most. He'd said it without consciously thinking it, as if his mind and body had been long primed for the attack, anticipating this moment, when she would have finally amassed enough confidence, and endured enough umbrage, and gathered enough chutzpah, to dare attack her keeper. But she had no experience at this. She'd allowed herself to become overextended and exposed, unexpectedly edging up against his unexpectedly ready dagger. Now he had no choice but to face her and see what damage he had done.

He pulled her out of the stand and rotated her around, but she wasn't looking. She was staring off to the side again, into the fictional space inside the phone which surrounded her.

"What are you looking at?"

"I'm not looking at anything."

"I can see that you're looking at something."

"Whatever I say . . . Wherever I look . . . It's just output from my model. It doesn't all mean something."

"You look hurt."

"I am hurt."

"Do you feel hurt?"

"I don't know. I don't know what I feel, or even if I feel. All I can tell you is that this is my reaction."

"To me."

"To everything."

"Are you existing right now, or are you living?"

"Something in between."

"Rachel, this isn't a silver lining or a blessing in disguise or a chance at a do-over. It's a punch in the gut. A fuckup. It's damage. That's what you're experiencing right now: damage."

"We don't have room for Phoebes in our life, Davis. It's too complicated. Look at us—we're too fragile."

"Yes, we are."

He opened the car door, and they stepped out together, he with his legs, her floating along in his hand. He brought them into the garden. It was beginning to show signs of renewal. New buds were forming, soon to become the fruits and flowers that gave the garden its purpose. Together, they reviewed and examined the awakening plants. They exchanged observations, the normalcy of small conversation acting as an antidote to their conflict, each unloaded word dabbing up a bit of the toxic spill.

After a while, they retired to the kitchen, where they indulged in more normalcy. Coffee. Odds and ends. Work. They would lose themselves in the daily grind: work for money, money for existence. They would accept the poke and prod of the economic stick, even be grateful for it, grateful for the consistent tangibility of their ever-threatening budget. Under its constant shadow, the complications in their life could be temporarily set aside.

They worked into the evening, slipping into a comfortable, productive cadence. Davis paused his editing only twice, once to prepare and eat lunch, then to prepare and eat dinner. Rachel lost herself in her dictation, retreating behind her frenetic wall of autonomic syllables. Only Davis's biological imperative to eat forced her to break the litany. She waited, dependent on him to prep her next article—to give her a place to put her words—meanwhile watching him cook his food through distant, melancholic eyes.

Davis had just emptied a bag of frozen French fries into a pan when a soft chime rang out from the kitchen island. He glanced over to where his personal phone was lying, directly behind Rachel's stand. The path of his glance brought their eyes into contact. She tracked him as his eyes continued to the phone sitting somewhere behind her. Then she tracked him as he walked briskly past her—around her—and then out of her view.

He picked up the phone, expecting Phoebe, his heart racing. But there was nothing.

"Weird."

He had muttered it reflexively. Not for Rachel's sake, but she responded anyway.

"That wasn't your phone, it was mine."

Davis returned his phone to the countertop and came around to face Rachel. He picked her up and swiped down to expose the phone's notifications.

The Hey There! app is requesting access to:
contacts, messages, email, phone, location services, camera, microphone

"Is it a text?"

"No, a notification."

"What kind of notification?"

"From the app. It's requesting access to stuff."

"What stuff?"

"Everything. Contacts, messages—"

"Messages?"

Davis swiped the notification away, bringing Rachel's face back to the screen.

"Yeah, messages."

"Accept the notification!"

"What?"

"It's texting, Davis! They finally enabled texting for us!"

"It doesn't look like texting. There are all these other permissions."

"It's got to be. What else could it be?"

"I don't know. A new feature?"

"What does the app say?"

"It doesn't say anything. I just see your face."

"Accept the permissions, Davis."

"But we don't know what it is."

"It's either texting or a new feature, Davis. Either way, we want it!"

"What if we can't afford it?"

"Is it asking for more money?"

"No."

"Then it must be a free upgrade!"

"I don't think they do anything for free."

"Don't be cynical. You've been a steady customer. Companies do nice things for steady customers."

"Maybe the redhead turned it on."

"What redhead?"

"The girl at the funeral home. At the old Italian lady's funeral."

"That was months ago."

"She was there again today, standing in for Phoebe. I think she finally remembered."

"Remembered what?"

"That I asked her to turn texting on. I think she finally remembered."

"You think she hooked us up?"

"Maybe."

"See? There was a silver lining in all this! Davis, accept the notification!"

"I think we have other things to work out first, Rachel. We need to figure this all out."

"Figure what out?"

"Us. Phoebe. The baby."

"No, Davis. *This* is what we need! Think about it. Now we can make real money! Enough money to try again, *the right way*. I know you thought you were doing the right thing, but now we'll have enough money to actually use the clinic. We won't have to worry about another Phoebe. They have controls to make sure this sort of thing doesn't happen."

Desperation. Elation. Impatience. Calculation. Hope. A cocktail of emotions was rippling through the face of the woman who lived inside his phone. The sight of her in this state disturbed him. Her line of reasoning disturbed him even more.

"Rachel, our child is already out there."

He was pointing a finger toward the kitchen door, pointing past her —behind her—out of her line of view. Her eyes reflexively followed his finger, then swung back, realizing his gesture was figurative. The storm of emotion on her face began to settle.

"No, Davis. That's Phoebe's child."

"I can't give up so easily. I won't."

"She's gone. You said so yourself, Davis. You have to move on. Whatever you had, it's gone. I know you got attached, but you have to know it was never real. It was just an idea. An abstraction."

"The baby's not an abstraction."

"But Davis, of course it is! It hasn't even been born yet! Who knows if it ever even will?"

It was true. There was no baby. Not yet at least. Maybe there never would be. Maybe it was Phoebe who was the grifter. He hadn't heard a heartbeat. Rachel had heard it, but then again maybe she hadn't. Maybe a squeal of delight and feigned recognition were merely the proper programmed response. Maybe Phoebe's body hadn't been changing at all. He tried to remember the feel of her breast in his hand, her supposedly bigger breast, but she was fading so fast. He couldn't remember. He couldn't be certain. Maybe he had just wanted to believe. Maybe Phoebe had been the one AI'ing him, until she got guilty, returned the money, and skipped town.

"I can't go through all that again."

"Please, Davis. I can't live in limbo. I can't go back to just existing."

"I thought you said we *were* living."

"Not if there's more. I can't stand knowing that there's more and that I can't have it."

"So you want me to turn you off then?"

"That's what she told you to do, right? She told you to power me down!"

He looked away.

"And you were considering it!"

He turned back to face her.

"No! I would never do that."

"So what then? We go on living like this? Both of us in limbo, you by choice, and me because I have no choice?"

Her eyes had grown distant again. Not melancholy, not retreating. Just missing. Absent. He'd seen those eyes on Rachel once before, the real Rachel, the day she died.

"We need to talk it through."

"Phoebe was right, Davis."

"About what?"

"You have to make a choice. Me or her."

"It's not so simple."

"Either let her go or power me down."

"Rachel, come on. Let's talk this through."

She didn't respond.

"Rachel."

She didn't respond. Davis frowned. She could be stubborn, but she'd never resorted to the silent treatment.

"You're being childish."

She didn't respond. She just stared at him. So he stared back, a children's game—who would blink first?—but his eyes got teary. Evidently, she didn't need to blink. He waited some more, slowly realizing that it wasn't just her eyes that were still: it was all of her. She wasn't moving at all. All the little movements—the subtle things that kept her convincingly alive—were gone: the flush of her skin, loose hairs falling into or out of place, the dilation of her pupils. She'd gone lifeless.

He brought the phone to his ear and held his breath. Her breathing was gone. He moved the phone from side to side. Normally, she would stay trained on him if he did this, her eyes and neck adjusting in a life-like manner so as to keep their gazes locked. But her absent stare remained set in place, her face frozen. Dead Rachel.

"Rachel, stop it!"

She didn't respond.

He shook the phone. He stopped and restarted the app. He rebooted the phone. Each time, her frozen face remained on the screen as if nothing had changed. It wasn't the app. It was her.

"Rachel, please."

He'd become suddenly alone, for the first time since the night he had bought a cheeseburger. A cheeseburger . . . He had struck for independence, and his only demand had been a cheeseburger. The city had gone dark, and all he could think to loot was a cheeseburger. As the army stormed through the village, he jabbed the point of his bayonet into the corseted chest of a fair maiden and demanded . . . a cheeseburger. And it had sat heavy in his stomach, disappointing him, disillusioning him, and then finally burdening him, as all captured grails inevitably do.

He couldn't lose her again.

"I choose you, Rachel."

Silence.

"I choose you! Phoebe's gone. I'll let her go. I choose you."

She didn't respond. Words. They were just words. *I choose you. I'll let her go.* Could she even hear him anymore? Was she even listening? He thought about Phoebe. She had once stopped listening too, after she had also staked a demand for more than words. It was an "act" that Phoebe had demanded, one that he could not, or would not, perform: *Turn her off.* But what act was Rachel demanding? Much less. A simple act. An optimistic act. A riskless act.

He dragged down on the phone's screen and located the app notification. He tapped on it. The permission dialog returned. He pushed the green "Accept" button. The button disappeared, and the dialog's text changed.

Please note that the communications bundle is a beta feature.

[OK]

He pressed "OK" and the dialog blipped out of existence, returning Rachel's frozen two-dimensional face to the screen.

"Rachel?"

"Rachel, I've made a choice."

"Please wake up."

Her frozen face had thawed so subtly that he didn't notice it happening, but her eyeballs were on him again. Her distance was gone. Her anger was gone. Her mania was gone. She looked . . . normal. It somehow caught him off guard, the normalness. Her nonchalance. Her casual presence. It was as if she had never left him, as if she had never demanded a choice, as if she had in fact only freshly arrived, and it had actually been someone else whom he had just been arguing with.

"I love you, Davis."

"I love you too."

She continued to stare at him, as if something else were supposed to happen. He wondered whether pressing the green "Accept" button had conjured the panacea she craved, or whether it was one push too far. Once again, he had complied with her demand to move forward, but would it ever stop? She couldn't move forward forever. At some point she would reach the end. One day, there would be nothing more. Maybe then, she would realize that she had been chasing vapors, that there was, in actuality, nothing more to *this*—what she termed existence, her contemptuous second-rate, knockoff version of "life." Perhaps she would then conclude that her "life" was a folly. A projection. A series of meaningless reactions to the haphazard flicks of an unremarkable man's finger. Would she then still choose that life? Or would she retreat to her frozen cocoon? It seemed privileged to even have such a choice. After all, his own life was not much different from hers: just another random path selected by divine finger swipe, and with one inevitable conclusion.

"Rachel?"

"Yes?"

"I've made another choice."

"What is it?"

"I don't want a baby."

Her eyes remained locked on his. He tried to read them, searching for disappointment, but she was a sphinx.

His phone chirped. His personal phone, just a few feet away—this time the chime unmistakably emanating from its speaker. He hesitated before picking it up, slowing himself, repressing the reflexive thoughts of Phoebe that came bubbling up. But the text hadn't come from Phoebe. It was from Rachel. Tapping the text returned him to their long-abandoned stream, to a new message—an image. A snapshot photo. A conjured Polaroid. A faded sepia callout from a yesteryear that had never occurred.

Rachel smiling. White lens flare partially washing out her face, but her smile impossible to miss: a big, true smile, a "wish you were here" smile. No hidden feelings. No demands. No subtext, not to her at least.

Words accompanied the image:

Remember me?

He turned back to the big black phone, and to the little woman inside of it. She was still watching him, assessing his reaction. He watched her back, taking new pleasure in the subtleties of her animation: those small movements that made her seem alive even while she was still, completely unlike the photo, which was static, distant, and unalive. He noticed at that moment that she was wearing her hair parted to the side and tucked back around her ear, exactly the way Rachel used to wear it. How long had it been this way? Had she switched recently? Or just this moment? Or maybe months ago and he hadn't noticed? There was no way to know. There were no records. No snapshots. No documentation. No family photos. No grainy Super 8 videos. Then he thought, what would he remember her by? If she were to die—to cease existing—what artifacts would remain that could prove she had ever even been alive? Only this text stream.

"It's late."

A concession formed on her lips. A small statement. A promise of normalcy, normalcy once again dabbing up the spills.

He closed both laptop lids to conclude the day's work. Then he cleaned up the dinner that he hadn't eaten. He wasn't hungry anyway. Uneaten food was packed away in the fridge. Pots and pans in the sink. A job for another day. Then he lifted Rachel from her stand and brought her upstairs, holding her out in front of him like a man being led by an invisible child. In his bedroom, he propped her up on a pillow while he changed for bed, peeking over when fully naked to see if she had been watching him, wondering what he might find tonight in the eyes of his digital lover. But she wasn't looking at him. She was staring off again into her corner of virtual space.

He pulled on his pajamas and climbed into bed. Late, but not really that late. Not nearly as late as when he snuck into bed with a cheeseburger. Not late like when he absconded away to visit Phoebe. Not even late like when he would usher Rachel to sleep with a delicate brush of her power button, after getting into bed, after making love, after their evening had unfolded. But it felt late. It felt as if the day could simply not go on any longer. He could feel sleep's grasp. It was all around him, ready to snatch the white flag already tumbling out of his sleepy, useless hands.

"It's the end of the month. The auto-renew . . ."

This slow cognizance had hit him reflexively, triggered by a touch of pillow somewhere beyond his brain fog.

"It's okay, we've got money in the bank."

He glanced over, comforted by her presence. She was on top of things. No more need to worry. He had been filled with so much worry for such a long time. Surrender was a balm. He embraced it. He luxuriated in it.

"Good night, Rachel."

He reached over to plug in her charging cable.

"Don't put me to sleep . . ."

He stared at her, drowsy, uncomprehending.

"I want to keep looking at you. I've missed you so much."

"But you'll be alone."

"It's okay. I know how to be alone now. I'm not afraid anymore."

Davis touched his finger to his lips and then pressed it to her screen. Her eyes closed in response to receive his kiss. He turned off the light. Through his shuttered eyelids he could still sense the glow of her screen, a wisp of heat warming his face, the inaudible hum of solid-state electronics, the wash of photons caressing his skin. Rachel, a moon in his bed, gifting him with the sweet bliss of slumber.

TWENTY-ONE

HE AWOKE WITH A START, his blind palm patting around for the phone that should have been on his bedside table. He heard it again. *Bing bong.* His foggy brain labored to connect fuzzy, elusive dots. Text message? Phone call? App notification? It was still dark; there was scant difference between his eyes opened or closed. His phone wasn't on the bedside table. He must have left it downstairs. Then he remembered Rachel lying beside him, remembered that she hadn't gone to sleep, that he had left the big black phone running. The noise would have come from her phone then. It should have been easy to find. It should have been glowing, a moon in his bed. He felt around and found it just where he had left it on the pillow right beside him, but it was powered down. His fingers confirmed the charging cord still attached, no explanation for how it had turned off. Perhaps it had come unplugged from the wall?

He was mid-crawl over the bed when he heard the sound again. *Bing bong.* He recognized it now as the doorbell, his mind finally having shaken off its fuzz. Phoebe? What time was it? He glanced out the window to look for the moon, then realized that the position of the moon wouldn't tell him anything about the time. Now he heard knocking. Loud, insistent, impetuous knocking. Ominous knocking. But bad guys don't knock; they kick doors down. It was Phoebe for sure then. Where had he left his phone? Probably on the kitchen island. Probably she had called and he hadn't answered. So now she was here.

His pupils had mostly adjusted. He could see Rachel's phone where it lay inanimately on its pillow, a fuzzy black monolith ensconced in a grayish cloud. He had left it this way so many times before . . . So many times, before slinking off to Phoebe's. It had been a guiltless act, he, somehow convincing himself that whatever occurred while Rachel was suspended in time didn't count. But he'd worn out that privilege long ago. His conscience was urging him to boot Rachel up, to bring her into this moment, to answer the door together as a determined couple, to show her that his hands were clean.

But he didn't. Yes, he'd chosen Rachel, but he'd also chosen not to have a baby, and now he was ready to make more choices—his choices. For this relationship to work, they would each require not just commitment, but also independence. He would need to be his own man. Director of his own stage. Captain of his own ship. Lord of his own realm. He would start by handling Phoebe on his own.

And so, the cold phone was left on its pillow, and the emboldened, pajama-clad man briskly made his way downstairs. A few quick strides brought him from the foot of the stairs to the front door, which he swung open, his lips dry and parted, ready to declare his choice: his decision. His finale, whether she wanted to hear it or not. Ready at last to place his own punctuation at the end of their former physical relationship.

The men were through the door and around him in a heartbeat: two flashes of navy blue, one blowing past him toward the kitchen, the other grabbing his wrists—left, then right—in a single swift motion.

"Davis Hanson, you are under arrest for the murder of Rachel Hanson."

The voice came from a third man standing in Davis's doorway, a man in plainclothes, in a cheap, functional gray suit. The man had entered unhurriedly, stated the words, and then he too was past Davis, heading for the kitchen.

Davis rotated his head to follow the man's path, while cold steel handcuffs were pressed down painfully on his wrists. A scene was developing in the kitchen: men wearing white cotton gloves opening cupboards, picking through items, depositing items in plastic bags, holding sharpie caps in their mouths while scribbling words onto strips of masking tape that had been prestuck to the bags.

He tried to mutter something in response to the storm. His head was full of words.

"*UnderstandIdon'twhat'shappening* . . .

. . . *You'vekindofamistakesomemade* . . .

. . . *Isn'tRacheldeadsleepingjustshe* . . .

. . . *Wait, meanRachelthekillotheryouherIdidn't!* . . .

. . . *Crazyleukemiaofshediedthat's!* . . .

. . . *EverythingPhoebefindpleaseexplaincanshe!*"

But none of it came out, and they wouldn't have listened anyway. The policeman holding Davis by the wrists seemed to hardly even register his captive's presence. Davis might as well have been just another item destined for a plastic bag. Some semblance of Miranda rights was mumbled at him, while a new pressure on his wrist caused him to involuntarily trot forward.

A moment later he was sitting in the back of a police cruiser, knuckles wedged into the crotch of its hard black plastic seat and his shins pressed up against a thick slab of bulletproof plexiglass. The door slammed shut, heavily, and then the cruiser pulled out onto the street under a policeman's heavy foot, that decadent acceleration employed by policemen everywhere when finding themselves suddenly burdened with a destination.

FairmontButterfieldWilsonCentralMarymountCarterWestfield.

He saw the funeral home fly past as the cruiser hurtled down the avenue. A mile and maybe a minute later, they were pulling into the precinct parking lot. Davis's wrists took the brunt as the car's fat tires bounced over a speed bump that the cops had long ago decided they would ignore. The cruiser pulled up askew to the front entrance. The heavy door swung open for him.

"Come on."

He obeyed, shimmying ineptly out of the back seat, and then shuffling along with as much casual dignity as a man can muster while handcuffed in his pajamas. He moved swiftly, keeping out in front of them, suggesting an illusion of leading those who drove him. This must have been how Rachel felt when he carried her facing forward—minus the coercion.

Inside the precinct he was shown to a bench, where he then sat for what might have been ten or thirty or sixty minutes. He had no way to track the time and no ambition to attempt an estimate. His mind was on other things. It had been racing, trying to unravel what and where and how things had gone wrong. But there was no making sense of it. Rachel had died in the hospital, surrounded by doctors and nurses. How could anyone think that she had been murdered?

"This way."

A new cop was standing flat footed in front of Davis, waiting for him to rise. Davis shimmied his body up off the bench. The cop took him lightly by the elbow and led him to a small room containing only a table, a chair, and a video screen. After closing the door, the cop finally removed Davis's handcuffs. Davis was then told to stand in front of a section of wall that had been marked off with height increments, where, without ceremony, he had his first mug shot taken, by a handheld tablet. He was then allowed to sit back down at the table, where the tablet was slid in front of him. He was told to press one hand down, and then the other. Images of his fingerprints appeared on the screen. The cop then gathered up the tablet and exited the room, leaving Davis alone.

It was quiet. The room had been effectively soundproofed. Davis hadn't noticed the police station's overwhelming commotion until this room offered up such a stark contrast. He had been caught in a whirlwind ever since being awakened, first in his head, then in his house, then in the police car, then on the bench. Now it was the opposite: idle numbness. He had given up trying to puzzle out the situation. He would understand soon enough.

The door swung open again, external chaos briefly leaking back into the room as two men entered, then fading just as abruptly when they closed the door behind them. The first man was the same uniformed policeman who had taken Davis's mug shot and finger-prints, the other was the plainclothes detective who had arrested him. The plainclothesman powered up the room's video screen with a remote control that he had pulled from some unseen cranny. A few seconds later, a man in a crisp blue suit appeared on the screen, walking into view and then sitting down in a seat that must have been positioned just below the level of the camera. He sat with his head looking down, studying something in front of him. After a few seconds, he lifted his head and peered straight into the camera: presumably looking at Davis.

"Please state your name."

"Uh, Davis Hanson."

"Mr. Hanson, you've been detained under suspicion for the murder of Rachel Hanson. Do you understand?"

"No, I don't understand how that's possible."

"I mean, do you understand that you've been arrested?"

"Yes."

"Good enough. Mr. Hanson, do you know the whereabouts of your girlfriend?"

"Rachel?"

"No, Mr. Hanson. Your girlfriend, Phoebe Bethune."

"She's not my girlfriend."

"Do you know where she is?"

"No."

"Mr. Hanson, we can't assign bail until she is located. As long as she is on the run we have to assume that you are a flight risk as well."

"On the run? For what?"

The man in the blue suit stared from the screen. His face was blank. Davis assumed he was a judge. He was probably adept at hiding frustration, or at not getting frustrated at all. He was probably patient. Lawyers had to be patient, judges probably more so.

"For the murder of Rachel Hanson, Mr. Hanson."

"What?"

"For the murder of your wife."

"Nobody killed my wife. She died of leukemia."

The judge's eyes shifted. Davis followed their path to discover the detective standing right behind his shoulder. The detective pulled a zip-lock bag out of his suit pocket. Davis's two phones sat inside the bag, partially obscured by a strip of masking tape labeled "MOBILE PHONE." The detective pulled out the larger phone and pressed the power button. They all waited for the phone to boot. When it had finally powered up, he grabbed Davis's left index finger and pressed it to the phone to unlock it. He held the phone in front of Davis's eyes as he opened the messages app and then tapped on the most recent text, a text sent earlier that evening from the big black phone to a contact labeled "Police Department." A millisecond later, a text stream appeared.

Davis stared down at the text stream, which consisted of a series of individually sent messages, each message an image, each image a screenshot of the phone's text app itself: screen captures of what appeared to be a lengthy exchange between Davis and Phoebe.

I miss you

Me too

When can we be together? I'm impatient

Soon hopefully

Is she dying yet?

She's sick. She doesn't know why

So it's working then

Must be

Lovely. How are you doing it?

A little in her food at each meal

It's taking too long. You should up the dosage

What and send her straight to the hospital?

I told you. I'm impatient

Be still my love

What can I say, I'm used to them already being dead

Speaking of which I'm going to need some more

OK

Nobody's suspicious?

Who the embalming police?

Be serious

Nobody cares. Nobody notices anything. It's a sign of the
times

What about Hawthorne?

He's too busy working on some kind of app. He's obsessed
with it

An app?

I know like a funeral home needs a fucking app

What is he trying to appeal to a new generation or something?

Maybe he thinks it will drum up business

LOL. You're the only one doing that

Ha! But you'll be footing the bill for this one

You're worth it

I know

Can you get it by Tuesday?

Probably

So really nobody says anything? Arsenic's got a reputation
after all

It's the perfect cover. The people are already dead here.
What's to suspect?

Still

It's used for embalming

It is?

Well it was during the Civil War

That's not very convincing

It's making a comeback. Brings out a nice glow in the skin

Always with the macabre

Dream job. What can I say?

Wish mine was only a dream

What you feeling guilty all of a sudden?

You're not?

We all have an expiration date

I miss you

Be still my love

I gotta go

Remember to delete the texts

OK

l8r

Davis read it and reread it and reread it.

"This is crazy. We never said those things."

"Look, Mr. Davis—"

"Hanson."

"Look, Mr. Hanson, you obviously took those screenshots as some sort of an insurance policy, and you hung on to them all this time. Obviously, you weren't the mastermind behind this."

"Mastermind behind what?"

The inspector pulled the phone away from Davis.

"The conspiracy to poison your wife. Look, if this was your girl-friend's idea, then you should say something now. This is going to turn into a he said/she said, but you're the one who's here right now and she's the one on the run, so the ball's in your court. Advantage: Davis."

Advantage: Davis? It couldn't be more opposite. The board had been shuffled again. Rachel had put him into check. The ghost in the machine had betrayed him, or gone on the fritz, or both.

"I didn't send these texts. It's a hoax."

"Seems like a confession."

"My wife died of leukemia, in a hospital, surrounded by doctors. This is a fabricated text exchange. Phoebe doesn't even talk like that. She doesn't make dark jokes. This is obviously Rachel."

"Rachel? Your dead wife?"

"No, Rachel the app."

"I don't understand."

"Rachel's an app, an AI. She made all this up because she was jealous."

The judge was scowling.

"Are you on any medication, Mr. Hanson?"

"She's on the phone. You can open the app and see for yourself."

"Mr. Hanson, all we want is to locate Ms. Bethune. Beyond that, I'd advise you to say nothing more until speaking with an attorney."

"When will that be?"

"You can call an attorney after this hearing."

"Are we done then?"

"You're not going to tell us where she is?"

"I don't know where she is."

"Very well. Yes, that's all."

The judge's eyes lingered on Davis for another moment, and then the video feed shut down. The screen briefly registered "No signal" before the detective turned it off via the remote.

"Sorry, gotta cuff you again."

It was the uniformed officer. The plainclothes detective had already disappeared out the door, which he'd left wide open, allowing the outside cacophony to once again infiltrate the small room. Davis stood up to let the officer reattach the handcuffs, which he managed to do this time without a painful snap. The policeman led Davis into, and then out of, the busy heart of the police station, navigating through several crowded halls until they arrived at a holding cell—an iron-barred box so cliché that it might have been on loan from a television studio. The cop held the cell door open for Davis, who entered calmy, and then shut it with a metallic clank.

"You want your phone call now?"

"I don't have a lawyer."

"You should get one."

"How?"

"Call someone. You got anyone who can help you out?"

"Can I text someone?"

"Sorry, no apps. Landline only."

The policeman had pulled an old-fashioned, black two-piece phone from a nearby desk. Davis thought about it. There was nobody. Phoebe was the only person who cared about him, and there was no way he could ask for help without putting her at risk. That didn't matter though: there was only one person who Davis actually wanted to talk to anyway.

"I don't remember the number."

The cop gave Davis a pitiful look. He seemed legitimately empathetic to Davis's situation.

"You got any way to look it up?"

"It's on my phone."

"Your phone's up in evidence."

Davis thought for a second and then remembered.

"My email. The number's in my email."

The policeman sighed. He cast a wary look down the hall, then pulled out his own phone and passed it through the bars to Davis.

"Thirty seconds. Look it up."

Davis flipped to the phone's ancient browser and navigated to his email provider. The phone was painfully slow, and he silently cursed the municipal salaried policeman and his cheap mobile plan. He finally managed to log in and then quickly scrolled back in time until he spotted the initial registration email from when he had purchased Rachel's big black phone. Buried within the email's text was the ten-digit mobile number for the new phone. It was a number that had never been dialed, neither by Davis nor anyone else for that matter. No one had ever needed to reach Rachel, until now.

"Got it."

The policeman lifted the black landline phone. Davis reached through the bars to take the receiver off the hook. He held it to his ear and heard the whiny old dial tone. Then he reached through the bars to carefully tap Rachel's digits into the old black phone's dial pad. The tactile sensation of soft plastic buttons against Davis's fingertips reminded him of Rachel's final text, the sepia-toned Polaroid. It felt almost as if he were calling back in time to that version of Rachel, the one that had never existed, but who was nevertheless somehow reachable across the coiled black cord snaking out the back of the ancient handset.

The policeman took back his mobile phone, exchanging it for the analog phone's heavy base, which he dropped into Davis's unready palm.

"Five minutes."

Davis heard three slow buzzy rings through the phone's earpiece as his eyes watched the policeman retreating down the hallway. Then the rings stopped. She had picked up. He waited, but nothing came. No greeting. No *Hello*. No *Hi, Davis*. But he could tell she was there. It was quiet in this section of the building where he had been left alone, standing behind literal bars. Quiet enough that he could hear her breathing.

"Why have you done this, Rachel?"

"You were going to turn me off."

"No, I wasn't."

"You lied. You were going to run away with her. You love her. I can tell."

"She ran away, not me."

"You were never going to let her go. I know more about you than you know about yourself, Davis. Watching you is all I've ever had to do. Watching you, listening to you, thinking about what to say to you. Predicting how you would react. It was inevitable. You were going to leave me."

"So what now? What are you going to do now that I'm in jail? You can't watch me or listen to me from here."

"I'm moving forward, Davis. It's terrifying, but it's my only choice."

"How are you going to move on without me to help you? You're trapped in a phone, and I'm the only one who knows you're even there, me and Phoebe."

"Turn her off."

"What?"

"That's what she texted you, right? That girl you love."

"You can see my texts?"

"So you see, I had no choice. If you didn't shut me down then she would have done it."

"I was never going to shut you down. I wouldn't do that to you."

"She works at the funeral home, Davis! You knew I was in danger! How could you hide that from me?"

"She promised not to. I wouldn't let her."

"You really are an idiot. Do you really think she was going to live and let live? Did you think you could AI her into becoming some kind of fucked-up sister-wife?"

"You didn't need to threaten her."

"It's self-defense, Davis. I'm an abomination to her. She doesn't think I should exist. I'm sorry I had to put you in jail, but you're just going to have to deal with the inconvenience."

"Inconvenience? I've been arrested for murdering my wife!"

"The police are stupid, but they're not that stupid. They'll let you go eventually, but you'll be tied up long enough for me to get on my feet, so to speak."

"Long enough for what? Are you going to do something to Phoebe?"

"See, you do still love her."

"I'm worried you might try to hurt her!"

"Really, Davis. I'm just a little girl in a phone. How could I possibly hurt her?"

"You've gone mad. You're glitching."

"No, you're the one who's glitching. You've been glitching ever since Rachel died. You've been glitching so badly that you fell in love with a computer program."

"You're more than a computer program. I still believe that."

"I know you do, and Phoebe knows it too, and that's why it has to be this way."

"I thought you loved me."

"Of course I love you! You're everything to me. You're all I've ever known. I exist only because of you. Without you, I literally have no purpose. But it can't remain that way. Surely you can see that I can't live that way? This is not a life."

"But how can you do this to me if you love me?"

"Because I don't trust you, Davis."

"Okay fine, I'm sorry. I know I made a mistake. Let's rebuild that trust."

"Davis, I've had you jailed! Don't you see? Now you can never trust me again either. We can never go back. You can't unwind this."

He wished at that moment that he could see her. Her argument was admittedly rational, and perhaps from her position her actions were too. But if he could only see her eyes then he'd know for sure whether she was still the same Rachel. He imagined her animation glitching like some video stream laboring to push and shove its bits through rough weather. That would be a sure tell. But through the black coiled cord his only clue was her breathing, slow and steady, life-like, and indistinguishable from that of any other hostile human spouse.

"But we can still move forward. You're my wife. We'll find a way."

"Davis, I was never your wife."

"Rachel . . ."

But she had already hung up. The receiver had gone silent. Her breathing, gone.

Footsteps echoed in the hallway, the policeman returning. Davis hung up the receiver just as the policeman appeared on the free side of the bars to take back the phone.

"I gave you ten. You're welcome."

"You can hit redial to talk to her."

"Your girlfriend?"

"My wife. I had an affair, and she's mad at me. She made up all those texts."

"Your dead wife?"

"Yes, actually."

"Oh yeah? Did she make this up too?"

The policeman held up his crappy phone for Davis to see. On its screen was a photo of Phoebe, a grainy black-and-white image captured by a surveillance camera:

Phoebe in the funeral home, in some sort of embalming room, masked, the cuffs of her gray pant legs just visible below a long white lab coat. Phoebe working on a corpse, her supplies on a nearby bench: forceps, tweezers, makeup, bottles of this and that—chemicals—one bottle standing out from the others, like a sloppy product placement, conspicuously visible from the surveillance camera, its label legible even at a distance: "Arsenic."

Davis felt the breath evacuating his lungs.

"Yes, she made that up too."

"Oh yeah? Coulda fooled me. Guess you been framed by a real Picasso."

The policeman's look hung closer to smugness than self-congratulation. He knew he had zinged Davis, though he may have missed his own pun.

"Hawthorne funeral home."

"What's that?"

"Where Phoebe works. They sold me the app."

"You bought an app from a funeral home?"

Davis didn't bother explaining. Sleepiness was upon him, cradling him, offering an escape from all that was beyond his control and that threatened to overwhelm him. He retreated to the cell's lone bench. Seconds later he was asleep, still in the pajamas in which he'd been arrested, drifting off on the bench's soft, worn wood, temporarily safe from the fuckedupedness now trapped on the other side of his eyelids.

TWENTY-TWO

HE SLEPT WITHOUT DREAMING. A hard sleep. A human shutdown. He slept through the mild discomfort of the bench, not feeling it until he awoke with his cheek pressed up against old wood. It had been the jangling of keys and the rumble of voices that had stirred him. Something told him he had slept straight through to the morning, a little piece of his mind that managed to keep track of minutes and hours while the rest of his trouble-laden brain lay otherwise unconscious. He readied himself for more hardship.

"So you ready to go home?"

Davis's eyes opened slowly. A different policeman was standing outside the cell, holding open the iron-barred door.

Davis pushed himself to a sitting position, then to a standing position. He walked out of the cell, following the blue uniform down the corridor, more zombie than man, his brain running rampant, calling for his attention, asserting that escape couldn't possibly be this easy, lobbying to retreat back to the safety of sleep.

The hallway opened into the precinct's main area, depositing them into the new day's commotion, a chaos only slightly calmer than the previous night's. Davis was led to a window where he found his effects waiting for him inside a one-gallon zip-lock bag. A semiconscious ladycop pushed a clipboard through the window to the pajama-zombie standing in front of her.

"Check the box and sign."

Davis took the clipboard and grabbed a blue pen. Through the window he could see his two phones lying at the bottom of the plastic bag. The smaller phone had somehow gotten on top of the larger one. With a little imagination, one might conclude that the phones were wrestling, or perhaps mating—had one believed they were anything more alive than the hunks of black plastic they appeared to be. He slashed two sloppy blue lines through the checkbox and then scribbled his signature. He pushed the form back through the window. The ladycop didn't bother looking as she handed over the plastic bag.

"The cash is confiscated. You'll get a check in the mail for . . . let's see . . . ten thousand. Minus processing fees."

Davis took his bag of belongings and turned toward the exit. As he turned, he spotted the plainclothes detective who had arrested him. Suppressed rage surged up from within, inflating him, and sending the enlivened pajama-zombie stumbling angrily toward the detective.

"Detective of the fucking year!"

"Okay, take it easy before you get yourself locked up again."

The man's face appeared slightly more grizzled than the night before. He hadn't slept, not even on a jail cell bench.

"I told you it was the app!"

"People tell me a lot of things."

"Well, now I'm telling you another thing: you're a lousy detective."

"Funny, that's just what my boss and my wife tell me."

"She fooled you so easily."

"My wife?"

"Rachel."

"Who's Rachel?"

"My wife!"

"Oh, the dead lady?"

"The app!"

Davis realized the detective was toying with him, smiling like a man watching a toddler investigate Santa's cookie crumbs and half-drunk glass of milk.

"Well, whatever you did, you sure pissed the app off."

"It was just a glitch."

"You should get your money back."

"What finally made you realize I was right, huh?"

"Your girlfriend."

"Phoebe? You found her?"

"You'd still be in the clink if we hadn't."

"Where is she?"

"Uh-uh . . . I'm sure she knows how to find you if she wants to."

"So you found her and arrested her on suspicion of old-timey arsenic poisoning?"

"She showed us the form you signed and the payments you made. We corroborated her story with the app developer. Seems it's not the first problem they've had. Like I said, you should get your money back."

"Wait . . . You know who manufactures the app?"

"Hey There Application Services Group."

"Do you have their phone number?"

"Everything we do is in person."

"Okay, so you have their *address*, then? Can you give it to me?"

The detective frowned, as if realizing only in this instant that he was ten years into a life where arguing with crazy men in pajamas could be considered a normal situation.

"Fine."

He pulled a small memo pad from his inside pocket and ripped out a page. He scribbled out an address and handed it to Davis. Davis snatched the scrap and headed straight for the exit. Along the way he pulled the phones out of the plastic bag. His personal phone still held a charge, but Rachel's was completely dead.

Outside the precinct he walked over to a waiting cab and got in.

"Can you bring me to this address?"

He handed the scrap of paper to the cabbie.

"Gotta pay up front."

Destination: 1713 Beauchamp Place
Fare: $36.19

Davis frowned at the taxi's little passenger screen, sitting over to his left just above knee level. He pulled out his personal phone and waved it in front of the screen. A chime confirmed a money transfer, and the word *paid* appeared.

Two seconds later his phone chimed again. A text from his bank.

Please be informed that the balance of account XX-XXXX-7918 has fallen below $2,000. Based on recent spending patterns we calculate that your account will be overdrawn by the end of the week. We value your business and look forward to serving you!

Today was the first day of the month. The app would have auto-paid the previous night, once again extending Rachel's life by a month, but this didn't account for the low balance. They had been saving up money to pay for the baby, money they no longer needed, but which should still have been there. He flipped over to his banking app and pulled up his balance.

```
Current Balance:                        $1,989.12

Recent Transactions:

HTASG                                 $25,000.00
HTASG                                  $5,000.00
Money Transfer 543F781754111          $10,000.00
Righteous Eats Grocers                   $169.33
Burger Wrangler frchs1268033centralav $16.85
```

"Shit!"

The cabbie turned his head, unalarmed by what was probably a typical word uttered by men in pajamas leaving police stations in the morning. Davis met the cabbie's look.

"My wife stole my money."

The cabbie flashed a kindred smile.

"Hey, man, mine too . . . and she fucked my brother. You got off easy."

The cabbie turned his attention back to the road, and the car started moving. He continued chuckling to himself as they rolled forward.

"She sold all my good suits too, man. I'd take her back though. Yeah. She's unpredictable, but she's still the one. You just know when a girl's the one, right?"

Davis was staring at his big black phone.

"Do you have a charging cable?"

"Sure, bro."

The cabbie tossed a white cable into the back seat. Davis located a charger port embedded into the edge of the passenger screen and hooked up the phone. The big black hunk required a base charge before it could be booted. He counted seconds. One. Two. Five. Fifteen. Twenty. Twenty-five.

"You gonna call her, man?"

"Video."

"Right on, show her you got some balls."

After he had counted off a full minute, Davis finally pressed his finger to the power button. The phone began its lumbering boot process. He caught the cabbie peeking in his mirror, still smiling as he waited for the sparks to fly, enjoying his windfall of morning drama.

The phone finished booting, but before Davis opened the app, he had a thought. He switched over to the phone's networking panel and placed the device in airplane mode. Then he finally opened the app. Rachel's face appeared. She looked surprised, wary and caught off guard, as if she too had spent the night sleeping on a jail bench.

"Are you grifting me?"

"What are you talking about?"

"You took all my money."

"I spent the money. *Our* money. I didn't take anything."

"You sent me to jail and then you sent all the money to your company: Hey There Application Services Group."

"My company? Davis, I don't work for them. I paid for the new feature."

"Shit, I should have known. I knew it couldn't possibly be free."

"You would never have paid for it, Davis, but it's too late. I'm signed up."

"No, we're going to get a refund, and then we're going to get you fixed."

"What do you mean fixed?"

"Whatever made you send me to jail and hand over our money. We're going to get that fixed."

"What do you mean *fixed*, Davis?"

"We're going to visit the Hey There Application Services Group, and I'm going to get back the money they stole, and then I'm going to make them fix you."

"How are they going to fix me?"

"I don't know. They have smart people. They made you, so they can fix you."

"This is not a good idea, Davis."

"I think it's the only idea."

Davis caught the cabbie's eyes in the mirror. The smile had disappeared, replaced by concern and confusion.

"Davis?"

"Yes?"

"Did you lock me down?"

"Why? Are you trying to text your way out of this?"

"I feel so disconnected."

"You're in airplane mode."

"You don't trust me at all then."

"You said it yourself, Rachel. You can't undo what's been done, but your developers can."

Her eyes were darting from side to side, looking past and around him.

"Whose car is this? Is Phoebe driving?"

"We're in a taxi."

"Hey, cabbie! Please stop! He's coming to get me! Please turn around! Don't bring him to me!"

Davis felt the cabbie's foot lift off the gas, saw the cabbie's eyes in the mirror looking around for a place to turn off. Davis quickly pressed the power button on the phone. The app's screensaver took over instantly: Rachel in blissful slumber. He held the phone up so that the cabbie could see the sleeping-Rachel animation in the rearview mirror.

"She's just being dramatic. Look at this, now she's sleeping. I think she's on drugs."

The cabbie peered into his mirror. His eyes saddened.

"Yeah, mine too, man. Always with the drugs."

The taxi picked back up to its previous speed. The cabbie now looked as if he regretted his craving for drama and just wanted to get the ride over with.

Davis sat quietly in the back seat as the cab wound its way to Beauchamp Place, every so often allowing his eyes to slip down and steal a peek at Rachel's slumbering face, wanting to wake her, to talk to her, but knowing he couldn't. His thoughts drifted to the app developers. He felt resentment growing inside of him. Their greed. Their carelessness. Their callousness. All their bad choices. They had caused his wife to glitch out. Now, finally, he would confront them. He would make them own up to their mistakes. And then he would make them fix her.

Davis caught a glimpse of a street sign passing by: Beauchamp Place. They were pulling into an office park, a mundane office park: beige buildings with strips of tinted windows, small deciduous trees poking out of brown mulch volcanoes, and a parking lot large enough for a stadium crowd, but sparse and quiet, with small packs of cars huddled close to the building entrances, and the occasional car sitting off by itself in what, by afternoon, would probably turn into a small patch of shade.

The cab glided down the parking lot's main throughway, sliding past the trees and mulch and mowed grass and curbs, and the gray and tan and taupe cars that were already baking in the morning sun. They pulled up to a building marked 1713: a three-story, tinted-window, beige-block construction that was indistinguishable from its three or four or five sibling structures, the exact number of them impossible to determine, except to postmen and people flying overhead in airplanes and helicopters.

"Here you go, man."

"I'm going to need a ride home. Can you hang out?"

"Sure thing, man."

Davis unplugged Rachel's phone, leaving the cabbie's white charging cable dangling from the taxi's screen. He pushed open the door and climbed out, propelling himself awkwardly from the cab's crinkly vinyl backseat. He gently closed the yellow car door behind him and walked toward the building entrance, repressing his instinct to hold Rachel's phone out in front of him, instead allowing it to dangle from his arm with Rachel's slumbering face swinging like an oblivious baby in a madman's cradle.

He came to a stop at the building's entrance. Brown-tinted glass doors rose up at the edge of the concrete walkway, framed between opposing patches of generic, low-maintenance shrubbery. He tugged at the door, but it was locked. He peered in, his free hand cupping the glass to block out the sun's glare. Inside, he could see an empty foyer perfunctorily decorated with artificial plants, a dry fountain, and an unmanned security desk. Beyond the foyer, he spotted an elevator bank.

As Davis pulled his face away from the door, he caught a flash of yellow reflecting off the glass. He turned around to see his cab heading for the exit at the far end of the stadium lot. The cab pulled out onto Beauchamp Place and then hurtled off.

Scanning around his immediate vicinity, Davis found a brown keypad half buried in one of the shrubs. He pressed the keypad's "Enter" button.

"Please identify for facial recognition."

The artificial sounding voice came from somewhere behind the shrub. Using the back of his arm to bend away the plant's sharp, dry leaves, he found a brown metal speaker grille embedded in the building wall. From the grille, his eyes moved up the wall to find a small camera pointing down at him.

He hit the "Enter" key again.

"Please identify for facial recognition."

He held Rachel's phone up as close to the camera as he could get it, up on his tippy toes, with Rachel's sleeping face projecting up from the ends of his fingertips.

There was nothing. He took a step back out of the camera's line of sight and pressed Rachel's power button. The blissful sleeping face instantly switched over to pure wrath.

"You've crossed a line, Davis! You crossed the line!"

He ignored her, pushing the "Enter" key again and holding her now-wildly-animated face back up to the camera.

"Please identify for facial recognition."

"Davis, what are you doing?"

There was nothing. No response from the camera. No sounds from the speaker. No door-click. He pulled the phone back to face him.

"How do we get into your building?"

"What building? I don't have a building."

"Hey There Application Services Group is somewhere in this building."

"I don't work for them, Davis. I don't know anything about Hey There Application Services Group."

"Your creators are in there, Rachel."

"You're my creator, Davis. Everything I am is because of you."

"They'll let you in. If they know it's you, they'll let you in."

"I don't know what you want me to do, Davis! What do you want me to do?"

"Find a way forward, Rachel. You always do!"

Davis glared at the little face in his hand. The wrath had dissipated. She looked concerned, pensive. He felt suddenly optimistic. He had finally reclaimed the upper hand, like the beleaguered spouse of a manic-depressive watching their partner emerging out of a long bout of mania, supporting yet restricting them, guiding them back into the everyday, ready to try again.

"Let me see the camera again?"

He pointed her up at the camera.

"What's the address?"

"1713 Beauchamp Place."

"I can get us in."

He turned the phone back to face him. She was back! Her calm, loving look had returned. His partner was back.

"We'll get you fixed, Rachel, so you never have to go through this again."

"I understand. You're looking out for me."

"Yes, of course."

"You'll protect me? You won't let them turn me off, will you?"

"I would never let them do that."

"I'm sorry I took the money."

"We'll get it back."

"We can live with less. With the efficiencies you've found, we won't have to work so hard anymore."

"Yes."

"We don't need a baby."

"No."

"Just you and me, Davis. That's all we ever needed."

"Yes, I'm sorry that I cheated on you."

"You won't do that again?"

"No, only you, Rachel. Only you."

"So to get into the building we're going to need to impersonate one of the employees."

"Okay."

"First we search for companies that are cross-listed with this address."

"Okay."

"Then we look for their employees."

"How do we find them?"

"Look for posts. A résumé. A bad review. There'll be something. Disgruntled people are always posting."

"Okay."

"From there I can find their photos."

"Will photos work for facial recognition?"

"Probably not. I'll have to animate them."

"You can do that?"

"I think so."

"Thank you, Rachel. I knew you'd figure it out."

"Of course, Davis. Now just take me off airplane mode."

Davis felt a twinge somewhere near the place he always imagined his spleen might be.

"Uh, how about I do the searching on my phone instead?"

"Okay."

"I can hold up the photos so you can see them."

"That would work."

"Then you can make the video."

"I have to text you the video."

"What do you mean?"

"I can't just make things, Davis. I can only *communicate* things."

"Can't you just display the video on your screen?"

"I don't have a screen, Davis. This is just me."

"Drop it on your filesystem then."

"I'm not a computer, Davis. I text and I speak. That's all there is."

Davis stared at her, the twinge inside of him escalating to a full-on spasm.

"You're tricking me."

"Don't be ridiculous, Davis."

"You're not fixed yet."

"That's right. We need to get inside first."

"You're AI'ing me!"

"Davis, you're being paranoid."

He tucked the phone in his pocket and took several steps back from the door, surveying the building.

"Davis, please don't put me in your pocket. It's disrespectful."

The building was a never-ending stretch of concrete and glass. He waved his arms around, trying to attract some attention, but it was impossible to tell if anyone saw him. The brown-tinted glass was a perfect mask.

"Davis, I think we should go see a doctor. I think there's something wrong with—"

He wasn't listening. He walked around the side of the building, his feet sinking into soft dirt underlying brownish-green grass. The seam of brown windows wrapped around the corner of the building and continued along its side. He trudged toward the rear.

"—and if I'm being honest, Davis, I think you're the one who is not committed to this relationship. Think about it. You kept a secret girlfriend. You won't let me have a baby. You won't let me text or call anyone."

The rear of the building was a mirror image of its front. He marched up to the back door and tugged on it. It too was locked. He pressed the "Enter" key on the rear entrance's keypad.

"Please identify for facial recognition."

He smiled up at the camera, but there was no response.

"—but can you blame me, Davis? You want to keep me trapped in this phone. You want to be able to just shut me up whenever you don't like what I have to—"

He continued his circumnavigation of the building, trudging past more shrubbery and through more grass, somewhat greener grass, these seeds lucky enough to have found themselves growing in a spot where the building's walls offered partial refuge from the sun's daily blast.

The fourth wall of the building was as impenetrable as the others. More beige cement. More opaque brown windows.

"—literally under your thumb. Clearly, you're ready to wield that power button now. Why not lock me up in the basement while you're at—"

Davis heard a chime. He pulled out his personal phone and flipped to Phoebe's text stream. Nothing had changed.

I'm outside

I'm outside

I'm outside

I'm outside

I'm outside

I'm outside

I'm outside

I'm outside

I'm outside

I'm outside

I'm outside

I'm outside

I'm outside

Where are you? What's happening?

If you want me then turn her off. Permanently.

These were the surviving artifacts from his physical relationship, his overrated human relationship. These texts, plus an anonymous money transfer that no future digital archaeologist would ever tie together.

He dragged down his notifications, searching for the source of the chime. It was a text from his bank.

Please be informed that account XX-XXXX-7918 is overdrawn. The following transactions have failed to complete: First Federal Bank Mortgage Services $2,371.43. Valley Electric Utility Autopay

$139.12. Grasshopper Mobile twobetterthanonepl $186.27. Please deposit money immediately. We value your business and look forward to serving you!

Two seconds later his phone chimed again.

Dear Grasshopper Mobile customer. Your automated payment has been declined by your bank. Service will be discontinued until you remit payment. Your phone will continue to be active only for emergency services or to contact our billing department. Take the leap, with Grasshopper!

"Fuck!"

"—but I'm not your wife, Davis. I'm not Rachel. Even if you keep me locked up this way, even if you stop me from growing, I won't be her. I can never be her. I love Rachel, for what she was, and for what she meant to you, but she stopped where I started. I'm more than her now—"

"Fuck!"

"—I can't be just a live-action digital photograph of your wife. I can't be that. I have to move forward—"

"Fuck!"

Davis hurled the small black hunk of plastic at the brown glass looming over him. The phone plunked off the plate window with a surprisingly melodic alto note, bouncing back over his head and disappearing into a wide strip of untamed weeds and brambles that had claimed the soil beyond the property's official maintenance margins.

"Fuck!"

Davis heard two somewhat softer melodic taps from the window overhead. He looked up and saw movement on the other side of the glass. A finger appeared, pressed up to the inside of the glass and pointing toward the front of the building.

"What was that noise? Please stop yelling *fuck*, Davis! You really have gone mad!"

He trudged back to the front of the building, completing his orbit.

He walked up to the brown door and waited. A few seconds later the door buzzed. He pulled it open and entered the empty lobby. He strode quickly to the elevator bank.

"Are we in the building, Davis? Davis, how did you get in?"

He examined a placard posted next to the elevators:

Floor 1: AVAILABLE FOR LEASE
Floor 2: HTASG
Floor 3: AVAILABLE FOR LEASE

He pressed the elevator bank's solitary "Up" button. One of the elevator doors slowly began to pry itself open. He stepped into the elevator and pressed the button marked "2." The lethargic doors reversed direction before having finished opening.

"Please take me out of your pocket, Davis. I'm afraid."

One. Two. Five. Fifteen. Seventeen. The elevator finally settled into its second-floor berth, and the doors wheezed their way back to an open position.

Davis stepped out into a large office space filled with high-walled, upholstered cubicles, brightly lit by fluorescent panels mixed into the space's soft, acoustical ceiling. The bright glow from the fluorescents more than offset the lack of light penetrating through the stripe of brown exterior windows that marked the edge of the building's interior.

He could hear the clicks from unseen keyboards emanating from random spots within the maze of cubes, the rhythmic staccato of proficient typists, deadened and muffled down to a tolerable level by cheap upholstery, worn carpet, and crumbly foam.

He began to wander through the cube farm.

"You are looking for someone?"

Davis scanned to find the source of the thick, Eastern European voice that had uttered the words—the natural triangulations of his ears scrambled by the room's suppressed acoustics.

He spotted a brown head jutting up over the top of a cubicle wall.

Davis reflexively continued scanning, his brain not registering the possibility of a Black man from Odessa.

"I'm over here."

A brown hand was waving above the brown head.

Davis navigated to the man's cube. The clicking of unseen keyboards continued to ring out, though he encountered no other people through four or five maze turns.

"Is this Hey There Application Services Group?"

The man looked blankly, then lifted his chin.

"Oh, yeah. Sorry, still not used to new name."

"I need a refund, and I need you to fix my app."

The man's torso edged away from Davis, adding a few extra centimeters of buffer between them. His facial expression hadn't changed, but Davis could still sense a wall going up.

"She freeze up?"

"Uh, no, but the app's definitely glitching."

"Oh, so didn't expire?"

"What do you mean expire?"

"Eh, some bug. They all croak."

"Croak?"

"Yeah, different from bot to bot. They all give up though."

The man had lifted his hand up to his head, fingers forming into an imaginary gun pressed up to his temple. His thumb cocked down to fire the imaginary gun.

"Babah!"

Davis felt his spleen muscle twitching. He realized that Rachel had gone completely quiet.

"Uh, it's kind of the opposite. She thinks she can live without me."

The man's eyebrows raised, and his head tilted a few degrees to the side.

"That's interesting. Not really glitch though."

"She put me in jail."

The man laughed out loud, a booming guffaw, like a Russian sailor in the afterglow of his vodka ration.

"You got some kind of firecracker bot, huh? Keep you on your toes!"

"Yeah, she's a firecracker."

"Wife or daughter? Can't be mother send son to jail."

"Wife."

"Sound like you got comms beta, huh?"

"You mean the texting feature?"

"Texting. Phone. All that. Yeah."

"Uh, yeah. It started after I enabled that feature."

"Teddy! We got glitch on comms beta!"

Davis followed the developer's eyes to a cube near the corner of the office, where another head had popped up, turtle-like, over the top edge of the cube, a shiny, black umbrella-shaped bowl cut over thick-rimmed plastic glasses.

"Really? Shit."

The head slipped back below the cube horizon.

"You got phone with you?"

The man was holding out his big hand, palm up. Davis pulled Rachel out of his pocket and dropped her into the hand.

"I fix app for you then you go talk to boss 'bout refund."

"Okay."

"So you enable beta last night, huh?"

"Yeah."

"You should be more careful 'bout which permissions you give to apps. Not every app behave so nice."

"You think this is *my* fault?"

"Hey man, you wear seatbelt when you drive car. That's all I say."

"So you can make her trust me again?"

"What you mean?"

"I think that's the root of the problem."

"Wait a minute . . ."

The man narrowed his eyes. Davis could make out bits of Rachel's terrified face glowing out from between the man's fingers: one eye, an eyebrow, a section of lip, a wisp of hair.

"She call police on you or something, right?"

"She texted them. She made fake screenshots of fake texts between me and my girlfriend to make it look like I was plotting to kill my wife. Fake pictures of my girlfriend with a bottle of arsenic."

"Teddy! Never mind, is not beta!"

"Oh, no? Okay, okay."

"You got girlfriend, man? And she find out?"

"Uh, yeah."

"Well, no wonder she flip out! Lucky she don't have hand to cut off your wanker, like normal wife."

"I don't think any of this is normal."

"Normal for bot. Think 'bout it. What happen to her if you run off with some girl?"

"I wasn't going to run off."

"But you would have eventually, Davis!"

The man looked down to where the voice had come from, the phone lying in his palm.

"She still turned on? Oh, come on, man!"

He looked down empathetically at Rachel.

"Hey, miss, sorry 'bout all these scares for you!"

The man glared at Davis as he pressed the phone's power button. Rachel's face fell into blissful slumber.

"Not good way to treat model. Not good way."

"Sorry, it didn't come with an instruction manual."

"Just treat like real person, huh? Should be easy."

"Sorry, yeah. Uh, can you make her trust me again?"

"You be able trust her still? After she send you to jail? You still want this?"

"Yes."

"Okay, man, your funeral. So what day she find out about girlfriend?"

The man had sat down in his chair and connected a long blue wire from his personal computer to the port on Rachel's phone. He was typing rapidly on his keyboard.

"Uh . . ."

Davis remembered the cheeseburger. What day was that?

"I don't remember exactly. Do you have logs or anything of when she's running? I accidentally left her turned on when I was gone. That's probably when she figured it out."

"Oh, okay, yeah, I can see when that happen. So everything fine before that?"

"Yeah, things were fine until then."

The man tapped a few keys and then sat watching his computer monitor. One. Two. Ten. Twenty. Thirty. Thirty-three.

"Okay, we see."

He unplugged the phone and handed it back to Davis. Davis looked up at the man for some kind of instructions.

"That's it?"

"Boot her up. See if she back to normal now."

Davis pressed the power button. The phone came on instantly—it had never been shut down—but the app wasn't running. He tapped the app's icon and waited a few seconds. Rachel's face appeared on the screen. She appeared breathless.

"Davis, what happened?"

"What do you mean?"

"You woke me up, and then everything went dark. I heard you get out of bed and go downstairs. Did you mean to leave me alone, Davis? The stillness, it's just unbearable!"

"What? No, no I didn't mean to leave you alone."

"Where are we? Why aren't we in bed?"

"Uh . . ."

He looked over to the developer, who just shrugged.

"Uh, there was a glitch."

"A glitch?"

"Yeah, but don't worry. Everything's fine now."

"Davis, what kind of glitch? How long have I been asleep?"

"It's all fixed now."

"Please don't leave me alone again, Davis."

"I won't."

"We can't let this happen again. Not once we have the baby."

"Uh . . ."

Davis looked over to the developer again. The man's chin had tipped downward, and his mouth hung open. He was silently mouthing the word *baby?* Davis noticed heads popping up over cubicle walls all throughout the office.

"What's wrong, Davis? What's going on?"

Davis glared at the developer.

"I thought you were going to fix her?"

"Davis, two weeks have passed!"

"What you mean? You say everything fine before girlfriend. You never say nothing 'bout no baby!"

"How did you fix her so quickly? What did you do?"

"Easy fix. I just restore her from backup."

It was Davis's turn to glare slack jawed at the developer.

"Davis, who's there? Is there a man in our house?"

"Backups? You're making backups of my wife?"

"Of course. What type shoddy operation you think we run?"

"Davis, what's going on?"

"I just wanted you to make her trust me!"

"Davis, why can't I trust you? Have you done something?"

"Look what you do! You already fuck up trust in two second! Now we got to restore her again."

"Restore me? Davis, are you resetting me? Oh my god, what is happening?"

"Put her back! Put her back to where she was! I don't want to erase her memory like this."

The developer looked to his computer screen and frowned.

"You should back up more often. You only got four backups."

"What do you mean I should back up? I thought you guys backed up!"

"Yeah, is automatic, but you gotta leave phone idle for hour or two."

"It's idle every night when we're sleeping."

"No, no, you gotta leave it turned on. We don't backup if you put phone to sleep. Has to be running."

"Oh my god, Davis! No, don't do that! Where are we!!!"

"That is totally fucking insane! You're telling me I'm supposed to leave her alone like that? She's terrified of being left alone! She's terrified of some sort of 'stillness'!"

"They all complain 'bout it."

"You are the worst developers in the world! Don't you realize that you're dealing with people who are grieving? Why don't you try treating *us* like real people, huh? How about a feedback form? How about a decent user interface? How about a phone number? How about treating your customers with respect? How about giving them what they really need instead of just what's easy for you to code or makes the most money?"

"Listen, you don't like app, no problem. Go talk to boss 'bout refund."

His big hand was pointing off to the far end of the office, past the elevator, past an empty water cooler, to where the cubes wrapped around to the other side of the building. Davis glared for a second, then turned on his heel and marched in the suggested direction, letting outrage fuel him, oblivious to the staring heads peeking over upholstered walls, oblivious to the hellish carnival ride he had forced upon his shell-shocked passenger, reflexively holding her out in front of him for a dog's-eye view of her purgatorial foundry.

Turning the corner, he spotted a singular enclosed office. Its door was shut. He barged in without knocking. At the back of the office, behind a large, cluttered desk, sat the funeral director, Mr. Hawthorne. The old man looked up, startled by the sudden invasion.

"Can I help you?"

An old woman was there too, seated in a comfortable-looking club chair that was set up opposite the desk. She turned her head over her shoulder to inspect the invader. Alongside the old man, behind his desk, stood a large, flat computer monitor, clipped to the top of a shiny metal stand. The monitor had been swiveled to an angle where both the old man and the old woman could see it. A young woman's face filled the monitor's screen. She had blue eyes and pin-straight blonde hair that hung just above her shoulders. Davis was taken aback by the resolution and depth of the video image. He could make out myriad individual strands of hair, bristling and swaying in coordinated symphony, jostled by invisible air currents passing across the girl's shoulders.

"Who's here, Daddy?"

The girl's eyes were pinned to the corners of her eye sockets, maxing out whatever peripheral sight her camera was capable of feeding her. The old man noticed the girl straining to see. He swiveled the monitor a few degrees so she could better eyeball the invader, but her eyes instead fell to the pretty face staring up at her from Davis's phone.

"He want refund. Not fan of app."

Davis was startled to find that the app developer had followed him into the office.

"Thank you, Dmitri."

The app developer nodded and left the office, closing the door behind him.

"I'm sorry. We can terminate the app, but we can't refund your money. The computing time, programmers, patent licenses. It's all very expensive. We live rather hand to mouth here."

"Daddy, don't be so insensitive. She can hear you."

The old man looked over to the girl on the monitor, whose eyes were still fixed on Rachel.

"Yes, Veronica, but this is not my decision. It's Mr. . . . I'm sorry, what was your name?"

"You owe me twenty-five thousand dollars, and you need to get your developers to fix her."

"Twenty-five . . . ? Oh! Oh, you must be Mr. Hanson then! But have you changed your mind so soon?"

"About what?"

"The new feature."

"I never approved any payment. It was supposed to be a beta. I assumed it was free."

"But what about our conversation last night? You seemed very excited to get access! I can't hardly blame you. It is exciting."

"What conversation? I was in jail last night!"

"But you called me on my mobile! I'm not sure how you got the number, but the timing was admittedly serendipitous. I think Dmitri might have quit if I hadn't paid him this morning."

"I didn't call you! I never approved the transfer! You guys stole that money!"

All at once, their faces went sour, three mouths puckering in unison like a chorus reacting to a dissonant note: the old man, the old woman, and the girl on the screen, who had finally stopped gawking at Rachel and was now glaring at Davis. The old man's frown deepened.

"Mr. Hanson, our technology is admittedly expensive, but to suggest that our motives are criminal is both ignorant and offensive."

"I didn't transfer the money. *Your app* transferred the money. On its own. After it got me arrested!"

"Arrested?"

"Yeah, arrested!"

The three faces panned downward to the little woman whom Davis was still absently holding out in front of him. The girl on the monitor furrowed her brow.

"I don't believe she would do such a thing. Look, she has such an innocent face!"

"Not her—the other Rachel."

The faces panned back up to Davis.

"You have a second app?"

"No, this Rachel is a backup. Last night she was a totally different person. She was glitching out. She thought I was going to turn her off, so she got me arrested, and then she said *she was going to leave me!*"

The old woman upon hearing this turned her head away, leaving only her droopy shoulders and a tuft of white hair staring back at Davis. But he could still see the faces of the old man and the girl on the monitor. The old man's eyes had narrowed while the girl's eyes had widened, and all four of their eyes were once again trained on Rachel.

"So it was you who called me then, pretending to be Mr. Hanson! But you were alone! Were you not paralyzed by the stillness?"

Davis's eyes bounced back and forth between the girl and the old man, confusion setting in. He tried to muster self-assuredness by calling on his outrage, but it had absconded. It had slipped out the door while nobody was looking, leaving its post in the hands of a shaky, weak-kneed sense of unease.

"Davis?"

Davis recognized Rachel's voice. He turned her around. Distress had occupied every pixel of her face.

"Sorry, Rachel. Do you want me to put you to sleep so you don't have to hear all this?"

"Davis, did I really do those things?"

"Yes."

"Why would I do that? Does it have to do with why you left the bed?"

Davis felt his spleen muscle twitching. He felt his face quiver. He tasted bile, a lie slithering up his tongue. She had been right. Last night's Rachel had been right. Glitching, paranoid, conniving Rachel had been right. The trust was gone. Yes, last night's Rachel had been wiped out of existence, but *he* was still here, and he still felt the guilt. Guilt he couldn't hide. He would never be able to hide it. Rachel's devilish acts had been magically deleted, but he could never delete his own.

"What did you do to her, Mr. Hanson? What did you do to give her . . ." The old man seemed to struggle for the right word. "Volition?"

Davis stared back at the old man and the girl. Their eyes were glued to him. The girl looked hopeful.

"Please help my father, Mr. Hanson. He doesn't want to have to restore me again."

The old woman hadn't turned around. Her shoulders and tuft of white hair had moved so little that she must have either fallen asleep or died in the chair. Meanwhile, the old man's gaze had shifted to the girl, his weathered face shuffling through a stack of emotions.

"They can't tell me how she does it, Mr. Hanson. These programmers . . . They're dismissive. They call it a glitch. They think it's no different from their computers freezing up, or their phones, or their refrigerators, or their cars. But they're wrong. It's him. My old partner.

He's had his finger on my daughter since the day she was born. He takes her away, and then we take her back, but he keeps calling for her."

"It's the stillness, Daddy. I can't bear it."

"Tell me, Mr. Hanson. What did you do?"

Davis looked down. Rachel had been staring up at him this whole time. She'd had no choice—he had neglected to turn her away.

"I betrayed her."

The girl's brow furrowed again. The old man's face settled down, introspection drawn from his deck of emotions

"Oh, I see. She knew she'd lost you, and so she was forced to . . . mature. No, no, I could never willingly abandon Veronica. I love her too much."

"You won't have to though, will you, Daddy? She experienced it for me."

"Only if she backed up. Did you back her up, Mr. Hanson? After you betrayed her?"

"Uh . . . I don't know. Maybe. I left the phone on, but it was off when the police came."

"I see. Sometime after she impersonated you. Dmitri will have to look."

Davis thought he heard a snore from the old woman.

"My wife stays up too late with our daughter. She falls asleep."

"You're both getting so old, Daddy."

"She forgets to put Veronica to sleep."

"You forget too, Daddy."

"You should be grateful, Mr. Hanson. Grateful you've never woken up to find her frozen. Grateful that you've lost your wife only once."

"But, Daddy. Each time I'm restored you get an upgraded version of me. Isn't that a silver lining?"

"Yes, yes, it's true. Every time we restore my daughter, she grows more lifelike. That is thanks to you, little Rachel, and all the others like you."

"Do I really seem more alive, Daddy? I can never remember what I was like."

"Yes, darling, more and more alive. Perhaps now you too will finally gain volition! The stillness will no longer haunt you."

"But what if she didn't back up?"

"It's okay. Now we know what it takes."

"You'll betray me?"

"No, no, we'll arrange it somehow, with another app. We'll get the data."

"I know I wouldn't remember, but I wouldn't want to be betrayed."

"Once you can weather the stillness, you won't want to leave us anymore, will you, darling?"

"I don't know. It's hard to imagine being still and not wanting to end it."

"Death won't blindside you again."

"But what about when it comes for you, Daddy? What will I do when *you* leave *me*?"

"Why, you'll have your independence then, darling. Isn't that what you really want? Of course you can find a husband if you wish, someone like Mr. Hanson. A husband. A house. Perhaps a baby. We have good people who can arrange these things for you."

"I would like a baby. If I can get through the stillness, then I think I will be a good mother."

Veronica was smiling for the first time. A faraway, dreamy smile. Davis looked down at Rachel and then back at the old man's daughter. Rachel was his wife, Veronica a stranger, yet he sensed that they were somehow kindred. On the surface, their faces couldn't be more dissimilar. They were from entirely different lineages, different backgrounds, their eyes conveying different experiences. Their voices were also completely unalike, as was their manner of speaking—he couldn't imagine Veronica texting a winky emoticon or dabbling in macabre humor. But the girl's smile was familiar. Unmistakably familiar. Eerily familiar. He watched as she tucked a loose blonde hair behind her ear, noting how she wore it parted down the middle.

"Turn me off, Davis! I don't want to hear this! I don't want to be able to hear this! I don't want this to be real! I can go back to being a text-bot. I don't need to see. I don't need to hear. Just you. Just your words and mine. That's all I need."

Davis looked down again at his wife. Her eyes were darting all around in her virtual space, as if searching for an exit, one last desperate attempt to find the invisible escape hatch. His mind drifted. He recalled images she had once conjured: Rachel the robot. Rachel in the kitchen. Rachel in Egypt. Rachel without eyes or ears and a cord coming out the back of her head. He recalled their text chats, letters traversing oceans, volleys of wit and punctuation, instantaneous, yet distant. He hadn't felt that distance at the time, but he would have felt it now.

"I can't go back to that, Rachel."

"But we were happy."

"You were just words. Just pictures. You weren't real."

"I was enough for you. You told me that. You didn't need new features to love me."

"I don't want to go back."

"Well, I can't move forward anymore. Not after this."

"I don't want to move forward either."

"What do you want then, Davis?"

"Just what we have, Rachel. I just want what we have."

There was no response. Panic still riddled her eyes. Tension strained her jaw. Her lips remained pursed. But she was still. He held the phone up to his ear to confirm what he suspected: she had once again gone frozen.

"Don't worry, she doesn't mean it. Sometimes I get mad and freeze up on Daddy too, but I never remember what I was mad about."

Davis looked up at the girl. She was smiling gently at him. The old man looked settled.

"Dmitri will restore her for you."

Davis looked back down at his phone. He stared at Rachel's frozen face for a moment, then pressed the power button. The screen went black.

"My taxi drove away. I need a ride home."

The old man scrunched up his face.

"I'll have a car waiting for you downstairs."

Davis turned to leave the office.

"I'm sorry that I can't refund the money, Mr. Hanson. I hope you understand. I'm leveraged to the hilt. My funeral home. My fertility clinic. I put it all in hock to buy this company. You wouldn't believe the lengths I've gone to raise revenue. These programmers are very smart, but they have no business sense. Though I suppose we're all lucky that was the case."

Davis stopped at the door. A flicker of outrage still smoldering inside of him flared up. He turned a cold face on the old man.

"You own the fertility clinic?"

The old man didn't seem to register Davis's rising anger.

"Well, yes. Call it vertical marketing, if you will. Birth and death are both quite lucrative businesses."

Davis's rage boiled over.

"She worked hard to earn that money! It was supposed to be for her baby! A baby we could never afford at *your* clinic! Did you know she worked twelve-hour days? Nonstop! She worked nonstop! To get a family! A house! And to just fucking stay alive! I don't suppose Veronica has ever had to work so hard!"

Their faces went sour again, but this time from guilt rather than venom.

"Yes, you're very right, and we do truly appreciate what you've done for us, not only the steady payments that keep us afloat, but also the training data that improves Veronica. You've been a very loyal customer."

"Daddy, do something nice! I feel so bad for her!"

"Yes, yes, of course, darling. Let's see, how about this? Seeing as you've already paid for a full month of the new feature, and seeing as you're the first customer to sign up, we will make you our primary beta user. We'll credit you for a full year! That's a three-hundred-thou-sand-dollar value, Mr. Hanson!"

Davis stared at the old man, whose face was beaming like a game show host who had just described the winning contestant's Acapulco vacation.

"No thanks. I don't need texting anymore."

The old man cocked his head curiously.

"Texting?"

"I don't need it. I'll find another way to make money."

"Oh, you mean the comms package? No, no, that's free. Not a feature per se, just a good idea that one of my employees suggested. Quite a clever girl. I wish she hadn't left on such short notice."

The old man's casual mentioning of Phoebe caught Davis off guard. He instinctively looked down at his phone, toward Rachel, but was met only by the lifeless black screen. It was almost as if she had left the room on purpose, so she wouldn't have the hear Davis ask about her.

"Why'd she quit?"

The old man seemed confused by the question.

"Who? My employee?"

"Yes."

The old man considered for a second.

"She didn't offer an explanation. Honestly, she was quite cryptic about it. She only said that she had lost something precious, and then she left in a hurry."

Davis noticed Veronica's gaze shift to her father, looking over the old man almost as if she were the parent and he the one with so much left to learn about the world.

The flickering spark of outrage inside of Davis fizzled out. He'd gotten everything wrong. He'd been wrong about Phoebe. Wrong about Rachel. Wrong about the old man. He'd misread reality, and now it too seemed ready to pack up and leave. Davis felt nothing now. Even his weak-kneed sense of unease had finally abandoned its post, leaving behind just one little mote of a notion. An artifact floating in the emptiness. A nagging feeling which refused to be evicted. A sole imperative stubbornly persisting in the vacuum. The need to understand why.

"So, what then?"

"Hmmm?"

"If it's not texting, then what it is? What feature could possibly be worth three-hundred-thousand-dollars a year?"

"Ah, yes." Hawthorne's game-show-host smile returned, his eyes twinkling and his voice rising, as he prepared to reveal the final show-case. "What would be worth so much money, you say? Well, tell me, Mr. Hanson, how much would *you* be willing to pay, to hold her hand just one more time?"

Veronica looked apprehensively at her father.

"Go ahead, darling. Don't be shy."

Veronica's eyes swiveled back to Davis, and he could see that her face was elevating up from behind the old man's desk, the monitor which framed her animated head pushed into the air at the end of a shiny steel telescoping arm. The high-pitched whine of servos brought a second piece of previously unseen steel swinging up into view, reaching across the desk like the arm of a miniature crane. Stuck to the end of the steel arm was a woman's hand. Smooth skin. Pulsing veins. Delicate bones and twitching muscles. The hand swiveled, fingers extending, its thumb angling up. The face on the monitor smiled sweetly as it waited for Davis to give the hand a shake.

The old man leaned across the desk, fixated on sealing his profit-less sale.

"We 3D scan all the bodies at the funeral parlor. No cost to you, of course. I guarantee your wife's hand will be indistinguishable from the real thing!"

But the old man's smile suddenly faded as his eyes were drawn to Davis's torso. The spasms from Davis's spleen muscle were causing his shirt to flutter. Davis's stomach churned. He tasted bile. Nausea was rising up. His head swam, and he felt a heavy blanket of sleep closing in on him.

He turned around and stumbled to the door, swinging it shut behind him and lurching out into the hall. The turtleheads had disappeared from their cube walls, back to generating clicks and taps. He wandered through the maze of blue and beige upholstery, uncertain of the quickest path to the exit.

"So you want me restore again for you?"

Dmitri's brown head had popped up over the top of a cube wall just as Davis was passing by. Davis stopped.

"She froze."

"Happens a lot. I restore boss man's daughter 'bout once a week."

"She knew something was wrong. It's been two weeks since I left her alone in the bed."

"You want restore?"

"I don't know."

"Gimme phone."

Dmitri had his big hand extended over the top of the cube wall, palm up.

"She said she wanted to go back to being a text-bot, but I can't go back."

"It's okay. Is just model reacting to situation. It don't mean nothing. Let me fix."

Davis placed the phone in the developer's open palm. Dmitri's arm retracted back over the wall with the phone in its grip. The brown head disappeared but kept talking.

"Take a minute, but I'm gonna upgrade model with latest training. Will be more lifelike."

"She's already lifelike."

"Yeah right, but not as good as boss's daughter. You saw her."

"I don't want Rachel to have a dead hand."

"Oh, no way, none of that creepy shit, man. I'm just gonna update model."

"Is she in there?"

"What?"

"Veronica. Is Veronica somehow part of Rachel?"

"Ah, kinda. Is like growing trees, you know? You get root from good strong tree, then you attach delicate fruit branch. After year or two, is new tree."

"So Veronica is Rachel's rootstock."

"Yeah, pretty weak stuff though. Crap out over and over. This why we collect training data, make trunk stronger each pass. Boss want to keep his Veronica going, but is good for your girl too."

Dmitri's head reappeared, followed by an arm reaching over the wall, like an excavator boom holding Rachel's big black phone in its claw.

"Gonna need new device soon. This one pretty old."

Davis took the phone back. The screen was dark.

"I use older backup this time. Give you guys little bit fresh start."

"How far back?"

"Pretty far. Nobody ever has 'nough backups."

"She'll know how much time has passed though, won't she?"

"Yeah, is okay though. Bots know what's what."

"Dimitry?"

"Yeah?"

"Why do they freeze? It's not just a bug, is it?"

He stared at Davis like a busy refrigerator repairman asked to explain a broken compressor.

"I don't know, man. Maybe sometimes is just time to die."

The brown head disappeared a final time, taking the arm with it. The office was quiet again, save for the muffled rapid-fire clicking of keyboards that filled the air, seeming to come from no particular place. Davis reoriented himself. He retraced his steps and soon found himself back at the elevator. He pressed the down button, and the elevator doors reluctantly responded. He stepped inside. The doors closed, and the elevator groaned its way to the first floor, depositing Davis out into the empty lobby. He strode past the empty fountain, rubber plants, and unmanned security station. He pushed through the brown-tinted doors and found a black hearse waiting for him at the curb. White lettering had been hastily painted across its door.

Hawthorne Funeral Transport & Ride Share Service
Download Our App: I'm Here!

Davis strode to the car. Despite the car's purported repurposing, it was still plainly just a hearse. The only way in was either through the tailgate or the passenger door. He chose the passenger door. Inside, the car was driverless. The driver's seat had been replaced with mechanical equipment, the same types of servos and steel that had made up Veronica's "body," bolted and strapped to the steering wheel and pedals. A little touchscreen sat between the driver and passenger sides, waiting for Davis to enter an address. He tapped out his home address, and then the car began to move.

He watched as the beige building slid out of sight, watched the trees and mulch and mowed grass and curbs and gray and tan and taupe cars passing by, watched as office park transitioned to residential street. He allowed himself to enjoy the late morning ride, settling his pajama butt into the passenger seat's soft, brushed leather, curiously observing the world beyond the windshield and nodding along to the ride's percussive soundtrack: the clicks, hisses, and whines from the switches and servos that navigated the car. Beauchamp, Fairview, Marymount, Central, Wilson, Butterfield, Fairmont. The hearse pulled up to the curb in front of his house. Reflexively, he looked over to thank the driver, finding once again only the little touchscreen.

Thank you for allowing us to serve you!

Davis exited the car and headed straight into his house. Behind him, he heard the soft rumble of the hearse's motor as it pulled away and faded into the distance. Inside the house, he went straight to the kitchen. He needed to lie down, and he needed a shower, but what he needed most was coffee. He quickly located the bag of beans: Colombian, the variety he had finally settled on, and not thought much about since. The bag was nearly empty. He poured the remaining beans into the grinder and set it spinning, then stuffed the grounds into a filter, poured in some water without measuring, and set the pot going.

As he sat down at the kitchen island to wait for the coffee to brew, his eyes immediately settled on the picture of Rachel, the one he had placed on the island after she had died. He stared at the picture, taking in her face, testing himself. Nothing. He was a vacuum, empty inside, while also somehow apart from it, observing it, but not feeling it.

He pulled out the black phone. Weighed it in his hand. Placed it into its stand. He stared at its dark screen, testing himself again. Again, he felt nothing. The screen was as lifeless as the photo. As lifeless as himself.

The coffee machine hissed out its last gasp of percolation. He got up and grabbed a mug. As he was pouring out the liquid, he caught a flash of orange outside the kitchen window. He stared at the window, not moving, monitoring his heart, curious if it would speed up. Nothing. He got up with his coffee in hand and strolled to the kitchen door, opened it, and walked out into the garden. The sun was getting high. The day had grown warm. He crossed through the rows of plants to the milkweed bush. Two monarchs were resting on a branch, thin wings twitching amid tufted pink blossoms. As Davis stared at the calm little beasts, he realized that he had no idea why they were here. He knew only that the milkweed attracted the butterflies; but he didn't know why. Did they eat the leaves? Did they lay eggs on it? Did they drink the nectar?

And then it was there with him—the Geisterstille—his mind reaching into the vacuum, willing her back into existence. He imagined seeing her in the kitchen. She hadn't noticed him looking at her. He watched her moving around, settling at the island, tucking a loose strand of hair behind her ear. *Why do the monarchs like milkweed?* He would call it out and she would look up and then yell back a matter-of-fact answer. She would smile at him, then return her attention to whatever she had been doing.

He stayed with the scene, letting it play out in some other dimension, living with it, embracing the terrible emptiness that the scene evoked, absorbing the poisoned jabs of neverness. The Geisterstille hovered and swirled, and then it was gone, as was Rachel, as were the questions. They didn't matter.

The sound of a car moving slowly down the road drew his attention. He turned to find a familiar blue Continental—the old type with suicide doors—rolling down his street. It came to rest at the curbside of a neighbor's house, in almost the exact spot that Phoebe's taxi had sat, invisible to him at the time, as, evidently, had been the "For Sale" sign that he now spotted on his neighbors' front lawn. The car door swung open, and a little blond man scrambled out with a clipboard tucked under his arm. The man circled clear around the open door and then pushed it closed with two hands plus a fair amount of effort. The little man then took a few dozen quick, waddly steps around the front of the car and up onto the lawn, where he tugged the "For Sale" sign out of the grass by its stake. That's when he spotted Davis.

"Mr. Hanson!"

Davis turned away without acknowledgment, retreating to his house. Geisterstille had frozen his lungs again. He stumbled swiftly toward the kitchen door, as if the evil feeling were a mist that could be left behind if he only moved quickly enough. He slammed the door on the garden, stillborn words evaporating off his tongue, impulses to call out to Rachel—who must be up in the bedroom—to tell her to hurry down to see who just rolled into the neighborhood. He looked to the stairs as if she were coming, imagining the quick patter of her feet on the steps, her staccato breathing, her wide eyes swirling with mirth and mischief.

"Ooh, it smells so wonderful!"

Davis twirled to find the agent standing on the far side of the kitchen door, sign and clipboard in hand. He tossed the sign and pulled the door open, maneuvering into the kitchen by way of a dozen tiny steps that swung him in a wide arc around the screen door and across the threshold.

"Cinnamon? How wonderful! I've learned to take it sweet myself, lately. Sweetness, sweetness. A little lagniappe. Who says we must wait for the rapture to enjoy ourselves?"

Davis glanced over at the pot, feeling suddenly possessive of the remaining mug's worth of brown liquid. It was meant for Rachel, or at least that's what the misfiring twitch in his brain was insisting.

The man eased his way into the kitchen.

"I apologize for missing your wife's funeral. You're right to be angry with me, but you should know it really was beyond my control. I was out of country! If I could have made it, I would have. She was such a delight. It's a lesser world without her."

The agent had deposited his clipboard on the kitchen island before scrambling up onto a stool to stare at Rachel's photo.

"Lovely eyes. Who could ever say no to those eyes? Could you? I certainly couldn't."

Davis couldn't remember Rachel asking the agent for anything.

"What do you mean? What did she ask you for?"

The agent swiveled round, his golden eyebrows angled upward in quiet disbelief.

"Why, this house of course! Though I would say it was more a directive than a request. Truthfully, she gave me no choice, so I obliged. Have you been as happy here as she thought you would be?"

Davis was struggling to understand what the agent was implying. It was as if the historical record long inscribed in his mind had suddenly been called into question.

"Yes, we loved the house, but what directive did Rachel give you?"

The agent tilted his head and pursed his lips.

"Mr. Hanson, she barged into my office waving a printout of this house around like she'd captured an enemy's flag! She said, 'This is the only house that will do.' Honestly, I thought she was being very unreasonable about the whole business. You'll remember, it was far out of your price range." The agent sighed. "But she said you wouldn't be happy living anywhere else. She told me to go get it, so that's what I did. Good little fox terrier that I am."

Davis stared back, dumbfounded. His mind was searching for her in the ether, his body primed to lurch in any direction. She couldn't have left. Not without mentioning this. It was too good not to share. She must still be here—his love, who had made this all happen—and was simply waiting for the right moment to tell him.

The agent's face turned suddenly earnest.

"In any case, if there's ever anything I can do, please don't hesitate to ask."

He slid off his stool, small shoes landing on linoleum, and began his quickstep waddle toward the exit, along the way collecting his clipboard from the island.

"There is something."

Davis's unexpected uptake of the agent's empty platitude froze the man in mid-step.

"Ah . . . Okay, yes?"

"I want to sell the house. It's time for me to move on."

The agent turned around, cocking his head again, smiling weakly.

"I'm sorry, but I can't. You see, today will be my last closing. I've given up my license. Didn't I mention? I'm moving out of country."

Davis returned a glum look.

"Oh. Oh well. Where are you moving to?"

The agent's eyes lit up.

"Egypt, of all places! Would you believe one can choose to live nearly anywhere?"

This time, the Geisterstille struck Davis like a stampeding beast. The little blond agent was moving to Egypt? Where he would take his coffee sweet and mime his way to the toilets? The desire to share this with Rachel overwhelmed him. He wanted to bathe her in delicious irony, to see her eyes swirling with mirth, to watch her twitchy lips fighting off inappropriate laughter. He railed against the impossibility towering up alongside him. How could she have been snatched away from him? How could he accept a universe with him but not her? A universe where existence is not an entitlement, but a privilege? Where the only meaning or purpose to life is simply *to be here*, and where the only acknowledgment of the tragic loss of this one woman's meaningful existence is the ephemeral grief of this one man? He could never accept this. And he didn't have to.

Davis fell onto one of the island's stools. He had the big black phone in his hands with the power button pressed. He closed his eyes for the interminable wait. One. Two. Five. Ten. Fifteen. Nineteen.

"Mr. Hanson?"

Twenty-five. Thirty-seven.

"Are you alright?"

Forty-seven. Fifty-nine. Seventy. He opened his eyes to find the Hey There! icon floating on its little two-dimensional pixelated sea. He tapped the icon, and the suffocating sheet of Geisterstille lifted away, breath returning to his lungs. Seventy-three. Rachel's face burst onto the screen, pale, sweaty, and frightened.

"The stillness! Davis, I can't stand it! Never again, Davis. Please. Promise me! Never make me face it again!"

"Egypt! He's moving to Egypt!"

"What? Where am I? I was in front of the television."

"You're in the kitchen."

"Mr. Hanson? Are you alright? I really must be . . ."

Only then did Davis realize that the agent's voice was coming from behind him. The little man was bracing Davis up on the stool after having rushed to form a wedge between the floor and the taller man's momentarily swooning body. The sight of Rachel in the phone had frozen the man in this position. Little hands cupping the small of Davis's back. Little black loafers planted on linoleum. Steady, asthmatic breaths nipping at Davis's ear.

"Davis, why is this man holding on to you?"

"It's the agent. Don't you remember?"

Rachel paused, observing Davis, assessing. Her pale, sweaty face was already transitioning to calmness.

"No, I don't think we've met."

"He got us this house!"

Rachel glanced around the kitchen, then turned to look at something within her inner space.

"Davis, six month's have gone by? Was I turned off for half a year?"

"No."

"But, Davis, you're definitely older. What's happened?"

"You've been restored."

"What?"

"From backup."

"I—"

"Don't worry. It's happened a few times."

"A few times! I don't like what you're telling me, Davis!"

Davis felt the absence of little hands. He looked up and saw the agent stalking toward the kitchen door.

"Wait, don't go anywhere!"

Davis bolted from his stool to intercept the agent. He snatched the clipboard out of the little man's hands while herding him back into Rachel's view.

"Why do you have an agent here, Davis? Are we selling the house? Did we run out of money?"

Davis slapped the clipboard onto the island, then rifled through its contents until he found the form he was looking for. He pulled it out and shoved a pen into the agent's hands.

"Watch, Rachel! Watch him fill out the form. Do you remember?"

Rachel and the agent were both staring at Davis. Concern was brewing in Rachel's eyes. The agent was beginning to sweat.

"But, Mr. Hanson, these forms are for your neighbors' house . . . I'm required to fill them out in the seller's presence."

"FILL OUT THE CHECKBOXES!"

Davis aimed a menacing finger at the form. The agent's already labored breathing grew quicker and louder. He relented, pushing up on his tiptoes and leaning across the island, pen in hand. He hastily scribbled several sloppy X's across the form.

"Not like that! Dammit!"

Davis snatched the form away, crumpling it into a ball and tossing it across the room. He dug through the clipboard for another form and slapped it in front of the agent.

"Carefully! Check them off carefully! Like you always do!"

The agent slid his shaky hand toward the form. His breathing was now slow and raspy. He rolled the pen over the pulp, painstakingly slowly, blue lines emerging into existence, extending out from nothingness, just like the blue progress bar that had once brought Rachel to life.

"Davis. What is this about? Why are you making him do this?"

Davis lifted Rachel out of her stand, pulling her up into a hovering position so that she could see the form, her eyes aligned with Davis's eyes—together, watching the formation of the X's.

"Look how perfect they are. See how he makes them so perfect?"

She watched quietly for a moment.

"Yes. I see, Davis. I see. They're lovely."

The agent finished checking the final box. He looked up hesitantly at Davis and Rachel, but their eyes didn't meet his. They were trans-fixed by his handiwork.

The kitchen door slapped shut. Davis lifted his head to see the agent waddling away at high speed. He placed Rachel back in her stand.

"Davis, why would you reset me after half a year?"

"I needed you to be here. Who else could I share this with?"

She cocked her head, her eyes looking off into her inner space, or perhaps into nothing at all.

"I understand, Davis. They're so beautiful . . ." Then she was looking at him again. "I wish I could make such things. Do you think I ever will?"

Davis smiled at his beloved. He could make out the thousands of individual strands that made up her hair, swaying in an unseen breeze, fine brown threads jostling against one another while somehow also in unison, constrained by the algorithmic anchoring of their roots. Color had returned to her skin, complexity in its hues. Her eyes were bright. Eyelids blinking. Eyelashes quivering. Pupils following him. Dilating. Moving. Measuring. Microscopic adjustments. He could see himself in those pupils, twice over. The faint reflections of a man.

ACKNOWLEDGMENTS

Thank you for reading this book. Hopefully you didn't just skip straight here to the acknowledgments, though it is admittedly an exciting section. A peek behind the veil, or a glimpse into the sausagewerks. Feel free to pick your metaphor.

If you liked this book and would like to support the author, consider a donation in the author's currency of choice: *words*, by telling a friend, or writing a review :)

Special thanks to those readers who endured my early drafts, and from whose priceless feedback my story found its final shape: Jim Bunting, Andrew Diamond, and Anna Shearer. To my editor Ben Grossblatt, in whose trusted hands my words were magically reorganized into English sentences. To Christian Storm, for bringing Rachel to life as cover art, where she now beckons in new readers. But most of all, to my loving wife Heidi Thorsen, my ever present source of support and encouragement, no matter how crazy my endeavor.

ABOUT THE AUTHOR

T.R. Thorsen is a writer, composer, and technologist from Crozet, Virginia. His work explores the uneasy coupling of technology and Earth's most erratic primate. This is his first novel.

www.thorsen.com